TERRAFORMING MARS

Mankind is on the brink of achieving a second planet to live on: Mars.

Vast corporations spend fortunes to compete to transform the Red Planet into an environment where humanity can thrive. The potential rewards are enormous, the risks colossal.

As the biosphere becomes habitable, immigration from Earth increases, and social and political pressures stress the already fierce corporate rivalry. While scientific advances are daily miracles, not everyone is working toward the same future.

In a savage place like Mars, the smallest error can be lethal.

T0020820

BY THE SAME AUTHOR

TERRAFORMING
MARS™

EDGE OF CATASTROPHE

JANE KILLICK

ACONYTE

First published by Aconyte Books in 2022

ISBN 978 1 83908 161 3

Ebook ISBN 978 1 83908 162 0

Cover art by René Aigner

Distributed in North America by Simon & Schuster Inc, New York, USA

Printed in the United States of America

9 8 7 6 5 4 3 2 1

ACONYTE BOOKS

An imprint of Asmodee Entertainment Ltd

Mercury House, Shipstones Business Centre

North Gate, Nottingham NG7 7FN, UK

aconytebooks.com // twitter.com/aconytebooks

CHAPTER ONE

It was two hundred years since humanity had sacrificed Mars' smallest moon as part of its mission to terraform the planet. Deimos had lit up the night sky in a streaking fireball which crashed into the dusty, red surface with such energy that it warmed the bedrock below. Hundreds of other asteroids followed in a bombardment big enough and sustained enough to push the temperature of Mars a few degrees higher.

Humans had pumped millions of tons of carbon dioxide and other greenhouse gases into the atmosphere to trap the warmth they had created and capture the heat from the sun. But even at the equator, the average temperature was still only minus twenty Celsius. Not enough for liquid water to flow or for humans to survive on the surface. With oxygen levels barely reaching five percent and atmospheric pressure only a tenth of Earth's, there was much still to be done on Mars.

The early morning sun filtered through the dome of the city built into the Deimos crater and chased away the gloom of artificial lighting. Stripped of its harmful radiation by the silica gel in the dome membrane, the light bounced off the natural construction materials of the buildings to give everything a rusty-red haze.

Mel's shoes tapped on the tiled ground in a metronome that ticked through the moments before she could see how her experiment had progressed over the weekend. She was days away from declaring her viral enhancers a success and the excitement of it filled her with a nervous energy. She picked up her pace and her footsteps played out an upbeat rhythm.

The closer she got to the laboratory, the more populated the streets became and she had to dodge some of the slower commuters. Invariably, these were Earth-borns. Developing in a gravity three times that of Mars, they were naturally more muscular than Mars-borns, but also around twenty percent shorter. A characteristic made more apparent on a planet where furniture, buildings and doors were built to accommodate a taller native population.

Easily passing one Earth-born couple with her longer, Mars-born legs, Mel overheard their discussion of where to meet for lunch. Her father had once told her that it was possible to detect which nation an Earth-born had come from by listening to the sound of their voice. It was one of the skills that had made him an effective, if notorious, diplomat for Earth. His forthright views that Mars should be subservient to Earth were so divisive that Mel had chosen to adopt her husband's surname when she got married in order to distance herself from her father's legacy.

Nevertheless, in that moment of eavesdropped conversation, she tried to differentiate the nuances of sound to discern their background, as she had been taught. But all she could tell was they didn't speak with a Mars accent. She knew her father would have been disappointed that she hadn't learned the lessons he had tried to pass on. Although he had always been supportive of her and her brother, he had never truly reconciled himself to the reality that moving to another planet and starting a family had meant his children grew up to be Martians.

Approaching the research district of Deimos City, she could see the glass EcoLine building where she worked towering above the rusty red of its surroundings. Everyone knew it as the Tall Greenhouse because of the climbing plants that wound their tentacles around the inside of the windows and pressed their leaves against the panes to soak in the available natural light. It was a mottled green beacon reaching up through the haze as an advertisement for the corporation's expertise in botanical sciences.

Mel was forced to slow as she reached the bottleneck of the entrance with the other early arrivals. Passing through the wide-open doors, the security scanner studied her facial features and matched them to the official employee list. She jostled for the elevator and stepped inside. The doors closed and the crammed box lifted her closer to her lab.

Anticipation rose with it. Soon, she would have the proof that her experiment could be a vital element in maintaining the burgeoning population of Mars. With more babies being born and the continual arrival of workers from Earth, the need to keep everybody fed was paramount. To her, it seemed wasteful to expend energy to grow crops like wheat when only the head of the plant contained the kernels of nutrition.

Her potatoes were different.

Grown for centuries for their carbohydrate-rich tubers, the species provided a perfect base on which to make improvements. She had used a virus to insert the genes of a soya plant into its DNA to create a potato rich in protein. Another virus removed the toxins from its leaves and replaced them with essential vitamins. A third virus enhanced the foliage with genetic material from an olive tree to generate essential fat for the human diet. She had created a complete food source with next to no waste which could be prepared in a variety of ways and absorb a range of flavors.

Once her final field trial had reached maturity, she would have the evidence she needed. With further tests and approval from the Science Board, it would only be a few short years before her potatoes were the staple of the Martian diet, much like bread had been for early Earth farmers.

The elevator jolted to a stop at the fifth floor and Mel's thoughts returned to the present.

Her shoes tapped down the corridor to the lab and she look-ed forward to the solitude of getting some work done before the distraction of others arriving. But, that morning, the lights did not sense her presence and flicker on to greet her. They were already on. Which meant someone had arrived before her.

Mel breathed in the clean air of the windowless laboratory and listened to the whir of automated DNA sequencers. Among the regimented lines of benches with their array of computer screens and white boxes of equipment, she saw the empty places where her colleagues Raj and Ben – the most likely candidates to have beaten her here – liked to sit.

Movement caught her eye near her own preferred

computer screen. In the white of a lab coat, and with her back turned towards her, the Earth-born woman had been almost camouflaged against the furniture.

Mel felt the rumble of annoyance that someone had decided to invade what she considered to be *her* desk. Until the woman turned and smiled with the defined red lips of precise makeup – and Mel saw it was Kaito.

It took her a moment to process the surprise at seeing her old friend.

The two of them had known each other since their first jobs at EcoLine. Both had been bottom-rung botanists with Mel fresh from Mars University and Kaito straight off the spaceship from Earth. They had maintained their friendship over the years even though Kaito had climbed the promotion ladder into management, while Mel had pursued the excitement of science.

Mel noticed that, despite the lab coat which gave Kaito the veneer of a scientist, underneath she still wore the smart suit of the corporate world she inhabited.

"What are you doing here?" asked Mel, pleased to see her, but taken aback by her unannounced appearance.

"I have a meeting on the top floor this morning," said Kaito. "I was running early and thought I would stop by."

Kaito, she knew, often had meetings in the Tall Greenhouse and had never before used them as an excuse to stop by. Which brought back that rumbling feeling. This time, it was a rumble of suspicion. Kaito, as well as her friend, was also her project supervisor.

"You're not here on an official visit?"

"Do I need an excuse to come and see you?" asked Kaito.

"Usually, yes," said Mel.

Kaito chuckled. "Well yes, I suppose that's true. I'm sorry, I always seem to be so busy."

They both did. Each time they had met over recent years, they had promised to be in touch to plan a social gathering, but it had never happened. If Kaito was guilty of being too busy to arrange something, then Mel was too.

"The truth is," said Kaito. "I'm here because I want to tell you some news."

"Work news or personal news?" said Mel.

"Personal." Kaito's face flushed like a teenager. "I've met someone."

Mel took another moment. Kaito had sworn herself off men after an exceptionally unpleasant breakup. The man had been older than her and worked in finance for the Mining Guild which, as far as Mel was concerned, set new records for the realm of dullness. After ten years, it was probably time she got over it.

"What's this 'someone' like?"

"Instead of me telling you, why don't you meet him for yourself?"

"Meet him? I'm not your parents, Kaito."

"They're on Earth and you're my oldest friend on Mars. I need to show him off to someone. What do you say?"

Mel's discomfort at not knowing what to say was interrupted by the arrival of two booming male voices. She turned to see Raj and Ben in mid-conversation about an upcoming intercity basketball tournament.

She nodded across a "good morning" and silently thanked them for giving her a get-out clause.

"While you're here," Mel suggested to Kaito. "Do you want to look at my field trial?"

"You make it sound like I had an ulterior motive."

"You're telling me you didn't?"

"I'm curious to see your progress, I have to confess."

Mel led Kaito to the back of the lab where a corridor provided access to the test rooms.

Her experiment was being conducted in the largest of the rooms, which replicated the conditions found on the vertical farms used to grow food on Mars. Although called a field, it was more like a warehouse of stacked shelves with live plants growing out of trays of soil. Each layer was lit by its own strip of LEDs to provide the precise wavelength of light preferred by the species of plant, while an irrigation system snaked through the stacks to deliver an exact amount of water. It was, effectively, a whole mass of fields placed on top of each other.

Kaito, despite saying she wasn't going to tell Mel about her new boyfriend, couldn't stop herself from talking about him. "His name's Felix and he works for Teractor."

"He's a lawyer?" said Mel.

It didn't make him sound anywhere near as exciting as Kaito seemed to think he was. Mel concentrated on typing her code into a number pad beside the entrance to her field trial and tried not to let it show.

"Teractor don't just do corporate lawyer stuff these days," said Kaito as the outer door opened. "Not that it makes any difference to Felix. He's in charge of personnel."

They stepped into the confined space of the antechamber which acted as a barrier between the corridor and the field.

"I was wondering," continued Kaito, "if you and Isaac want to come over for dinner to meet him on a sort of double date."

The outer door slid shut again and nozzles above and at the sides blasted air to shake free any loose particles of dust and other contaminants.

Mel had to shout over the artificial wind tangling her hair and ruffling her clothes. "I don't know if I can get a babysitter. How about my place?"

"Of course! How is Daniel?"

The air shower abruptly stopped and Kaito's second sentence bellowed around the small room.

"He's saying new words every day," said Mel, smiling at the thought of her little boy as the inner door released its seal. "Last night he–"

The hint of a foul smell stole her words.

The wisp of decay drifted in through the gap between the opening inner door and its frame. The hair on her arms under her lab coat prickled like the fur of an animal sensing danger.

"What's that smell?" asked Kaito.

The more the door opened, the stronger the odor became. A moldy, acrid smell that caused her eyes to water and made her want to breathe through her mouth. She tasted a bitterness on her tongue.

Powerless to do anything else, she stood statue-still while the door continued on its oblivious journey. Moment by moment, centimeter by centimeter, it revealed row upon row of black, withered leaves stacked on top of each other. Each layer was a forest of decaying plants emitting the stench of death.

"Mel…" breathed Kaito. "What happened?"

Mel, shaking with incomprehension, took a step out of the antechamber to be closer to the plants. Before the weekend, she had stood in the same spot and breathed in the freshness of their green foliage. It had been a life-affirming feeling. Three days later, she felt like she was standing on the edge of a battleground where an unknown enemy had slaughtered innocent victims.

Kaito pulled the sleeve of her lab coat down over her fingers and used it to cover her nose and mouth as she stepped out to join her.

"Mel, we should go back inside and enter decontamination."

"This makes no sense." Mel approached the first stack.

"Don't touch anything!"

Ignoring her, Mel reached out for the nearest leaf and rubbed it between her fingers. Oil slid from its broken cell membranes and covered her skin in a rancid film.

Taking a shallow breath to avoid drawing the foul air deep into her lungs, she plunged her fingers into the soil beneath the plant. They sank into its cool, moist particles.

"Mel, what are you doing?"

She had to see if the potatoes had survived.

Digging frantically with her fingers, she scattered soil out behind her and onto the ground until she sensed she was deep enough. Cupping both hands, she scooped up as much material as she could to lift out a nest of soil containing a clutch of bulbous, egg-like tubers.

The potatoes were small, but appeared to have survived unscathed. She flashed Kaito a hopeful glance before selecting one, half the size of her palm, and letting the others fall away. She brushed off the dirt to reveal the unblemished whitish-brown skin of a fresh potato. Allowing herself a moment of relief, she felt the reassuring weight of the tuber in her hand.

She squeezed ever so slightly to confirm that at least she had grown a firm and viable crop. For an encouraging moment, it withstood the pressure, but then the brown skin gave way with the fragility of an eggshell. The potato collapsed beneath her fingers into a black mush which burst a wave of pungent air up into her nostrils. In horror, she dropped the decayed mass into its tray and backed away.

Kaito placed her hands on her shoulders and she felt her friend's warm breath at her cheek. "There's nothing you can do."

Mel resisted Kaito's gentle motions to pull her away. She had spent years perfecting the technology and was certain there was no way her field trial could have failed. But, as a scientist, she could not ignore the evidence.

Eventually, with ruined flesh still clinging to her fingers, she allowed herself to be drawn back into the antechamber. Kaito operated the controls to seal them inside for decontamination and she watched the landscape of her failure disappear, moment by moment and centimeter by centimeter, behind the closing inner door.

CHAPTER TWO

Alex snoozed to the rhythm of the multi-terrain farm transporter traveling away from Deimos City. The airtight bus with its single, solitary window at the front was little more than a collection of regimented two-seater padded benches lined up on either side of a narrow aisle and driven by an automated system. The aging vehicle felt every bump and hollow they drove across. Years of sweaty workers climbing aboard after a hard shift had seeped into its fabric, so even first thing in the morning it smelt of stale body odor mixed with the earthy smell of soil trodden into it by contaminated boots.

Sitting beside him, next to the aisle, Alex's best friend among the farm workers was absorbed in his WristTab. Kurt, four years older than him at twenty-two, had an aptitude for the job which Alex didn't have and didn't want to have. While Alex's spindly frame struggled with planting and harvesting crops, Kurt's tall and broad physique became more muscular with each year he worked the fields. Kurt also didn't seem to understand the concept that work was what you did to earn money in order to have fun. He enjoyed his job and had ambitions to move up within the farming industry, whereas Alex's plans were to get out as soon as possible.

When he said he had plans, what he actually meant was, he had dreams.

"Hey, Kurt!" Alex jogged Kurt's arm so his WristTab juddered out of his field of view.

Kurt looked up wearily from beneath his heavy brows. "What?"

"What are we doing today?"

"Don't you ever look at the schedule before you come to work?"

"Not when I have you to do it for me."

Kurt continued to look unimpressed. "We're harvesting potatoes."

Alex groaned. The thought of lugging around those heavy, misshapen lumps was enough to make him wish he'd stayed in bed. "I hate potatoes."

"You hate every crop," Kurt pointed out.

"I like to be consistent," said Alex.

Kurt shook his head in disapproval and went back to his WristTab. But Alex could see the hint of a smile on his lips. It was a challenge to make Kurt laugh in the morning when he was at his grumpiest, and Alex enjoyed trying.

Except, if Kurt was going to sit glaring at his WristTab all through the journey, he was going to be no fun. Alex stood up and clambered over him to get into the aisle, unapologetically sticking his bum in Kurt's face as he passed.

"For goodness sake, Alex," Kurt grumbled.

Alex ignored him. Served him right for being boring.

Standing up afforded him a better view out of the window. He saw the same Martian landscape that he saw on every trip out to a farm, regardless of which direction they took when leaving the city. Rusty red dirt with the occasional patch of green where hardy lichen clung onto sheltered spots behind boulders or in depressions in the rock.

Two hundred years of terraforming and that's all humanity had to show for it. An acne outbreak of green pockmarks on the face of the planet.

The bus took a sudden turn to the right and Alex put a hand on the back of Kurt's seat to steady himself. A shaft of bright light streaked across the window. Too bright and narrow to be from the early morning sun, it had to be a beam from the new space mirror being constructed in orbit.

Curious, he moved toward the front of the bus.

"Hey, big head!" someone shouted from behind. "Sit down!"

The voice sounded very much like Kieran. Alex turned and glared at the Earth-born pest who, as usual, was sitting in the back row with his irksome friends.

"If you wanted to look out the window, you should have sat at the front," Alex told him.

"Go live in the asteroid belt!" Kieran spat back at him.

"Step out an airlock!" Alex retorted.

He turned away again, deliberately standing to his full Mars-born height so his head almost touched the roof of the bus.

It provoked a multitude of other complaints from others who he actually liked and Alex faced the dilemma that being considerate to them would mean yielding to Kieran.

"Sit here, Alex."

Yolanda, a young woman sitting alone on the front seat, shuffled up to make room for him. She had only been part of the working party for less than a month and had yet to attach herself to any particular set of friends.

Alex sat, considering it the best way to compromise without losing face in front of Kieran. "Thanks, Yolanda."

"Yule," she corrected.

Through the window, the light from space shone across the dreary Martian surface. In the center were the myriad rectangles of a solar panel array. Their glassy blue surfaces glistened like water to capture the energy beamed from orbit. Beside them, a translucent dome sat like a half-submerged bubble. Too small to be a city, it had to be a research station. Around it, the scraggy green shoots of plants he couldn't identify reached out to bathe in the sunlight focused from the mirror. Probably the result of germinated Earth seeds spilled accidentally or dropped deliberately into the dirt.

He must have traveled that route hundreds of times before and never noticed. He only saw it because it was highlighted by the spotlight of the space mirror.

The sun was more than two hundred million kilometers away and was never going to provide Mars with the same amount of energy as Earth. Unless projects like the space mirror could harness more of its warmth.

It must be so exciting to work on such a project, out in orbit and free from the constraints of gravity. Not as if he would ever truly know. He'd never had the aptitude for science the recruiters demanded and his school report showed he had fooled around too much in class for corporations to consider him for the more desirable jobs.

The bus turned again and the light from the space mirror disappeared from view, to be replaced by the ugly, utilitarian box of the farm complex. Its standard red brick construction only stood out from the landscape because it was tall enough to reach high above the horizon.

Timeless minutes passed while the bus followed its programmed routine to link with the building. The airlock doors secured themselves to the walkway and the farm workers stood from their seats. Like automatons, they shuffled forward to make their way to whatever field they were due to work that day.

Most of them could be replaced by robots and no one would even notice. But the rapid expansion of the Mars colony meant construction and manufacturing had priority over agriculture. With raw materials limited, it made no sense to invest in expensive robots when people were cheap, plentiful and adaptable.

At the end of the walkway was an embarkation room which acted as a break between the individual field and the rest of the complex. The workers shuffled into the six-meter square, airtight enclosure and Kurt joined Alex at the front.

"Yolanda, eh?" he said, nudging Alex's arm like Alex had done to him on the bus.

"Yule," Alex corrected.

The door closed behind them and the seals secured the workers inside.

"I think she likes you," Kurt teased.

"She had a free seat next to her, that's all."

Yule was standing a meter away from Alex, waiting for the inner door to open. He decided the next time there was a free seat beside her on the bus, he would try to talk to her.

The door to the field released its locks and a brief hiss of gas equalized the pressurized environments before the soft whir of a motor began to slide it sideways.

A breath of air drifted in and Alex wrinkled his nose at the unpleasant smell.

"Euw!" he said. "Who had eggs for breakfast?"

He laughed and some of those standing around him laughed too. Alex looked up at Kurt in the hope he would share in the joke. But Kurt looked troubled. He kept his eye on the opening door while the smell grew stronger.

As soon as the gap was wide enough, Kurt pushed Alex through. He stumbled inside and Kurt stepped in after him.

Alex came to a complete halt as he stared at a field of death.

Thousands of plants in hundreds of trays stacked from floor to six-meter high ceiling had perished, their leaves slumped over in the black of mourning under the illumination of their LED strips.

Alex gasped and the rotting smell clawed at the back of his throat. He pulled his shirt up over his mouth and nose to filter out the foul air, but it wasn't enough to block its putrid taste.

The rest of the workers spilled out of the embarkation room and looked aghast at the dead plants. Concerned and confused mutterings broke out around him.

"What happened?" Alex asked Kurt. "Did they forget to water them?"

"Or watered them too much," he replied.

Kurt accessed his WristTab and made a call to the onsite supervisor.

People's eyes were watering from the decay in the air and

some looked like they were actually crying. Others turned to go back into the embarkation room and someone banged on the door in panic. "Let us out! Let us out!"

But Alex didn't care. The one thing a field full of dead potatoes wasn't going to need was a bus full of farm workers to harvest them. Because they turned up for their shift, they would still get paid.

Being paid not to do any work? It sounded like an excellent start to the day to him.

CHAPTER THREE

Alex dangled his feet in the forbidden water.

The bronze face of Bard Hunter looked down at him with disapproval. The statue of the long dead founder of Deimos City stood on a plinth above the lake, under the apex of the dome. While he was alive, he had asked for his effigy to be placed there so it could watch over everything he had created. From what Alex had been taught about him at school, he would have hated being powerless to control the generations who came after him.

The lake itself was a ten-meter diameter circular pool bordered by a half-meter high wall which citizens were not allowed to climb over. Hence Alex's rebellious decision to sit on it with his feet hanging over the prohibited side. Up above him, to his right, was his shirt. He had wrapped it around one of the four surveillance cameras that watched over the lake from atop a pole so it wouldn't recognize his face and report his misdemeanor to the Mars Security Service.

Citizens glared at him as they passed and he basked in

their contempt. He heard some of them talk about him in disparaging tones. One officious woman even shouted at him to get out, but he merely swore at her and she wisely went on her way.

He was lucky it was the quiet hour between the end of the working day and the arrival of the evening crowd or he would have had more people to swear at.

Alex swayed his feet in the water and felt the cool swim through his toes. His jeans were rolled up to his calves and he was a little cold without his shirt, but he enjoyed how his display of nakedness added to his disrespect of the Bard Hunter statue and all it represented.

"Hey, Alex!" A deep masculine voice called from Central Avenue.

Alex turned to see Ivan strolling toward him. His muscular mineworker's body looked even more impressive than usual when compared to Alex's exposed torso. He wore one of the expensive tailored jackets he suddenly had a penchant for and swaggered with the confidence that came with being a few years older and being sure of his opinions.

At his side, Elea was an unusual match for Ivan. Younger and more academic than him, her quiet intelligence sat in contrast to Ivan's often impulsive personality. It made her life more exciting, she had once told Alex, and she would rather hang out with the gang than socialize with her intellectual college friends.

The couple jogged up to greet him.

"Can I join you?" said Elea, looking jealously at Alex's feet dangling in the lake.

She hopped up onto the wall and was about to swing her

legs over when Alex stopped her. "There's only a narrow area where the cameras can't see. You don't want to be reported."

Elea followed Alex's gaze up to his shirt, then across to the other three unshrouded poles with their motion sensors and facial recognition cameras still scanning most of the water.

"That's a trick I taught him," said Ivan.

With that, he took off his tailored jacket and handed it to Elea. He pulled his shirt up over his mouth and nose to disguise his face and jumped up onto the wall by the adjacent pole. He grabbed onto it with both hands, wrapped his knees around it and shimmied up to the top. He made it in seconds where it had taken Alex minutes.

By the time Ivan had blinded the second camera with his shirt and slid down the pole again, Pete and Sammi had arrived.

They were more like Alex in that they were trapped in a life of serving the Martian corporate machine. Pete, clever enough to turn his hand to most things, but easily bored, had been drifting from job to job since Alex had met him. Sammi worked for the Mining Guild and had met Ivan when they were briefly assigned to the same shift. Sammi had loved the camaraderie of mine work, but he wasn't much good at it and was soon moved to an admin role, which he hated.

All of them were Mars-born and proud of it.

"How did you get off work early?" asked Sammi.

Alex leaned back with his hands on the outer edge of the wall to emphasize that he had been relaxing there for some time. "I applied my cunning and my intelligence."

"You told me someone screwed up the propagation program in the field you were supposed to be working on," said Pete.

"That was one theory," said Alex. "Anyway, who cares?"

Ivan, who had walked along the top of the wall to join them, bent down and rolled up his jeans. He jumped into the lake at the edge where the water came up to his knees and his movement created ripples that lapped at his legs.

"Can I come in?" said Elea.

"As long as you stay within this area." Ivan drew a semicircle in the air with his index finger to indicate a safe zone which the blinded cameras couldn't see.

Elea swung her legs over the wall, pulled up her tight-fitting leggings as much as she could and slipped into the water. She winced at the cold.

"A bit too chilly, is it?" said Ivan, scooping up a palmful of water and splashing it over her face.

"Hey!" Elea splashed him back, but her aim was off and only his forearm got wet. So she made a second attempt, scooping up a double handful and launching it in his direction. Water struck Ivan directly in the chest and ran down the contours of his stomach muscles.

A tit for tat water fight ensued with both splashing each other as they squealed and laughed. Pete and Sammi sat on the wall alongside Alex to watch and inevitably suffered collateral damage from wayward splashes.

By the end, they were all almost entirely soaked with forbidden water.

"If we were on Earth, we could do this every day," said Elea. "We could swim in the sea, paddle in a lake or lay back in a whole bath of water."

"Because we're born on Mars we have to break the rules to even touch the sacred lake," said Ivan, making a rude gesture at

Bard Hunter. The statue seemed to intensify its disapproving stare.

"It's because Earth-borns make the rules," she said.

"Exactly," Ivan agreed.

He walked around the inner edge of the safe zone he had indicated earlier as if to test its boundaries.

Elea hopped back up onto the wall and sat slowly drying next to Alex.

"We grow up to serve the terraforming project and that's our only purpose," said Ivan. "They want us to be their mineworkers, their scientists, their industrial laborers – all to turn this planet into a new Earth because they've done so much damage to their original one. They got rich on exploiting the natural resources of where they came from and now they want to do the same on Mars by exploiting us."

His words stirred the feelings of injustice that Alex had always had, but never understood. Until he met Ivan. It was what made hanging out with Ivan's gang more than just a fun way to kill time. "They know the gravity of the red planet traps us here," he said.

"Of course they know!" said Ivan. "On Earth, our bodies would crumble in their gravity, our muscles would struggle, our bones could break and even our lungs would fight to breathe in their plentiful oxygen. So we are kept inside this dome, knowing that death awaits us if we step outside. Mars is a prison and we are its captive workers."

Alex shivered and not only because of the chilling thought. He was wet, semi-naked and sitting still.

Around them, more people were approaching Central Plaza as the surrounding restaurants, holographic and other entertainment venues opened to welcome the night-time crowd. Some of them had stopped to stare at the miscreants trespassing in the lake. He thought he saw at least one of them report it on their WristTab.

"I'm going to get my shirt," said Alex.

"Good idea," said Ivan, moving to follow suit.

Ascending the pole was easier with the grip provided by the naked skin on Alex's arms and the bottom half of his legs, but Ivan still reached the top of his pole first.

"MSS!" yelled Pete.

Alex looked down from his vantage point to see his friends scatter and the dark blue uniforms of two MSS officers approaching from the north side of Central Avenue. He glanced up at his shirt still wrapped around the camera. Calculating it would take too long to climb the last fifteen centimeters to unravel it, he reached up and his fingers brushed at the dangling material. He stretched until he could grab hold.

He tugged and the material ripped free.

Clutching the torn shirt to his face, he loosened his grip on the pole and slid down to the wall. The sharp pain of friction burned his skin.

"You!" bellowed the voice of a male MSS officer.

Alex swiveled his head. The officer narrowed his eyes, but he was an overweight and middle-aged man who was at least twenty meters away – which gave Alex a good chance of getting away.

He jumped off the wall, calculating he had time to grab his shoes from where he left them, and made a run for it. He dodged startled pedestrians on the south side of Central

Avenue and heard the thumping shoes of the overweight man following behind. But, even in bare feet, Alex was faster and more nimble.

He glanced behind to see the officer was giving up already. His colleague, a younger woman who might have had a fighting chance of getting near him if she could be bothered to try, had also slowed to a walk. Alex could have stopped running, but it was exhilarating to feel the air flowing over his skin helping to dry the last droplets of water.

After too many people had stopped to stare at him, Alex turned into the relative privacy of a side street. His heart thumped as he put on his ripped shirt and his salvaged shoes. Like he was slipping back into the guise of being an ordinary person.

Because being with Ivan made him feel like he was more than ordinary. One day, people like him and Ivan would show the whole of Mars that young people need to be listened to.

CHAPTER FOUR

The steady breathing of her husband in the bed beside her suggested Isaac was still asleep. Mel longed to be in that comfortable world where her brain could rest and recharge. But even the warm cocoon of her bed could not tempt her mind away from the problem it was trying to fix.

She had found nothing wrong with her potato plants. Early analysis revealed no bacteria, no virus and no obvious reason for them all to die within the space of sixty-four hours. The DNA sequences she had run, although preliminary, had revealed no major alterations to the genome, which meant she still didn't know what could have gone wrong. The only thing she could think of was a mistake she had made six months before. She had dismissed it at the time as unimportant, but now the memory of her own carelessness continued to deny her sleep.

A click broke through the stillness of the bedroom. Mel opened her eyes and looked down the end of the bed to where the door had opened a crack. A growing shaft of light spilled into the room to chase away dark thoughts.

Daniel had managed to open the door all by himself for the first time. He stood in the doorway with his hand clinging onto the door handle for support and staring at his parents with wide eyes.

A sense of pride, more comforting than pleasant dreams and soft bedclothes, warmed her. At the same time as she realized this new milestone meant their life in the apartment was going to be different from now on.

"Hello, Daniel," said Mel. "What are you doing here?"

The mattress moved beneath her as Isaac groaned and turned over. "What's going on?" he said, his words muffled by the bedclothes.

She glanced at the semi-awake man at her side with his dark hair all tangled after a night's sleep and the stubble on his chin giving his face a dark shadow.

"Do you want the good news or the bad news?"

Her question pulled him out of sleepiness and he lifted himself up on his elbows to see beyond the foot of the bed. "I think I know what you're going to say."

"The good news is…" said Mel. "Daniel has learned to open doors."

Isaac focused on his son. "And I suppose the bad news is… Daniel has learned to open doors."

"Yeah."

The boy's hand slipped from the handle, his little legs unable to support him anymore, and his bum dropped to the ground with a soft thump. He blinked and turned his head as if trying to work out why he was suddenly looking at everything from a different angle. Then, almost as quickly, the moment was forgotten and he raised his two arms into the air. "Daddy!"

Mel laughed and allowed her head to flop back onto the pillow. "I think he wants you."

Isaac grumbled and Mel felt the mattress stir again as he pulled himself out of bed and grabbed a robe from the side. "All right, Danny boy, what do you want? Do you want some breakfast?"

"Festbust!" said Daniel.

Isaac had put only one arm into his robe when his WristTab bleeped with the sound of a call coming through. "For goodness sake," he mumbled to himself.

Isaac waited until he had put both arms into the robe before lifting his wrist to look at the display. His expression wrinkled into a frown. "Sorry, it's work." He gave Mel an apologetic smile. "I've got to take it."

Mel groaned to the inevitable and pulled herself out of bed. "How about Mommy gets you breakfast instead?" she said to Daniel before reaching for her own robe.

The boy's face looked confused rather than upset about the change around of parents and she scooped him up from the floor to head to the kitchenette. Isaac answered the call and, even though she couldn't make out most of the words, she could tell he wasn't happy.

Isaac ran a delivery depot in Deimos City and was constantly frustrated by the complexities of moving stuff from one part of Mars to another. From what he had told her, the integrated world of logistics made extracting DNA from a plant and identifying its forty thousand genes sound simple.

Mel carried Daniel on her hip, cradling him around his waist with one arm while using her free hand to pull a bowl of softened oats from the fridge that she had prepared the night before. He was getting heavier each day which was another sign he was growing up.

Isaac came in, half dressed with his shirt on but not buttoned up, revealing the dark curls of his chest hair.

"I've got to go," he said, fastening the buttons as he talked. "Another farm says they don't want us collecting supplies from them today and it's screwed up the whole schedule. I have no idea what they think they're playing at."

Mel put the bowl of oats down on the worktop. "How many has that been now?"

"Three."

"What are these farms doing?"

"They've got some new person in charge who doesn't seem to understand that everything is finely balanced. It's called 'just in time logistics' for a reason. I don't know how many times I've tried to explain how supply chains work – they can't suddenly decide to change their dates without it having a knock-on effect on everyone else. I have vehicles in the wrong place, staff not knowing what they're doing, businesses expecting supplies which don't arrive…"

Isaac ran his hand through his unbrushed hair which did nothing to improve his disheveled appearance. In his haste, he had mismatched the buttons and buttonholes on his shirt so one half hung lower than the other.

"Do you want me to take Daniel to daycare this morning instead of you?" she asked.

"You're going to have to, I'm sorry."

He stepped over and gave her a quick kiss on the lips. A perfunctory gesture which had become a shorthand for them to express their love for each other.

"Isaac," she called him back.

"What?"

She tapped her finger in a line down the front of her own chest to indicate a row of buttons while she stared pointedly at his uneven shirt.

He glanced down at himself. "Oh, for goodness sake!" he mumbled, begun unbuttoning the shirt again and went out of the door.

"Daddy's very funny, isn't he?"

Daniel stared back at her with wide, uncomprehending eyes.

"It means Mommy's going to be late for work."

He clearly had no interest in her adult problems and reached out a tiny hand to the bowl on the side. "Oats!" he said.

"Yes, you're right," said Mel, picking up the bowl and feeling the cold, hard surface against her palm. "Oats are more important."

Mel typed her code into the keypad of the cold storage area, the lock released and she opened the door to step inside.

Low level lighting greeted her presence and revealed a line of white refrigeration units against the back of the room. The green glow of indicator lights showed they were functioning normally and they hummed with the monotone notes of machines with the singular purpose of maintaining a constant temperature. Even the room itself was kept cool, so in her shirt sleeves and lab coat, Mel felt goosebumps lift the hairs on her arms.

One morning six months before, she hadn't needed to type

her code into the pad. The door had been left ajar overnight and some of the warmth from the corridor had seeped inside.

An amber light on the unit where she kept her nuclear stock had warned her that the temperature was compromised. She had put her hand on the door to push gently and heard the kiss of the seal secure it shut. It hadn't let in enough warm air for the indicator to turn red. But it had been enough to make her want to stand there for half an hour to make sure the light turned back to green.

The guilt of the memory chilled her more than the cool of the room. Most working days, she had been the first person in and the last person out. Which meant she was almost certainly the person who forgot to shut the doors properly. She wondered if her carelessness could have introduced a fatal flaw into her experiment.

Mel pulled at the handle of the refrigeration unit to check on her virally enhanced microplants. Inside were the shelves of specimens in racks of test tube-like jars. Visible through the glass were their white lace roots topped with the green specks of leaves that had the ability to become a mature plant.

They were the grandparents of all her potatoes which had been tested to be sure they were free of pathogens. Their cuttings had produced healthy microtubers in the lab which she had used to cultivate seed potatoes. A second generation had been grown from them to multiply the number of seeds, as was common practice in commercial farms. It was that second generation which was planted in her field trial.

Trying to make sense of the conflicting information in her head, Mel shut the door to the refrigeration unit and took an extra moment to ensure it was properly closed.

Behind her, on the opposite wall, were the three storage bins where she had kept her seed potatoes before planting them. She opened the first one and stared down into its black, empty well. Her thoughts fell into it as she tried to understand what could have possibly gone wrong.

The sound of someone typing in a code from the outside pulled her from her trance. She dropped the lid of the bin shut.

Raj's bearded face peered around the door. When he saw her, he stopped in the doorway.

"There you are," he said. "I need to show you something."

"Show me what?" said Mel.

"You have to see it for yourself."

There was an urgency about him which suggested she should do what he asked. Not that she had time to question him further because he was already back in the corridor and heading to the main lab. She made certain to close the door behind her and jogged to catch up with him, his unfastened lab coat billowing out behind him like a flag leading the way.

Five of the lab techs had gathered around the desk where Raj usually sat. Her unease grew on seeing their serious expressions in the somber quiet of the room.

"What's going on?" she said.

"An anonymous video has been made public," said Raj.

The others moved back just enough to allow Raj and Mel to stand in front of the screen. Raj instructed the video to play.

The screen was filled with the blackened leaves of potato plants. The shock of the unpleasantly familiar hit Mel like the blast of air from a decontamination chamber. The images zoomed out to show the plants were among racks of dead and dying foliage.

"Somebody leaked a video of my experiment?"

Mel turned to look at the faces of her colleagues behind her. But if one of them was responsible, they hid it well beneath their stunned faces.

"I thought that's what it was at first," said Raj. "But look closer, it's not your field trial."

Feelings of betrayal dissolved as she turned back and noticed each small detail of the field that differed to her own. A higher ceiling with even more stacks of plants than she had grown, a rear wall made of red brick rather than the metal one she was used to and someone she didn't know – possibly a farm worker – walking in front of the camera.

"It claims to have been taken at a farm on Mars within the last week," said Raj.

The images evoked the smell of decaying plants, and bitterness returned to her tongue. "Could the same thing that killed my experiment also have killed farm crops?"

"If the video is genuine, it has to be a possibility," said Raj.

The cold returned to her body as Mel thought back to her conversation with Isaac. Three farms had cancelled their collection of supplies in recent days. If they had been forced to do so because their crops had died, it meant not only was the video genuine, the death was spreading.

CHAPTER FIVE

Hidden at the edge of the dome, behind a red brick perimeter wall, were the maintenance systems that almost everyone in Deimos City took for granted. They provided oxygen to breathe, heat to keep them from freezing, light so they could see at night and electricity to power it all. Silently, the systems filtered carbon dioxide from the air to extract the carbon for use as a fertilizer on the planet's farms and recycle the oxygen. They reclaimed water vapor and extracted moisture from sewage and waste water, impurities such as dust were removed and garbage was recycled. At the same time, fresh oxygen and water were pumped in to replace what had been removed and the whole thing ran in a continuous cycle.

Access to the area was strictly limited to maintenance technicians and robots. It required a specific electronic key which could open the hatches cut into the wall at strategic intervals approximately one hundred meters apart. Apart from one vulnerable door on the western side of the city which Ivan had shown to Alex.

It lay down an almost forgotten walkway between the perimeter wall and the backs of apartment buildings used to house families. Virtually no one went down there other than the children who liked to play out of sight of their parents. Alex believed Ivan must have once been one of those children. He imagined how Ivan might have discovered the door had a weakness. Or, more likely, he had been the one to weaken it.

It was late in the evening and the sounds of playing children had long since faded. Alex stopped at the door and listened. Even though the silence told him he was alone, he still glanced around to check no one was watching before pulling a knife from inside his jacket.

The ordinary dinner knife, blunt rather than sharp, had a blade thin enough to slip into the crack between the door and the wall. Once far enough in, he slid it downward until the faint clink of metal on metal meant it had found the bolt. With a quick jerk, the knife exploited the door's weakness and it sprung from its frame with a satisfying click.

The unventilated space released a puff of stale air. Alex allowed it to drift over him, savoring the contrast with the filtered, odorless air of the dome he breathed every day. Then he stepped into the gang's secret space.

There was only room to stand fully upright in a narrow strip before the roof of the dome sloped away to become a second wall some three meters from his feet. Beyond the glass, in the fading light outside, it was possible to see the wall of the crater into which the city was built, laying like a horizon several kilometers away. The tubes that linked the city's ventilation ducts to its oxygen tanks or drew in air to be filtered and recycled snaked around the dusty recess above him.

He heard his friends' voices traveling around the curve of the perimeter wall. Dominant among them was Ivan's booming voice which provided an easy beacon to follow. Alex picked his way past the banister of supporting struts, which gave the edge of the dome extra stability, to join them.

Pete was the first one he saw, standing in his usual spot with a hand leaning against the outer armored glass panel, followed by Sammi who was leaning against the opposite wall.

Elea was sitting in Alex's preferred spot, on an old ventilation box which must have been discarded years ago by a lazy or absent-minded technician. Normally, she would glance away again, but this time she kept watching as he approached. So her glance became a prolonged stare. Followed by the stares of Pete and Sammi.

Ivan was resting on one of the supporting struts with his back to Alex. He was the only one who didn't turn to look. He just stopped talking and the echo of his booming voice died away so Alex joined his friends in silence.

"What?" said Alex, under their uncomfortable gaze.

"Is it true?" said Elea.

"Is what true?" said Alex.

"Are crops dying?" she said. "Are we running out of food?"

He didn't realize the rumors had spread beyond the farms. Everyone was talking about the video, but the supervisors had said it was taken of the dead field that they'd witnessed after they had left, which was why no one recognized the farm worker walking past the camera.

"We were told it was an isolated incident," he said. "Someone screwed up the watering schedule."

"And you believe what you were told?" said Ivan.

Alex thought back to his last few days at work. He had harvested a field of wheat and another of soya without a problem. Kurt complained about last minute changes in the schedule, but Kurt always complained about that sort of thing. It hadn't occurred to him that their shifts were being moved around because more fields were dying.

Embarrassment at being naive flushed at Alex's cheeks. "The rumors might be true."

"I knew it!" said Ivan. He sounded almost pleased.

"If they are true, what are we going to do?" said Elea.

"I've been stocking up on supplies," said Pete.

"Me too," added Sammi. "I already can't get some of the stuff I want."

Alex had the sudden, horrible thought that supplies at the apartment he shared with his mother were running low and neither of them had done anything about it.

Ivan pushed himself away from the strut he was leaning on and paced up and down the narrow strip with nervous energy. "They're lying to the people of Mars as usual," he said.

"Some people are organizing a march down Central Avenue," said Elea. "We could go."

"A march!" Ivan scoffed.

"It's better than sitting here talking among ourselves," she said.

Ivan's expression softened as he considered. He turned to Elea and she shuffled up on the ventilation box so he could sit beside her.

"Maybe you're right," he said. "A march – a show of strength – could be what we need. Not just walking down the street, but really making our voices heard."

She lifted her WristTab. "I'll send you the details."

Ivan looked round at the others. The excitement in his eyes was infectious. "Let's make some plans to ensure they can't ignore us."

CHAPTER SIX

Mel watched the Chair of the Terraforming Committee lift her eyes from the podium and look straight ahead down the lens of the Interplanetary Cinematics News camera. Farah Sharif's tailored suit, in the cerulean blue of the ruling Unity Party, was immaculate, while her subtle makeup and precise, short haircut emphasized her serious expression. Behind her, the Terraforming Committee crest, encompassing two sheaves of wheat cupping the globe of Mars, endorsed her authority.

Raj and Ben were the only people in the lab with her, looking at their individual screens, but Mel had a sense that the whole of Mars was watching. No one could have escaped the shortages of food which were becoming apparent in the shops and the circulating suggestion that crop failures in multiple farms were to blame.

"I want to address the rumors that have been spread around Mars by a small number of irresponsible people over the last few days," said Sharif. "I want to assure you that we have plenty of food to feed ourselves. Crops are thriving and supplies are at their optimum level.

"I have seen, as you all have, the images of dying plants. They have been presented to you as shocking, but that is a misrepresentation of the facts. Mistakes have been known to happen in the farming industry, like we all sometimes make mistakes in our own lives. In this case, there was an error in the watering program and the field couldn't be harvested. But this example was one field in one farm among hundreds on Mars. Our robust systems can withstand such minor blips. In fact, they are designed to make allowances for one-off events like this.

"Someone has taken this isolated incident and blown it out of proportion. I understand that people are scared and I understand the human desire to make sure you have enough to eat, but it is individuals stocking up on that little bit extra which is putting strain on the system."

She looked from her notes back to the camera with concern. "The experts who advise the Terraforming Committee tell me it's panic buying. But I tell them, people aren't panicking, they are doing what they think is right for their family. However, if everyone buys a little bit extra all at once, the system is taken by surprise. It's distorting reality to make it appear that supplies are running low when they are not.

"So, I urge you. Please return to your normal behavior. There is no need to panic. Mars has plenty of food to feed everyone."

Sharif ended with a smile. Mel found it cold and calculating. She turned off the ICN feed in disgust.

Raj, who had been watching at his own screen, silenced

the babble of ICN commentary and turned to Mel. "Do you believe her?"

"No." It depressed her to admit it, but she had spent the previous evening listening to Isaac tell her about the disruption of farm delivery schedules.

Ben also cut the ICN feed to his screen. "She's right about panic buying. If everyone hoards twice as much food as they need, they're going to *cause* the shortage they were scared of in the first place."

"Sharif's wrong about it only being one farm, though," said Mel. "Isaac's had multiple farms cancel collection of supplies. No one will give him a straight answer as to why."

"The more pertinent question is," said Raj. "Could the problems at the farms be connected to the death of Mel's experimental plants."

"I've been thinking about it ever since I saw that video and I don't see how," said Mel. "I can't find a trace of a pathogen in my potatoes and the farms must have been struck by some kind of virus or bacteria. Crops which have grown quite happily on Mars for two hundred years don't suddenly die for no reason."

"So, what do you think killed your experiment?"

She was about to put forward her theory about epigenetics when the door to the lab opened.

Mel expected to see one of the lab techs arriving for the start of their shift and was surprised when Kaito entered. Seeing her friend made her realize she had done nothing to fix the dinner date they had talked about.

"Kaito!" she said. "Coming to see me twice in two weeks, that has to be a record."

Kaito did not return her smile. "Morning, Mel."

Two men, looking uncomfortable in lab coats stuffed over the top of their clothes, followed her in. The first was Earth-born, in his early thirties and with tightly cropped hair. His companion – with the height and slight figure of a Mars-born man – was older and starting to go gray.

"You are Doctor Melanie Erdan?" said the Earth-born man in the familiar accent she associated with her father.

Mel threw a pointed glance at Kaito, irritated she'd brought strangers to visit when she had so much to do. "And you are?"

"These men are from the Mars Security Service," Kaito explained.

Tensing with guilt, even though she knew she had done nothing wrong, she understood why Kaito looked so serious. "MSS?"

"I'm Inspector Deverau," said the Earth-born man. "And this is Sergeant Jones."

The Mars-born man offered a smile, which Mel did not feel like returning.

"What is this about?" she said.

"You conducted an experiment that caused plants to die," said Deverau.

A cold wave of betrayal passed through her body as she realized someone must have told the MSS about her experiment.

Kaito, Raj and Ben looked as shocked as she felt, but if they hadn't passed on the information, someone else must have. If not directly to the MSS, then to someone outside of the Tall Greenhouse who wasn't bound by the same loyalty and confidentiality.

"Who told you?" she asked.

"That's not important," said Deverau. "We only want to ask you a few questions."

"OK." Mel stood ready to answer anything. She had nothing to hide.

"I think it would be easier if we did this at the station." He turned sideways to invite her to leave.

Mel did not move. "Easier for who?"

"Easier for everyone," he said.

"Am I under arrest?"

"Not at this time," said Deverau.

If his words were supposed to be reassuring, then they failed.

"Go with them and answer their questions, Mel," said Kaito. "It's the quickest and easiest way to sort all this out."

Kaito's supportive smile gave Mel the confidence to realize she was right. "If that is what you prefer," she told Deverau.

"When you get back, we can fix up that dinner date," said Kaito. "How about next week?"

"Sounds good," said Mel.

But she wasn't thinking about dinner. As she joined the two men, she rehearsed in her mind what she was going to say to prove her experiment had nothing to do with any other crop deaths.

CHAPTER SEVEN

Central Avenue was heavy with the anger of the people of Deimos City. They had taken their fear, their doubts and their fury and brought them out into the open.

What Elea had told them would be a gathering of a little more than a hundred people had turned into a thousand. Possibly many thousands. Alex sensed the emotions of them all joining with his own.

ICN hovercams buzzed around the heads of the protestors, occasionally zooming left or right to get the best pictures from the best angle for the live broadcast. Alex pulled up the scarf covering his nose and mouth to obscure even more of his face and tugged at the hat already pulled down tight over his ears so the edge came to rest on his brow.

With Ivan striding out a few paces ahead, Elea behind and Sammi and Pete at either side, Alex listened to the chatter of the other marchers. No one had believed Farah Sharif's denials. They, like him, knew she only wanted to keep control over the population and hide what was really going on. With so many people hoarding supplies, no one was at the point of going short of food. But every time he felt the normal, slight pang of hunger between meals, he became scared about what would happen if that hunger couldn't be satisfied.

Part of the crowd began chanting.

"What do we want?" cried a female voice.

Others responded. "We want the truth!"

The chant continued on a loop with more and more people joining in each time. Until their voices filled the avenue and became one resounding demand.

Ivan slowed a little so he fell back to be close to Alex. "Looks like we're heading for Central Plaza," he said, just loud enough to be heard over the chanting.

"That was the plan, wasn't it?" said Alex.

"Yeah, but I'm worried about what the MSS might do when we get there," said Ivan, looking around at the crowd.

Alex followed his gaze and saw the occasional dark blue uniform of the MSS standing on the sidelines, watching.

"There's only two ways in and out of the Plaza," said Ivan. "They could corral us in there if there's enough of them."

"They can't arrest us all," said Alex.

"Well, I'm not going to give them the chance."

Ivan jumped out to the edge of the crowd and reached up for a hovercam. The unwary machine was too cumbersome to escape Ivan's two strong hands. Its elevating propellers whirled faster to wrestle back control, but the machine was no match for him.

Alex knew what Ivan was about to do. They had discussed, back at the hideout, how they would address the planet by hijacking an ICN camera. And now, buoyed by the strength of the crowd and confident in his disguise, he wanted to be the one to vent his anger.

"Let me do it!" he said.

Ivan turned the hovercam to focus on Alex's masked face. "Make it good," he said.

Alex's eyes peered through the sliver between his hat and scarf to glare directly at the camera lens. "This is what we think of the call to behave as if everything is normal!" he yelled.

He turned sideways so the camera could focus on some of the protestors marching around him.

Alex turned back to the impassive camera lens and hoped Sharif was watching. "Because we know it's not normal. We were told the footage of a dead field was a one-off. A blip. Nothing to worry about. But it isn't – I've seen it. The truth is, the crop deaths are spreading. How much, we don't know, because no one will tell us."

The cries of "tell us the truth" resonated around him, elevating his sense of power. Like he was the choir master and they were his chorus.

"What's the truth, Sharif? How many crops are dying? What supplies do we have left? Were you expecting us to behave as if nothing was wrong when people fear they will starve?"

A crashing noise followed by a cheer caused Alex to turn. A large window at the front of a café had been smashed by someone in the crowd. The shattered façade fell away from the frame and rained to the ground in a myriad of sparkling splinters.

The crowd surged. People bumped into Alex and he was propelled with them. The hovercam was knocked from Ivan's hands and it wavered precariously close to the heads of the people behind him, with its propellers spinning wildly before regaining uplift to fly out of the way.

Opportunists crunched over the broken glass to loot the café's contents. They climbed over tables and chairs. Two people rammed their shoulders against a locked back door in an attempt to force it open. Others scrambled behind a counter to ransack shelves and drawers. A row of mugs was knocked off the countertop and fell to their deaths among the pieces of broken window.

To be part of the mayhem of destruction was exhilarating.

One man, clutching a stack of five boxes, pushed his way out from behind the counter and slammed into Alex's shoulder, in such a frenzy that he didn't notice the top box tumble off the pile. Alex picked it up and saw it was a box of cookies. The sort that were sometimes served with very expensive coffee in places where only the very rich could afford to waste their money. He tucked the illicit prize inside his jacket.

The sound of another shop window being broken somewhere further up the avenue caused another surge in the marchers. Two opposing forces pushing in different directions. The excited ones high on the thoughts of destruction and theft, the scared ones desperate to get out of their way.

Cries of "don't push", alongside the screams of those trapped in the middle, went unheeded. A woman was elbowed in the nose. Blood ran down her face and dripped off her chin onto the back of the man in front of her. The man didn't notice. No one around her noticed.

Someone tugged at his sleeve. It was Elea, suddenly beside him. "We should leave," she said.

Alex was reluctant. "Where's Ivan?"

"Don't know," said Elea. "Don't worry about him. He can look after himself."

An MSS van had appeared on the opposite side of the street, its dark blue livery ominous behind the continuing stream of bodies marching towards Central Plaza.

Its rear doors flung open and five MSS officers in riot helmets jumped onto the street. Their boots hit the tiled ground and each of them unholstered a shockgun.

Alex stared at the five barrels primed with paralyzing darts and the heat of excitement drained away.

"You're right," he told Elea. "We should go."

A man with a bulging jacket of whatever he had stolen from the shop ran out from behind him.

A shockdart zipped from the advancing line of dark blue and struck the man in the chest. Electricity discharged into his body and he shook as the dart robbed him of control of his muscles. Gravity claimed him and he collapsed to the ground in an undisciplined heap.

Convulsing, with confusion and fear in his eyes, he stared up at Alex for one chilling moment before he sagged into unconsciousness.

Alex staggered back into the crowd. The air was full of screams. He twirled around to look for his friends, but Elea had gone and there was no sign of the others.

Buffeted by bodies, Alex somehow found his way to a side street. Within a few hundred meters, the number of people around him had reduced to only a few. He removed his hat and scarf and adopted the disguise of normality.

Alex took a free city tram and sunk into a seat by the

window. The gentle side to side motion soothed him towards home, even though the contraband of the cookie box pressed against his chest under the veneer of his jacket.

Live scenes on his WristTab showed the crowd funneling into Central Plaza from the north and south approaches. Aerial views revealed a ring of dark blue surrounding them and he remembered Ivan's warning about being trapped.

If there was still part of him that wished he were there, it was dispelled when he saw the recording of his speech. Keeping it silent in the company of strangers on the tram, he saw the fervor looking back at him from his own eyes. If the number of people on the street gave the protest volume, then it was his words that gave it meaning.

It was a short walk from the tram stop to the apartment he shared with his mother.

He was old enough and employed enough to be allocated his own living space, but Alex was stuck on a waiting list struggling to cope with too many workers and too few homes. So, he and his mother were forced to work around each other to lead independent lives in a shared space. Which was why he was rarely home unless he was sleeping.

He walked in to see his mother staring out of the apartment's one and only window at the front. Like she had been there all day, nervously twirling the gold necklace that she always wore around her index finger.

"They're bringing in rationing at midnight," she said, still gazing out of the window.

"Since when?" asked Alex.

"Since a few minutes ago."

The announcement must have been made after he got

off the tram. It was an admission that either the authorities couldn't keep control or the shortages were serious – or both.

Alex reached inside his jacket and pulled out the box of cookies. It was a bit squashed, but had largely survived the journey from Central Avenue. "You can have these."

His mother looked at him for the first time since he had walked in. She turned the box over in her hand and regarded him with suspicion. "Where did you get these?"

"You're not supposed to ask when it's a present."

His mother's penetrating stare found the guilt inside of him. "Alex, I don't have to worry about you, do I?"

"Of course not."

It was a reflex response and he wasn't sure if it was a lie or not.

"Make sure I don't have to."

As a dutiful son, he was supposed to make her a promise, but his conscience wouldn't let him.

"Enjoy the cookies," was all he said.

He turned and headed for the solitude of his room where the only person he had to lie to was himself.

CHAPTER EIGHT

The windowless interrogation room was small, sparse and claustrophobic. Mel had been brought into the square box and told to sit at the far side of a single table in the middle. Opposite her sat the two MSS officers, Deverau and Jones. They appeared comfortable, even casual in the enclosed environment, while Mel was trying to suppress her nervousness with long, slow breaths.

Cameras nestled into the corners at the ceiling looked down on them, while microphones she couldn't see recorded everything. Beside her, a single empty chair was reserved for legal representation if she needed it. Which she was told she did not, as she was not under arrest. She was also certain that the science would prove she had nothing to do with whatever it was they were investigating. But, as she looked across the table at her interrogators, she couldn't stop doubts from creeping in.

"I presume you know why you are here?" said Deverau with a friendly smile. If that was supposed to reassure her, it didn't.

"You said it was about my experiment," said Mel. "Other than that, no. I don't know why I'm here."

Deverau looked down at the tablet he held, carefully tilted away from her so she couldn't see his notes. "Your experiment involves using viruses to infect plants and change them on a genetic level, have I got that right?"

"More or less."

"But I'm told something went wrong and the plants died."

"That's how science works. You test something to see what happens and you learn from the result. Whether it's the result you wanted or the one you didn't."

Deverau nodded and consulted his tablet again. "Do you pay attention to the news, Mel? You don't mind if I call you Mel?"

She shrugged. "It's my name."

If he was hoping that using her first name would make her feel comfortable, then it had failed. Her fingers tapped nervously on her leg under the table.

"If you pay attention to the news, you will know something has gone wrong on some of the farms on Mars and the plants have died. I'm no scientist, but it has been suggested to me that these two events could be linked."

"Suggested by who?"

"How I come to have the information is irrelevant," said Deverau. "Tell me why crops on Mars have suddenly succumbed to the exact same problem as the one which killed your experiment."

"What evidence do you have?"

Deverau shrugged his ignorance. "As I said, I am only an MSS officer, but they look the same to me."

Jones, who had been sitting quietly all that time, tapped his finger on his own tablet and passed it across the table for Mel to see. "That's an image from one of the affected farms."

It was an enhanced still taken from the leaked footage. In the center were the blackened leaves of a potato plant sagging in the soil, surrounded by other similarly afflicted plants. Some of them still had streaks of green on their stems as if hanging onto life.

Jones swiped his finger across the tablet to bring up a different image. A chill passed through her as soon as she recognized it. It was one of her own photos of a specimen from her field trial. The dead potato plant, complete with decayed tubers, was laid out like a corpse against a white background. A ruler alongside measured its length at thirty-five centimeters.

"Where did you get that?" Mel tapped on the screen and the stolen image responded by zooming in to the dead potato. "Those images haven't been released – to anyone."

"It doesn't matter how we have the images." Deverau raised his voice for the first time. "What matters is the similarities between them. How did what happened at your laboratory also happen at the farms?"

"You can't make that judgment by looking at pictures!"

"How should I make a judgment?"

"By doing the science. You need to examine the farm crops to discover what killed them. If it's a virus or bacterium, that should be easy to find. Possibly spread through the fields by workers going from one farm to another, or brought in by suppliers of seed or fertilizer. DNA sequencing can determine which strain."

"What strain killed your experiment?"

"None – that's what I'm telling you." The man's naivety was infuriating. "I had success in the lab, but when I moved to a field trial, the plants didn't reach maturity. My guess is something happened to the seed potatoes while they were in storage. Or something about the shock of being grown outside the lab, in the equivalent of a vertical farm, caused them to die."

She could tell by his blank expression that he didn't really understand what she was talking about.

"Surely you don't believe it's a coincidence that your trial died at the same time as the farm crops."

The patronizing way he phrased his statement only fueled her anger. "It has to be. Even if I were to find some sort of hidden pathogen was responsible for the failure of my field trial, my experiment was grown in a sealed lab, in a separate complex, inside the sealed dome of Deimos City. The farms exist in their own self-contained units out on the planet surface. The suggestion that whatever killed the farm crops invaded my lab is next to impossible."

Deverau threw a glance across to his colleague. Jones looked decidedly unimpressed.

"Interesting," said Deverau. "Because we don't think it happened that way round. We think you created something in your lab which escaped."

"What? Even if my experiment escaped from the enclosed field trial, even if it got out of the lab, even if it – somehow – made its way out of the research building, it would still have to escape the confines of Deimos City. It simply wouldn't happen by chance."

"So you're saying it had to have been deliberate?"

Anger turned to fear as she realized what he was implying. "You think *I'm* responsible?"

The impassive faces of her interrogators continued to watch her reactions without allowing her to read their expressions.

"Do I need legal representation?" she asked. "Because if you're accusing me, I think I do."

"We're not accusing you of anything. Just asking questions." Deverau consulted his tablet again. "Erdan is your married name, is that right?"

"What of it?" said Mel, wary of his sudden change in questioning.

"You were born Mel Walker, the daughter of Frank Walker the diplomat."

Her muscles tensed. She had worked hard to pull herself out from under the reputation of her father and the last place she wanted to be reminded of it was in an MSS interrogation room.

"He was a very vocal supporter of the interests of Earth, if I remember correctly," Deverau continued.

"He came from Earth to work as an Earth diplomat. It was his job," said Mel.

"Except, according to his reputation, he had a notorious zeal for it. He believed the interests of Earth outweighed those of a mere colony on a neighboring planet."

"I'm not my father," Mel insisted.

"Because the latest I hear is that the Terraforming Committee is appealing to Earth for help. Supplies will take months to get here, but with rationing and other measures, it might be enough to get us through."

Mel glared back at him, daring him to come to his conclusion so she could point out how ridiculous it was.

"That's a stark reminder of how reliant we still are on Earth, isn't it?" suggested Deverau. "One little problem and we go running back to the mother planet to bail us out. If someone wanted to send a message, then sabotaging a few fields of crops would be an easy way of doing it, wouldn't you say?"

"I wouldn't do that!"

She could feel the argument slipping away from her. Her body's natural defenses made her heart beat faster and caused heat to rise to her face, but they couldn't help her.

Deverau looked square across the table. "It would be easy for someone with your scientific knowledge, and not unexpected for the daughter of Frank Walker."

It was like she was back at school with the other Mars-born kids taunting her about her Earth-loving father. Long-buried feelings of injustice woke to rage inside. She had not stood up to the bullies then, but she was an adult now. She had to stand up for herself and for the science she had worked so hard to develop.

"I was born on Mars, I've lived my whole life on Mars," she told Deverau definitively. "My work is on Mars, my friends are on Mars – my *family* is on Mars. You think I would risk the stability of this planet to send a message I don't believe in? My son is only one year old. When I heard about the farms, don't you think I was worried for his safety? If Mars struggles to feed itself, then I struggle to feed my son and I…"

Tears welled in her eyes as she thought about Daniel, but she was determined not to lose herself to emotion in front of the supercilious MSS officers. "I didn't do this terrible thing that you're accusing me of."

Mel pushed the tablet with the image of her lab experiment

back across the table at the men and sat back in her chair. She folded her arms and resolved not to say another word.

Inspector Deverau stood watching Mel on the live video feed from the adjoining room. The screen showed her alone at the interrogation table, having barely moved from her resolute position sitting back on the chair. If she had been of a criminal background, holding back the tears might have been a nice touch, but for a woman whose file clearly showed she had worked all her life in biological sciences, he felt it was genuine. If he had a young child and listened to all the hysteria circulating around Deimos City, he might have been moved to tears as well.

The door opened and Sergeant Jones stepped inside. "Hey, Dev," he said. "You still here?"

"No," said Deverau, giving him a blank look. "I've gone home for a well-earned rest. What you are seeing is merely a figment of your imagination."

Jones rolled his eyes at his boss' attempt at humor. "Right," he said, closing the door behind him.

Jones sat at the table, on the chair nearest to the video screen, reducing his towering Mars-born height to something a little shorter. Which was how Deverau preferred it. Talking to Jones for a long period of time while he was standing up gave him a crick in the neck.

Jones nodded across to the screen with its image of Mel. "What do you think?"

Deverau considered for a moment. "Innocent until proven guilty."

"You don't think she did it, then?"

Deverau didn't know. He was a little bamboozled by the science, he had to admit. "Do I think there's a connection between her dead experiment and what's happening at the farms?" he asked himself. "Yeah, I think there has to be. But do I think she deliberately poisoned the means of food production on Mars? That's a stretch, Jonesy."

"Except," said Jones, "she said it herself. For something to get out of the lab and into the farms by accident – well, it's virtually impossible. Which means someone did it on purpose. Which is a crime, which is why we were instructed to bring her in."

Deverau looked at the image on the screen again. Mel had finally moved and was leaning forward on the chair with her arms resting on the table. He had met many criminals in his time in the police force on Earth and, subsequently, in the MSS, and she wasn't behaving like a guilty woman. "Why would she do it, though?"

"Her father," said Jones. "She grew up in a household where Earth was considered the supreme authority. Now Mars is pushing back with increasing murmurs about independence from certain people and she wanted to teach the colony a lesson."

Deverau understood the animosity many Mars-borns still felt toward Frank Walker, even some five years after his death. But that prejudice risked clouding their judgment. "There's no evidence for that. I mean, how do you feel about your father?"

"My father?" Jones shrugged. "I love him, I suppose. Even though he drives me mad."

"Precisely!"

"What do you mean, 'precisely'?"

"You're your own man. Just as, I imagine, a daughter with intelligence enough to get a doctorate in biological sciences and run her own scientific project for EcoLine is her own woman. The influence of her father isn't a strong enough motive on its own. We certainly haven't got enough evidence to hold her, let alone charge her. Can you sort out the paperwork to release her under investigation?"

"We can't release her," said Jones.

Deverau gave his sergeant a skeptical look.

"I mean, that's partly what I came in to talk to you about. We have orders to send her to Noctis City."

"Orders?"

"MSS HQ were trying to get hold of you, but there's something wrong with your WristTab."

Deverau lifted his arm and saw the communication device was turned off. He always turned it off in interrogations because being interrupted just as his prime suspect was about to make a confession could put a real dent in his crime clear-up rate. He was supposed to turn it back on again when he left the interrogation room, but he was usually still processing what he had heard and would often forget.

He switched on his WristTab and a flurry of messages tumbled through.

"They want a more senior team to interview her and take over the investigation," said Jones.

Deverau confirmed what he was being told as he scrolled through the messages. "A 'more senior team,'" he repeated, irritated that his authority was being undermined. "Do you think they mean someone who wasn't born on Earth?"

"They said the investigation is too high profile to leave it to a regional MSS office. They say the increasing unrest in Deimos City means we're going to have our hands full dealing with that. We've been told to arrest her. That'll give us twenty-four hours to hold her while they figure something out."

Deverau turned his back on the live video feed. It seemed that figuring out Mel's motives was no longer his concern.

"Then I suppose you better find a reason to arrest her," he said. "I'll still need you to handle the paperwork, if you don't mind, Jonesy."

Jones stood from the chair, reaching his full height. "You do know we don't use paper on Mars, don't you?"

"It's an expression," said Deverau. Police forces on Earth didn't use paper either, but the terminology from centuries past had stuck around and that's how all the officers on his old beat had talked. It was one of those words that, when he was tired and stressed, came out of his mouth to remind people that he was an immigrant.

"Look at it this way," said Jones. "If, after twenty-four hours, they take over the investigation, it'll be one less thing to worry about."

"Yeah," said Deverau.

Except, interference by his superiors at Noctis City only ever increased his worries.

CHAPTER NINE

Sapped of the green of their youth, the desiccated grass-like blades of soya had given the last of their energy to nurture the seeds in their pods. Tired under the pinkish glow of LED lights, they had reached the end of their useful life and were ready for the reaper.

Swarms of farm workers on Alex's shift had descended on their quiet field to rob the mature plants of their beans. The crisp, dried-out stems would then be salvaged for their valuable fibers and, in the afterlife of the plant, would become unrecognizable as textiles and packaging.

Almost the entire field had succumbed to the harvest. Leaving behind stacks of dark brown soil trays primed to receive the next crop rotation.

Like the empty shelves of a food warehouse.

Only one unharvested stack remained. A towering swish of yellowed foliage at the back of the field, waiting for the forklift robot.

The machine reached up high with its prongs to pluck the

top layer. Lifting it free, the robot reversed and turned to face the production line of workers near the end of the field. It lowered the tray to chest height as if holding out an offering to the humans and trundled down the aisle. With each imperfection of the path, the tray juddered and the heavy pods of soya nodded their way to the harvesting machine.

Alex's job was to guide the tray onto the conveyor belt that fed the harvester. He suspected Kurt had put in a quiet word to ensure he was paired with Yule. Not as if working at the conveyor provided much scope for matchmaking. Goggles protected their eyes from flying stalks and dust, while masks over their mouths and noses covered up most of the rest of their faces.

Alex's feet ached from having stood there all day. His goggles kept steaming up and it was unpleasant to breathe in the humid atmosphere created by his own breath and sweat inside the mask. But it was energizing to be there, only three months since he had been in that same field planting the seed. With all the talk of food shortages, to be playing a role in harvesting a successful crop gave him a sense of achievement he had never experienced before.

The robot delivered its gift onto the conveyor. The belt sensed its weight and attempted to move the tray forward. But it was stuck on the prongs. Through the un-steamy portion of Alex's goggles, he exchanged unspoken communication with Yule. Together, they tugged at the tray, it was freed from the robot and propelled along the conveyor into the waiting mouth of the harvester.

Turning blades swiped at the soya stems and liberated them from their roots. The plants tumbled into the belly of the machine where unseen processes extracted the beans and salvaged the straw.

At the rear of the harvester, Kurt waited for the beans to drop into a hopper which he would guide onto another robot for onward transport. The fiber-rich bundles of leftovers fell into another bin to be taken away for processing. The rest of the workers ensured the soil was sieved of roots before entering a sterilizer. From there, it was enriched with fertilizer before being restored to the tray, offered back to the waiting forklift robot and returned to the stacks.

When the last tray had been fed into the harvester, Alex stepped out of the field into the walkway and relieved himself of the goggles and mask. Drawing in a lungful of clean air, he wiped his eyes with his sleeve to clear the sweat. Out ahead of him, at the end of the tunnel coupled into the airlock, was the delivery vehicle. Heading towards it was another forklift robot, this one carrying a silvery, cast titanium, sealed hopper of soya beans.

Alex jogged to catch up with it, then ran round the front so its sensors detected him and it jerked to a halt. He grinned. He loved the power he had over the automaton, even though it was childish. He put his hand in front of the sensor to make sure it remained immobile while he jumped up on the hopper and sat on it. When he removed his hand, the machine detected nothing was in the way and continued trundling, apparently ignorant that it had a passenger on board.

At the end of the walkway, Alex hopped off and watched the robot carry out its final delivery of the day. It maneuvered onto the liftgate at the back of the vehicle and was raised into a cargo hold already full of neatly stacked, cast metal, sealed hoppers.

As he watched the robot add its delivery to the stacks, he heard the voices of two men talking inside. "Is that the last hopper?" one of them was saying.

"That's it," said the second, an older man with a gruff voice.

Alex couldn't see them, partly because they were standing behind the hoppers and also because it was dark in there compared to the lights of the walkway.

"It's a shame," said the first one in what could have been an Earth accent. "This could feed a lot of people."

"Not seven million," said the one with the gruff voice. "That's barely a bean each."

"This lot should be contributing to the ration, that's all I'm saying."

"Don't be naive. You'll be saying next the Terraforming Committee runs the planet."

"Well, officially, it does."

The gruff man grunted.

The forklift raised the hopper it was carrying and placed it on top of a stack of two others at the rear of the vehicle. As it withdrew, two men – presumably the ones whose conversation he had overheard – appeared from between the rows.

Alex could see the first man had a closely trimmed beard that had turned almost entirely gray. Following him, the younger man wore his long dark hair gathered up into a bun on the top of his head.

The gruff one stopped as he saw Alex standing, clearly illuminated, in the middle of the walkway and staring up at them. "Is there a problem?"

"I've come to get the robot," Alex lied.

"It's a robot," said the gruff one. "It can get itself."

The robot, having deposited its cargo, returned to the platform and was lowered down to Alex's level.

"What did you mean, 'it's a shame'?" said Alex, still thinking about the men's conversation.

The younger one threw a glance across to his older friend and the way they seemed to tense at the unspoken communication suggested they were self-conscious at being overheard. "Nothing."

The forklift trundled away from the vehicle, but stopped when it sensed Alex in the walkway. Alex deliberately didn't move. "What did you mean, this isn't going to the ration? It's food. It's grown to feed people."

"All I meant was, there are 'people' and there are *people*," said the gruff one.

"Jake!" his friend reprimanded him.

Alex looked from one to another as his mind began to piece things together. "You mean corporations," he said. "It's the corporations who run the planet."

"I think the kid's got it," said the gruff one whose name, evidently, was Jake.

"And we've got to get going," said the young one, jumping down out of the vehicle. He glared at Alex. "Take your robot and get out of the airlock."

Alex stood his ground and looked up at Jake, who was still waiting beside the hoppers of soya beans. "What about the corporations?"

"They're rich, they're powerful and they're just as scared at the thought of starving to death as the rest of us. If you were them, what would you do?"

Alex contemplated, in silence, what the young man had said. He remembered his mother stuffing a month's worth of food into a cupboard which she had rushed to buy in the hours before rationing took hold. It had been understandable, it had been instinctive, it had been human. He imagined what that reaction might look like when scaled up to the size of a corporation.

"If I was rich and powerful," said Alex. "I would make sure I didn't starve to death."

Jake smiled and the gray hairs of his beard bristled with the movement of his lips.

The younger one strode up to Alex with such purpose that he thought he was going to hit him. Instead, he grabbed hold of his arm and yanked him sideways. "I said, get out of the way! I don't want to be taking this load back to the depot when it's dark."

The forklift, no longer sensing a human in its path, begun trundling back down the walkway.

The man deposited Alex on the other side of the airlock. "If I were you," he advised him as he let go of his arm, "I would forget the ramblings of a cynical old man."

Alex just stood watching as the younger one also retreated and jumped back up into the vehicle.

"Who are you calling old?" Jake said when his colleague joined him.

"You don't deny you're cynical, then?"

"I'm realistic, there's a difference. I've made more deliveries to corporation warehouses these last weeks than ever before."

"Get up into the driver's cab. I'll join you when I've sorted the airlock." The young one slammed his palm against a button on the inside of the vehicle and lights whirled red to warn that the door was closing.

"They tell me I'm transporting machine parts or construction materials, but I know–"

The rear shutter of the vehicle closed and the end of the man's sentence was cut off as the hermetic seals operated to ensure it was air tight. But Alex didn't need to hear it to understand what the men were talking about. The airlock door in front of him began to close in preparation for the atmosphere to be sucked out and the vehicle to depart, allowing the thin, unbreathable atmosphere of Mars to enter the embarkation space.

Alex turned and ran down the walkway to catch up with the returning robot. He didn't want to ride the slow, trundling machine on the way back and kept running. He had to get back to the bus as soon as possible and return to Deimos City to tell Ivan.

CHAPTER TEN

There was nowhere for Alex's anger to escape in the close confines of the maintenance area. It bounced off the glass of the dome and the brick of the perimeter wall to saturate the air.

Elea, sitting on the ventilator box, with Pete and Sammi standing next to her, listened to what he had overheard at the farm and added their own anger to the atmosphere.

Ivan listened quietly, leaning back against a supporting strut with his arms folded. When Alex had finished, his expression didn't change.

"Are you surprised?" he said, unmoved by Alex's tirade against the corporations and the system.

Ivan's arrogance angered Alex even more. "Don't you understand what the men were talking about? Corporations are stockpiling food for themselves! It doesn't matter if it's surprising or not, it matters that it's happening."

"Alex is right, Ivan," said Elea. "The rich should be on rations like the rest of us."

"Does that mean they're prepared to let ordinary people starve?" said Pete.

"If it's us or them, they might," said Sammi.

Ivan pushed himself away from the strut and unfolded his arms. "Do you want to do something about it?"

There was an enigmatic look in his eye.

"Ivan has a plan," said Elea, guessing rather than knowing.

Ivan's smile suggested she was right. "We hit their supply lines," he said. "Take back what they stole and return it to the people."

"How?" asked Alex, the energy of anger morphing into the electricity of excitement.

"I'll use my contacts to find out when the next shipment is," said Ivan. "They'll be almost certainly taking it away from Deimos City, and that's when it will be vulnerable."

He paced the narrow strip where there was enough headroom for his tall, muscular body. Thinking through his plan as he spoke. "Sammi, can you source me a Mining Guild truck? Fully equipped for work on the planet surface and big enough for the four of us plus a shipment of food."

Sammi stood up straight at the mention of his name. "I think so."

"We use explosives at work for mining. I know I can get access to those if I bribe the right people," said Ivan.

"Explosives?" said Elea, looking uncertain.

"You want to send a message to the corporations, don't you?"

"Yeah. But–"

Ivan interrupted her. "Not to hurt anyone, only to safeguard the food they're stealing."

"How do you propose to do that?" she said.

He grinned again.

Ivan outlined his plan over the course of the next hour. The rest of them threw in suggestions and refinements until the maintenance area was alive with ideas. By the time they left, Alex thrilled to think of what was possible.

If he knew one thing, it was that he would never become like Jake, the old and cynical transport worker. He would never blindly follow orders when he knew what was really going on.

He was going to fight for the rights of the ordinary Martian and Ivan was going to help him.

CHAPTER ELEVEN

Mel had been allowed one quick call with Isaac in which she had tried to be positive and unemotional, which was hard when she could see the concern in his face. After that, the call was terminated, her WristTab was confiscated and she was placed in a windowless MSS cell.

Focusing kept her emotions at bay. Fear, anger and frustration were locked out of the room as securely as the MSS had locked her inside of it. Two rationed meals, with the nominal titles of "dinner" and "breakfast", were delivered and she ate while sitting on the narrow bench which spanned the rear wall of the cell.

Only a duty lawyer, with even less understanding of science than the unenlightened Deverau, came to speak to her. The lawyer told her increasing unrest among the population had led Farah Sharif to enact legislation giving the MSS greater powers. The emergency measures allowed them to keep Mel in custody for up to a week without charging her. Enough time to transfer her to Noctis City.

Until then she could only sit or lie on the bench and force herself to maintain composure while she dozed, but never slept.

CHAPTER TWELVE

The jewel that was Deimos City sparkled in the afternoon sun as the train pulled away. Deverau had forgotten how beautiful it looked from the outside, with each panel of armored glass cut to perfection and catching the light at a different angle. From his vantage point twelve meters above the ground, looking through the window of the carriage, it was possible to imagine the haven of civilization that the first visionaries of Mars had intended it to be.

Mel, sitting opposite him at the back of the carriage, staring down at her cuffed hands, was not the sort of criminal he usually dealt with. She was an intellectual, for one thing, not out for personal gain, but acting on a wave of ideology – according to the theory put forward by his superiors at Noctis City.

Having questioned her and read her file, he wasn't sure he believed them. Which was why he had elected to oversee her transfer to Noctis City himself. The Noctis detectives – or noxious detectives, as he often thought of them – had banned him from questioning her further at the station, but if she happened to speak to him while they traveled on the train, then that couldn't be helped.

It was commonplace for the Martian Rails company to allow the MSS to requisition a passenger carriage attached to a scheduled cargo run for such transportation. It kept costs down, avoided interfering with the rail timetable and ensured prisoners were kept away from curious members of the public. If not always curious members of the skeleton staff that crewed the train on such journeys.

There was also a skeleton security detail with two uniformed MSS officers sitting at the other end of the carriage. Okoye, a jaded woman who had been with the service for at least twenty years, and Jeffries, a younger man who appeared equally as bored as she was with the job.

Deverau decided to lay out everything the farm crop deaths had caused. "Food shortages, rationing, rioting, global panic," he said. "You must be very pleased at what you have achieved."

Mel lifted her head and regarded him with disdain. "I'm not responsible, I told you."

"The detectives at Noctis City seem to think you are. Why would they think that?"

"Shouldn't you be asking them?"

That's exactly what he was going to do when they reached their destination. They could dismiss his calls, but they couldn't dismiss him so easily when he stood in front of them in their own office.

"I'm asking you," said Deverau.

Mel fixed him with a hard stare and he could sense her resentment. "I imagine I'm a convenient scapegoat," she said.

"That's not an argument that will stand up in court. Not when plants die in your lab at the same time as they start dying on farms."

"Then what do I need to say to convince you I'm not a saboteur?"

"You're a scientist," said Deverau. "Tell me about the science."

Alex attached the bomb to the rail as Ivan had shown him and felt the pull of the magnet as it hugged the metal. He flicked the switch on the detonator and a red light blinked to indicate it was ready to receive the signal.

He stood up straight and took in the landscape of Mars from the top of the Martian Rails. The vista of rusty red rock blemished with patches of green moss and yellow lichen was so vast that it made him dizzy, to the point where he could hear his own nervous breath within the confines of his rad-suit helmet. Even stepping onto the wide-open expanse of the planet's surface was unnerving for someone who spent his life inside the dome of a city, the enclosure of a bus or the walls of a farm. But standing on top of a twelve-meter-high structure built to carry trains between Deimos and Noctis Cities was beyond what he imagined.

They were too far away from either city to see them, even on top of the elevated track, but he could see the straight line of the constructed road that linked them, along with the winding paths made by rovers as they took less traveled routes off-road.

Rising up into the pink sky on the horizon were the cylindrical white towers of a processing plant pumping greenhouse gases into the air. Beside it, sitting in a natural depression, was the white, icy beginnings of a lake. The circular body of frozen water sparkled in the afternoon sun like a glistening white dinner plate nestled within an undulating red tablecloth. Tentacles of ice snaked from the edges of the lake where tributaries had formed when the temperature had crept enough above freezing to turn the top layers to liquid water, before they froze again.

"How are you doing?" said Ivan over the rad-suit's encrypted comms channel. He was standing about five meters further along the track, looking back at Alex.

"I've done two," replied Alex. "One more to go."

"Quickly. We haven't got much longer."

Alex reached into his backpack and pulled out the last of the bombs. Checking he had enough slack on his safety rope, he stepped across the track to place the package onto the rail. Its magnetic clip secured itself onto the metal, and Alex activated the receiver on the detonator and retreated.

"Done," he told Ivan.

They both made it back to the climbing cables they had used to ascend to the track. Ivan, as the more experienced, clipped on his harness first and began descending on the vertical zip wire. Alex saw Ivan's white-suited figure speed away towards the ground as he fumbled in the cumbersome gloves of his suit to fix himself to the wire. When he felt it click into place, he tugged at the harness to ensure it was secure. With a breath to restore his faith in the safety systems, he stepped off the track.

A moment of falling and a flash of fear. Then the braking mechanism cut in and slowed him for a brief, exhilarating rush to the ground.

Alex decelerated over the last meter so his feet alighted

softly on Martian soil. He turned to where Elea, Pete and Sammi stood at a safe distance by the Mining Guild truck. Unclipping himself, he ran as best he could in the bulky suit to join them. Within minutes, the train would arrive, carrying food supplies away from Deimos City.

The shame of being led, in handcuffs, out of an MSS van and onto the train had stripped away Mel's dignity. Martian Rails staff had watched with curiosity like she was an exhibit being displayed. It made her feel dirty. Even more so because she had spent two days in MSS custody without a shower.

She had told Deverau that restraining her was not necessary, but his only reply was that it was MSS protocol. He had secured the handcuffs without compassion, using a code on an electronic fob which he placed in his jacket pocket.

But he had offered a crumb. A chance to explain herself. The lawyer who had told her she was being transferred to Noctis City had warned her not to say anything to the MSS without legal counsel being present. But it wasn't the lawyer's future on the line.

"My work is supposed to help feed Mars," said Mel. "Entirely the opposite of what I'm accused of."

"You use viruses," said Deverau. "Viruses spread disease."

"My viruses infect cells to change specific parts of the genetic code. After they have done their job, they die. Their effect only lives on when the mutation is passed onto the next generation of plants through their DNA."

"But your experiment still died."

"I'm working on the theory it was an epigenetic failure."

Deverau's eyes narrowed with incomprehension and he

scratched at his temple with his index finger. "You'll have to forgive me, I don't have a degree in biology."

"It's like an extra layer of genetic regulation," said Mel. "Most people know DNA is the building blocks of life, determining everything from whether we're a human being to whether we have a big nose. But epigenetics doesn't use the standard four letter DNA code. Instead, it modifies DNA to switch genes on and off. Epigenic regulation can be triggered by altered environments, which could explain why my lab tests found no problems, but the crop failed when I moved to a field trial."

"What does that have to do with the farm crops?"

"Nothing." That was precisely her point. "Which is why I should be in my lab working on this problem, not locked up by the MSS!"

She had raised her voice in frustration and drawn the attention of the two MSS officers at the rear of the carriage who watched her with suspicious eyes.

"Unfortunately, my superiors in Noctis City disagree," said Deverau. "They suspect you're responsible for crop deaths on farms and, from what I've seen, the evidence backs them up. In my line of work, it pays to believe there's no such thing as a coincidence."

Indignation boiled inside her. "But I could be useful to Mars! You showed me images of dead potato plants – is it only potatoes, or has it spread? I'm the leading botanist in that area – I can virtually recite the potato genome off by heart. I need to be investigating this, not the one being investigated."

"And risk you manipulating the data to cover your own back? I can't see anyone agreeing to that."

The argument had slipped away from her. She scanned Deverau's eyes for a flicker of understanding or even sympathy, but his expression had hardened. She knew she could prove her innocence, if only if she was given a chance to unlock the scientific evidence.

The white-painted bullet of a train sped toward the six bombs, its Martian Rails red logo blurring with the movement.

With shallow breaths of anticipation, Alex waited for the inevitable. He glanced at Ivan, who stood with his thumb poised over the detonation device with its radio aerial extended to above his helmet. Elea, Pete and Sammi regarded him anxiously, their expressions clear through the visors of their rad-suits. Ivan kept his gaze fixed on the train.

"Ivan!" urged Pete over the comms, speaking for them all as they feared the train would pass.

"Not yet!" said Ivan.

Alex looked up at the train, now directly in front of him, mere meters from the explosives. He understood that firing them too early would allow sensors on the track to communicate with the train and give it time to stop before it reached the damaged section, making it too difficult for them to reach. But this was leaving it too close.

The nose of the train sailed over the bombs.

"Now!" Ivan yelled.

He hit the button on the remote.

Flashes of flame blasted from the ammonium nitrate under the belly of the train. The exhilarating fireworks ate up the oxidizing agent packed inside the bomb. Flares of orange escaped to find traces of oxygen in the atmosphere and burned for a brief, bright moment. Alex imagined the metal of the rails twisting with the explosion as Ivan had told him they would. From his position on the ground, it was impossible to see it actually happening.

The rumble along the track would have caused the railway's emergency systems to cut in. The train slowed, but did not falter.

"You fired it too late!" shouted Sammi.

Alex didn't want to admit Sammi could be right and willed the train on.

Until the central carriage hit the site of the explosion and jumped half a meter into the air.

"Yes!" he shouted. The squeals and thrilled yells of success from the others echoed over the comms in his helmet.

The carriage landed back down on the rails and, like a gymnast missing her footing on a balance beam, slipped and toppled. It threatened to take a suicidal plunge over the side and was only saved by its attachment to the rest of the train.

The carriage hung precariously over the edge, suspended improbably in the air with the carriages either side of it maintaining their fragile grip on the rail.

It swayed, then settled. Ripe for plundering.

CHAPTER THIRTEEN

The train jolted violently.

Mel was thrown sideways. She only stopped her face from hitting the window by slamming her cuffed hands against the glass. Brakes screamed from beneath them as the force of metal upon metal tried to stop the train.

Deverau jumped to his feet and craned his neck at the window to try to see what was happening.

The male MSS guard, who she had overheard being called Officer Jeffries, ran down the aisle and slammed his hand against the intercom by the side of the connecting door. "This is MSS in the central passenger carriage – what's going on?"

The female guard, Officer Okoye, left her post and rushed to join Deverau. "Can you see anything?"

Mel, still sitting, watched the panicking MSS officers with the increasing realization that, if something serious had happened to the train, they would care more about saving their own skins than thinking about protecting hers.

The train lurched again. Deverau fell backwards and hit

his head hard on the metal frame of a seat as he went. Jeffries was catapulted into the door, but remained standing. Okoye managed to make a soft landing on a seat, but Mel was hurled onto the floor.

She skidded along the aisle on her elbows and knees. The friction burned her skin. Her momentum stopped at the soles of Deverau's shoes where he lay on the ground. He was conscious but groaning from the fall. Deverau put his hand to the back of his head. When he removed it, there was blood on his palm.

Mel kept still, ignoring the stinging in her elbows and knees, denying the notion that she should be afraid. Thinking of how she could take advantage of the situation.

"Inspector!" Okoye shuffled off the seat she'd been thrown into and knelt down beside Deverau's chest. "Are you all right?"

As he groaned a noncommittal reply, Jeffries raced to the window. "The train's come off the track." He pressed his hands up against the glass as he tried to see more. "One of the carriages is hanging over the edge."

"What?" Okoye jumped up to look too, leaving Deverau to recover on the floor.

Which was when Mel noticed the flap of his unfastened jacket, laying at the side of his body, revealing his inner pocket. She pressed her grazed forearms into the floor, silently wincing at the grit pressing into the wounds, and shuffled subtly forward.

The carriage shifted suddenly. Mel took in an involuntary sharp breath. The short jolt was enough to imply they were resting in an unstable position.

"What do you think you're doing?" Jeffries yelled at Okoye. "Your body weight'll tip us over the edge!"

"It wasn't me," Okoye insisted, backing away from the window.

In the commotion, Mel reached out for Deverau's jacket pocket. Finding the presence of mind to focus, she slipped her cuffed hand inside. Her fingers touched something as smooth and small as a pebble. Scrabbling it into her palm, she withdrew her clenched fist. Glancing up to see Deverau emerging from his dazed state, she held on tightly to her prize and shuffled away from him.

Alex clipped his harness onto the climbing wire and hit the control. The mechanism propelled him up the side of the tower holding the elevated rail above the rugged Martian landscape. He took one last look at the incredible view before glancing above him as the harness automatically slowed his ascent as he reached the top.

Ivan was already up there, standing beside the rail on a narrow ledge never meant for people to walk on. He pressed himself against the body of the train, partly obscuring the letter T of the painted Martian Rails logo. Ivan reached out an arm to Alex. As he grabbed it, Alex felt the strength of his friend's grip which gave him enough reassurance to release himself from the climbing wire. Nevertheless, he was relieved when Ivan secured him to the safety line.

"Both up," Ivan reported to the others waiting on the ground.

Alex looked along the line of the stricken train, with the carriage precariously hanging over the edge. There was an eerie stillness about it. Like it was sitting securely on top of the track, held on by its connection to the rest of the train, while at the same time, it was prepared to fall with the slightest movement.

If it did, the safety systems would uncouple and sacrifice the one carriage to save the rest. Which meant Alex and Ivan should be safe enough in the less precarious sections. Until the emergency services reached the scene – and they had every intention of being gone by then.

The bombs may have damaged the rail and possibly blown holes in the body of the train itself, but from where they were standing, there were no obvious points of entry. Just an outline of sealed emergency doors cut into the steel fabric which could only be opened from the inside.

"We're going to have to blast our way in," said Ivan.

He reached into his backpack to retrieve the last of the bombs.

"Are you sure there's no one in there?" said Alex.

"No windows means it's a cargo section. I told you, a train like this is going to have a maximum of three members of staff on board. They'll most likely be up front with the steward or at the rear. Don't you think I made sure of all this before we stuck six bombs under the train?"

"I only wanted to check." He felt embarrassed to have even mentioned it.

Ivan edged his way along the ledge and shimmied past the *S* and the *L* of the logo to where the line of a door was cut around the letter *I*. He placed the bomb on the center, the magnet held it in place, and he began to shuffle back.

A sudden blast sent puffs of escaping air out into the Martian atmosphere. The door panel was blown off and tumbled end over end towards the ground. The force of it knocked Ivan off his feet and his body followed the falling door.

"Ivan!" Alex yelled.

Ivan fell a meter before his harness snagged on the safety line. He was left dangling on the line attached to his waist, slowly spinning as his arms and legs struggled to regain control. Beneath him, the door landed in a cloud of dust.

Alex breathed out a silent thank you as he tried to work out what had gone wrong.

His first thought was the bomb had gone off too early, but it was soon obvious the explosion had come from inside and was too small to have been a bomb. Someone had triggered the emergency evacuation procedure. An escape slide, bright green to show up against the red of Mars, burst out of the hole created by the discarded door and unfurled like a giant tongue down to the planet.

So much for there being no one inside.

A rad-suited figure emerged from the train and sat on the evacuation slide. The inflated cushion of air bounced a little as gravity took them and the figure slid safely down to the planet's surface.

Alex waited a moment, but no more members of Martian Rails staff followed.

Ivan had managed to grab hold of the safety line to stop himself from spinning and pull himself up vertical to sit in the harness. He was breathing heavily over the comms and Alex made a conscious effort to keep his own nervous breaths away from the microphone in his helmet.

Alex double-checked his safety line and pressed himself

against the body of the train. He edged his way along, as he had seen Ivan do. When he was close enough, he crouched down to reach out a hand. Ivan took it with a firm grip and Alex helped him climb back up.

"Here we go," said Ivan. He moved back along the train and stepped through the opening.

Alex followed, waiting until the last minute to unclip his safety line before slipping his foot inside and jumping down into the carriage.

Turning, he saw what they had come for: boxes and boxes of food supplies.

A pre-programmed female voice spoke clearly and calmly from speakers hidden in the carriage. "The train has stopped as a safety precaution. All passengers are asked to prepare for evacuation. There is no danger at this time, but passengers are advised to carefully make their way to an evacuation pod. Rad-suits are supplied for emergencies only. Please do not stop to put on rad-suits unless instructed by a member of staff."

Green arrows flashed on the floor, lighting the way to the front of the train.

Officer Jeffries picked Mel up by the arm. Roughly tugging at her ligaments so her feet barely touched the ground, he dragged her back against the direction of the arrows and threw her onto her seat.

"Stay there," he ordered.

He immediately turned his back on her and she considered running. But with no plan or place to run to, she elected to appear quiet and compliant while waiting for her moment.

Okoye helped Deverau to his feet. The inspector swayed a little as he grabbed hold of the frame of the seat he had hit his head on. A drop of blood from his wound dripped onto his white shirt.

Two overhead compartments above the seats where they were standing popped open and the arm of a rad-suit dangled down like it was reaching out to them. The pre-programmed voice repeated its message. "The train has stopped as a safety precaution…"

Behind her, the door to the next carriage slid open and a man dressed in the green of a Martian Rails uniform ran in.

"What are you doing here?" he shouted at Deverau and the officers. "Didn't you hear the announcements?"

"What's going on?" said Deverau, still woozy.

Air rushed past Mel's shoulder, being drawn through the open door into the next carriage where the same pre-programmed voice was making a different announcement. "The integrity of this compartment has been compromised. You are advised to evacuate immediately. Environmental conditions approaching safety limits. The integrity of this compartment…"

The voice became fainter, the air seemed in less of a rush and a glance behind confirmed to Mel the door was closing to seal off the breach. She had less than a second to decide whether to take the risk.

She decided to run.

Mel jumped off her seat and caught hold of the closing door before it met the frame. Pushing with her cuffed hands, she forced it back until there was enough space for her body to slip through.

She was in a cargo hold with beige fiber boxes of supplies stacked on either side of a narrow walkway. A single line of flashing green arrows told her to go back the way she had come. The cold was biting. The icy air clawed at her throat. She realized she was taking in faster and deeper breaths. Her lungs were working harder to find oxygen as the atmosphere in the carriage leaked out.

"Environmental conditions approaching safety limits. The integrity of this compartment..."

She needed to do something about the leak. The cargo hold wasn't meant for people, there were no overhead bins containing emergency rad-suits because there were no seats. But beside the door was a white cabinet with black and yellow hatchings around the edge. Very welcome red lettering on the front read: *Emergency Rad-suits*.

Mel pulled at the cupboard handle and it opened with little force to reveal four suits packed neatly inside, complete with helmets and air tanks. She yanked at the nearest one and it unraveled at her feet. But to put her arms into the sleeves and secure the helmet, she needed her hands free.

Mel fumbled in her pocket with her right cuffed hand and grasped the smooth, round fob which Deverau had used to lock her wrists together. It was a simple device with a number pad and a main enter key.

She pressed her thumb onto the enter key and wriggled her wrists. The jaws of the cuffs bit into her skin as tight as ever. Refusing to accept the rapidly advancing realization that the fob required a code to activate, she hit the enter key again. And again. The handcuffs remained locked.

She peered through the glass at the carriage she had escaped from. Deverau and the officers were still with the member of staff. At her feet, flashing green arrows urged that she return to them. The strain on her lungs, drawing in huge breaths to find enough oxygen, told her she didn't have much longer. The pain in her wrists reminded her she was not free.

She watched Deverau turn to realize the seat where Mel had been sitting was empty. He looked towards the door and she felt the chill of his anger as their eyes met through the barrier of the closed window.

Deverau stared at his prisoner, separated from him by the reinforced glass panel of a closed door leading into the next train carriage.

Furious that he had taken his eye off his charge, he rushed to the door and slammed his palm on the control. A display on the panel informed him the door was locked.

Jeffries and Okoye ran up behind him with their shockguns drawn.

Deverau must have communicated his anger at their incompetence because they both looked suitably embarrassed.

"Deverau!" It was Mel's voice over the intercom. "I'm running out of air in here. I need to get out of these to get into a rad-suit."

She held her hands up to the window to show the handcuffs locked around her wrists.

"Open the door!" he shouted into the intercom.

"No," said Mel. "Give me the code."

She twisted her fingers around to reveal the electronic fob she had stolen from him.

Deverau, in panic, plunged his hand into his left jacket

pocket to find it empty. Embarrassed at allowing himself to be pickpocketed, he checked the right jacket pocket just in case, but there was nothing there. He slapped his hand angrily against the door release.

The panel defied him. The sign continued to state it was locked.

Deverau turned to Jeffries. "Can you shoot it open?"

Jeffries shook his head. "With a mechanism like that, a shockdart's more likely to fuse it shut."

The man in the Martian Rails uniform shouted from behind them. "We need to get off this train! The carriage is stable for now, but I don't know how long that will last."

"I'll take 'for now'," said Deverau.

"It's not up to you. I'm putting myself at risk to make sure you're safe."

"You can leave if you want," said Deverau. "But first, I need you to get this door open."

The man frowned, maneuvered warily past Jeffries and Okoye's shockguns, and pressed exactly the same button as Deverau had done. "It's locked," he said.

"I can see that – get it open!"

The microphones were still active between the two compartments and he could hear Mel's labored breath. She had activated an air tank on one of the rad-suits and had wedged the helmet under her arm so she could keep dipping her face into it to breathe some of its oxygen-rich air. It would buy her some time, but it wouldn't keep her alive for long.

"The carriage has been breached, it's locked for safety reasons," said the man. "She needs to open it from the other side. It's to stop people going the wrong way in an emergency."

"There must be an override! What if someone was injured and incapacitated in there?"

"A rescue team could gain access or it can be overridden from the steward's cab."

"Do it!" ordered Deverau.

The man ran up to the intercom on the other door. Mel tapped the fob on the glass. "Code!"

"Come in here and I'll give it to you," said Deverau.

Mel shook her head. "No way. If I have to face trumped-up charges at Noctis City, there's no telling if I'll ever get out."

Deverau glanced behind him. The train man was getting no answer to his calls. He was running out of options.

"Come on, Deverau," said Mel from the other side of the door. "Where am I going to go? We're in the middle of the Martian plains."

Deverau swore. He suspected she was bluffing, but he couldn't know for sure. Swallowing his pride, he reeled off the set of memorized numbers. "Four, four, eight, nine, seven."

With each word, Mel pressed the corresponding number on the pad. At the last one, a massive grin formed on her lips as the cuffs opened, slipped from her wrists and clattered to the floor. She turned from the window and Deverau lost sight of her.

The man returned from his fruitless attempt to raise someone on the other intercom. "There's no reply, the steward must have evacuated. Like we should have done minutes ago."

"Inspector," said Okoye. "We need to get to the evacuation pod. You shouldn't put yourself at risk for her."

Deverau turned to the man. "You have evacuation chutes, don't you?"

"Every other carriage," he acknowledged. "But passengers are supposed to go to the pod. You need rad-suits to use the chutes and most members of the public haven't used one since training at school. People in a panic don't always put them on properly and you end up killing more passengers than if everyone had stayed on the train."

The man's unhelpful attitude was infuriating. "Do I look like a member of the public to you?"

Angry, with his pounding head adding to his irritability, he turned to Okoye and held out his palm. "Give me your shockgun."

"What?" She blinked in confusion.

Deverau clicked his fingers. "Your shockgun. Now!"

Okoye passed it over.

Deverau examined it. It was primed with five darts. More than enough to overpower his fugitive.

"You and Jeffries get to the evacuation pod," he said, reaching up to the open overhead bins and pulling down two rad-suits. "Train guy – whatever your name is."

"Liam," said the man.

Deverau looked at both suits, found the emblems which indicated one was more suitable for Earth-borns and the other more suitable for Mars-borns and chucked the larger suit over to Liam.

"Liam, get suited up, get to the steward's cab and get that door open," he said, kicking off his shoe and placing one leg in the smaller suit. "I'm going after her."

CHAPTER FOURTEEN

Alex lifted another box from the top of a stack in the cargo carriage, leaned backwards so its weight was closer to his center of gravity, and stepped carefully toward the chute leading out of the train and down to the surface. He placed the box on the edge and gave it a gentle push. The container slid down a couple of meters before its top half conspired to accelerate faster than its bottom half and it tipped over. It rolled end over end until it crashed at the bottom.

Alex rested against the doorway. The boxes were heavy and had probably been stacked by robots back at Deimos City. After moving only half of the ones they needed to move, he was feeling the ache in his arm muscles.

Ivan placed the next box on the chute without obvious effort. There was no apparent difference in the way he gave it a gentle push, but for a reason only a physicist could fathom, it slid down the inflatable slide without even looking like it might tip over.

Ivan slapped Alex on the shoulder as he stepped back from the opening. "No time to rest," he said over the comms.

Alex took a breath and turned back to the boxes. At least half of the freight compartment had been sent down the chute to where Pete and Sammi were waiting to load the boxes into the truck. It still looked a daunting task to move the rest.

"Ivan, I estimate you've got ten minutes before you need to get out of there to avoid us running into any rescue or investigation party," came Pete's voice over the comms.

"Thanks, Pete," replied Ivan. "How are you doing down there?"

"Just about keeping up," said Pete. "We've only seen two members of Martian Rails staff evacuate – you were right about there being a skeleton crew on a freight service. They're sensibly staying well clear of us, but Elea's keeping an eye on them in case they try to cause trouble."

"Good," said Ivan, carrying another load to the chute.

Alex wrapped his gloved hands around a box at the back of the train, ordered his tired arm muscles to brace themselves, and lifted. A sudden movement at the end of the compartment caught his eye.

A rad-suited figure ran in from an adjoining door.

He dropped the box in shock. "Ivan!"

The figure stopped short and Alex saw the two frightened eyes of a woman staring out from the visor. Her head turned from Alex to Ivan and back again.

"Steady," said Ivan.

"Is she one of the train staff?" said Alex.

"They should all have evacuated by now."

The woman appeared to be saying something, but if she had her comms switched on, her voice wasn't relayed across their encrypted channel.

Alex leaned sideways to check the carriage behind her. He saw no one else, only more boxes.

The movement startled her and she raised her hands. The universal sign that she was unarmed and was of no threat.

"I think she's alone," said Alex.

"Then we can overpower her if necessary," said Ivan.

The three of them faced each other. No one daring to move.

Deverau stared at the control panel beside the locked door.

"Come on, come on!" he said under his breath. He heard his own voice, unusually loud within the confines of his helmet, and remembered how much he hated rad-suits. It had been almost a year since his last MSS mandatory training in the things.

Even after five years on Mars, he found the restricted view inside them frustrating and the awkward way he had to move in them even worse. His only consolation was that Mel would be in the same predicament.

The display above the panel changed from *locked* to *unlocked* and the door popped open a crack. "Finally!"

Deverau flipped off the safety on the shockgun, readied his finger on the trigger, and stepped into the next carriage.

Rows of beige storage containers stacked up to the ceiling ran the length of the compartment, with only a narrow walkway down the center. Beside him, on the wall next to the door, a white cabinet had been wrenched open and a spare rad-suit lay on the floor, but there was no sign of Mel. He held out his gun and took careful steps forward, his back against one line of boxes, watching out for any hints of movement – as much as he could see in the wretched helmet – with both his weapon and his mind prepared to fire at a moment's notice.

He paced the length of the carriage, not really expecting his prey to still be there waiting for him. Which he confirmed when he reached the far end and found the door unlocked.

Peering through the window, he saw the adjoining freight compartment was mostly empty, other than a few stacks of boxes at the far end. A flash of something white moved out from behind one of the stacks.

Deverau ducked back from the window and turned from the door. He pulled the gun in close to his chest, with the barrel pointing to the ceiling, as he visualized how he was going to enter the carriage to confront the rad-suited figure. Instinctively, he quietened his breath, even though he knew no one could possibly hear him in the helmet.

Deverau turned, kicked the door aside, aimed his weapon out in front of him and burst his way in.

The same rad-suited figure he had seen through the window was carrying one of the boxes to a gaping hole in the side of the train where the fading light of the Martian day cast shadows over the uneven terrain.

The figure turned and, through their visor, Deverau saw it was a young man. The man's eyes widened in surprise and then fear as he saw the gun trained upon him. His mouth opened in a panicked cry Deverau couldn't hear and he stepped toward the hole. Deverau continued to aim his weapon, but the man wasn't his target and he held his fire.

The man dropped the box out of the hole and jumped after it.

Deverau ran forward and saw the man sliding to safety

down an evacuation chute. At least, he thought, he hadn't jumped to his death.

Another flash of white made him turn. A second figure he hadn't seen – lying in wait in his helmet's blind spot – threw one of the boxes at him. It must have been heavy because it fell far short of its mark, but Deverau still jumped back. The box landed on its corner and burst open, spilling packets of rice at his feet.

The rad-suited figure had to be Mel. She ran for the opening. Deverau fired. She leapt forward, diving head first onto the chute, and the dart whizzed past to strike the edge of the hatch.

Deverau raced to follow and paused at the dizzying opening, twelve meters up above the Martian plains. He gasped at the expanse below, but had no time to hesitate. Reminding himself of the need to catch up with the rad-suited figure, he subdued his natural anxiety and jumped.

He landed buttocks-first on the inflatable, which bounced with his sudden weight. It tipped him over backwards and he slid inelegantly sideways, flapping his arms to try to right himself as the gravity carried him down. Below, the fleeing figure skidded to a stop on the Martian dust and was helped to their feet by somebody waiting at the bottom.

As the person stood, they glanced up at Deverau and he saw it wasn't Mel, but another young man. The youth grinned as he turned and ran away with his companion to a waiting vehicle.

Deverau's boots struck the ground and he scrambled to his feet just as the vehicle sped off in a cloud of dust.

He looked around for Mel, but the only other people out on the planet's surface were a group of five in rad-suits sitting two hundred meters away on an outcrop of rock who paid him no attention. Presumably they were the evacuated train staff and the two useless MSS officers who didn't so much let the prisoner slip through their fingers, as turn their backs while she walked away.

Rad-suits were deliberately white so any lost person could easily be seen against the Martian landscape. But he saw no one else. With no cities or other buildings nearby, he had a full view of almost three-and-a-half kilometers in every direction before the curvature of the planet fell away at the horizon.

He turned his head at the flash of movement in his peripheral vision. Above, hanging off the edge of the elevated rail, teetered the stricken train carriage. Threatening to fall.

He ran on instinct. Struggling to move his legs fast in the cumbersome rad-suit, he stumbled on the uneven terrain. With a last glance behind to check he was clear, he lost his footing and belly-flopped to the ground. Skidding to a halt in the dust, he rolled himself over to see what was happening.

Less than twenty meters away, the carriage lost its battle with the pull of the planet. Metal pieces from the couplings on either side flew off like startled birds. It hung for a moment, half on and half off the elevated platform, as if scared to take the final step. But there was nowhere else to go. Defeated by its own weight, it tipped sideways and tumbled.

Falling in the slow motion of Martian gravity, its descent was almost graceful. A ballet of somersaults cut short by a sudden impact with the ground.

The crash reverberated underneath him. Smashed pieces spiraled from the wreckage and Deverau gasped as he saw a fragment of metal spinning towards him.

He turned just in time for it to ping off the back of his helmet. Followed by the clatter of raining dirt and debris. Then silence.

He sat up and the particles of dust which had landed on him slid from the surface of his rad-suit. Meters away from him, the carriage lay split open.

Deverau realized how close he had come to being inside of it. And how foolish he had been to dismiss Liam's warnings. If the carriage had fallen sooner, it could have been his body that broke on the hard Martian surface.

He stood to see a fleet of emergency vehicles rushing towards him. The plumes of dust sent up by their tires suggested a sense of urgency.

But it had come too late. The train had crashed and Deverau's fugitive was in the wind.

CHAPTER FIFTEEN

Having slipped unseen into the thieves' truck, among the towering piles of badly stacked boxes as it bounced across uneven ground, she was a free woman. At least for now.

The two men stealing from the carriage must have thought she wasn't a threat, otherwise they might have stopped her when she ran for the evacuation slide. They didn't know, of course, that she would stow away on their vehicle. And they wouldn't have to know, as long as she kept herself hidden behind the boxes and slipped out when no one was looking.

Whenever they reached their destination. Wherever that was.

CHAPTER SIXTEEN

Ivan drove the truck into the main Deimos City transport hub where buses came and went from the surface of Mars. It was the perfect place to open up the back, unseal the boxes and distribute the stolen food.

Within minutes, anyone who was traveling anywhere, along with half the transport staff, were clamoring to grab whatever they were offered. The word spread quickly and soon there was a horde of people with their hands outstretched at his feet.

The elation was like nothing Alex had ever experienced. Greater than walking out of school for the last time, greater than his dad returning from orbit with a gift for him when he was a child, greater than the first time he kissed a girl.

It was not the adulation, because he knew none of the crowd really cared who he was, but the feeling of giving back to the people what should have been theirs to start with. The gratitude on their faces sparked a warm excitement inside of him and he couldn't stop smiling beneath the scarf he had tied around his face to protect his identity.

Ivan, meanwhile, had taken center stage. He literally stood in the middle of the truck, with his toes on the edge, while the rest of the gang handed out food around him. He had brought two loudspeakers, which he had wedged into either side of the truck, and used his WristTab to transmit to them.

"The food we produce on Mars should belong to the people of Mars!" his voice boomed through the speakers.

Around half the crowd – their emotions already running high as they fought to get the handouts – cheered.

"The corporations think they can steal supplies for themselves," he continued. "They think they are protecting their interests, their rich chief executives and their privileged friends by stockpiling supplies. But we have shown them that we will not be denied what is rightfully ours. The workers who toil in the mines have just as much right to eat as the people in suits who sit in meetings all day – more rights, I would say! The child in school, the woman in the oxygen plant, even the man who cuts your hair deserve access to the food they need to live. Humans came to Mars for a better life. We were promised that life and we will not have it taken away from us!"

Alex had his back to the crowd, opening the next box to grab at the packets of bread inside, when someone pushed him out of the way. He assumed it was Pete or Sammi or even Elea being in a rush, but as he stumbled sideways, he saw it was a stranger. A skinny man, wide-eyed with both excitement and desperation. Alex was about to push him back when Pete was suddenly there.

"Oi!" Pete grabbed the man by his jacket and dragged him away from the box. His feet scrambled to find footing on the floor as he was virtually lifted into the air.

The last Alex saw of his face was the look of shock as Pete spun him round and flung him into the crowd. The man's arms flailing, he landed on the sea of bodies, their outstretched hands catching him like he was one of the food parcels they craved.

"This is getting out of control," Pete said into Alex's ear.

"Yeah." The transport hub was full of people now, all of them clamoring for free food and many of them whipped up by Ivan's inflammatory words.

A woman jumped up onto the truck and ran right past Elea. Elea tried to grab her, but her reactions were too slow and the woman was soon diving into the nearest box. Another person climbed into the truck where Alex had left it unguarded. Two more followed. It was the start of an invasion they couldn't hope to stop.

"We need to go," said Alex.

Pete nodded and rushed over to Ivan.

"We demand that all stockpiling stop!" Ivan was telling the crowd. "We demand–"

Pete yanked at Ivan's WristTab arm and his broadcast abruptly ceased. He looked like he was about to yell at Pete, but they were suddenly surrounded by the hungry masses. In the jostle to scramble onto the truck, one of the speakers was knocked to the ground and people started using it as a step.

It was ugly. Savage. The sophistication of the human race, with its ability to travel to other planets, reduced to the base instinct of feeding itself.

Elea and Sammi jumped down with whatever packages they still had in their arms. Alex, at the last minute, dove into two open boxes and grabbed a loaf of bread and a packet of something – he didn't know what – before joining them.

Among the crowd, he was turned from an exalted bene-factor into someone in the way. He forced himself against the flow of people and pulled off the scarf to meld into the sea of bodies.

He became like them. Pushing and shoving indiscriminately to selfishly make his way to safety.

Deverau stood halfway up the steps of the transport hub and looked down at the mess below.

The perpetrators of the riot were long gone, slipped out in the mass of the crowd, while a handful of MSS officers called late to the incident were powerless to intervene. Three injured people lay on the ground. One had twisted her ankle so far around her leg that the toe was pointing behind her instead of in front. It was a grotesque sight which a paramedic hid under a blanket while administering some medication to stop the poor woman going into shock. Two others had been taken to hospital with breathing difficulties from being crushed. Another five sat in various corners of the hub, clutching bleeding arms and faces, or simply staring out into the distance.

Deverau had got the call about the food riot while in the MSS vehicle that had picked him up after the train raid. Rather than going back to the station, or seeing a doctor as one of the officers had advised him, he had arranged to meet Jones at the scene of the crime.

"You think Doctor Erdan was here?" said Jones, standing beside him.

"Has to have been," said Deverau.

He had ordered an MSS team to search the vicinity of the

train crash, but he knew it was a waste of time. The jury was out on whether Mel was sprung from the train by a gang posing as thieves or whether thieves had targeted a cargo train and she was lucky enough to be caught up in the criminal enterprise. Either way, she must have escaped on the truck. The same one Deverau was staring at, abandoned in the hub.

"It was lucky no one was killed," said Deverau.

He began to contemplate how he was going to catch his missing prisoner. Which he would have to do on top of finding the reprobates who had staged the food riot. All while the increasing unrest in Deimos City sapped MSS resources.

"You should get that checked out," said Jones, indicating the back of Deverau's head.

Deverau tentatively touched the sore, swollen bump and felt where dried blood had matted into his hair. "So I've been told."

"You said you were dazed and nearly passed out. You might have concussion."

"Don't make a fuss, Jones. If I'd wanted to be made a fuss of, I would have stayed on Earth with my mother."

"Is she the reason why you left?"

"No," he snapped.

In truth, Deverau missed his mother. He missed his father, two sisters and the whole extended family. Leaving them behind was the hardest thing he had to do when he came to Mars and, although the MSS recruitment officer had told him receiving video messages from home made the separation easier, it was a lie.

Even so, he had to admit Jones was probably right about his wound.

"I'll stop by the MSS doctor on call on my way home, if that makes you feel any better. While I'm there, I'll see if I can figure out what I'm going to say to those charlatans at Noctis City about letting their suspect escape."

CHAPTER SEVENTEEN

Fate had landed Mel back in Deimos City. The arc of the familiar dome overhead, which had always been a symbol of safety, had become a canopy of vulnerability. With every step through its streets, every turn around every corner, she feared the MSS would be waiting to re-arrest her.

She wanted to return to Isaac and Daniel, but she knew the MSS would find her. Isaac would certainly put himself at risk to help her and she couldn't let him do that. She needed him to be safe and look after Daniel. So, even though she desperately wanted to hold her family close and tell them everything was going to be OK, it was too dangerous.

As she had told Deverau on the train, the key to proving her innocence lay in the science. Returning to the Tall Greenhouse was impossible. After her home, it was the next place that Deverau would think to look for her. Even if she was able to get in and up to her lab without being reported by one of the hundreds of people who worked there, she wouldn't have the days, weeks or even months to continue her work. So she went to see the only friend she knew might be able to help: Kaito.

She took a nervous ride on the public tram to the area of the city where Kaito lived, all the time wondering if the other passengers were looking at her. It made her so anxious, she got off a stop early and walked the remaining twenty minutes to Kaito's apartment building.

Kaito was not a creature of habit. She would work late if she needed to and stop off somewhere on the way home if she felt like it, but at some point she would have to come home. So Mel waited there, huddled against the corner of a building, until she saw Kaito's recognizable hurrying figure approaching from the other direction. Mel slipped round onto the main street and quickened her pace to catch her friend before she disappeared inside.

Kaito stopped mid-stride when she saw her. Her expression ran through recognition, surprise and shock.

"Mel!"

"Hello, Kaito."

Mel managed an apologetic smile, pleased to see her friend, but also guilty to be involving her.

"You're alive! Thank goodness!"

Kaito stepped forward and drew her friend into a hug. The warmth of Kaito's body was so unexpected and caring that she wanted to cling onto it. But if she allowed her emotions to surface, she feared they would eat away at her strength.

"You heard about the train?" said Mel.

"It's on every WristTab on the planet," said Kaito. "But I only knew you were on the train when Isaac called me. He had a visit from some MSS officers saying they couldn't find you after the crash."

The sudden, unexpected mention of Isaac drew the heat of tears to Mel's eyes. Her vision blurred, but she didn't let them fall. "How is he?"

"He thinks you might have been killed. He wanted to know if I'd heard anything. I said I hadn't, but I can call him now."

Kaito went to lift her WristTab to her mouth, but Mel reached out and grabbed her arm. "Don't!"

The shock on Kaito's face made Mel realize how tightly she was holding her and she released her grip.

"Mel, what's going on?"

"I escaped, Kaito. I'm on the run. You can't tell anyone. Not even Isaac."

"Even if he thinks you're dead?"

It was an awful thing to do to the man she loved, but it was necessary. "He'll know I'm alive when they don't find a body."

Kaito stared at her, aghast.

Mel wasn't sure what she could see. Perhaps her desperation. Or her exhaustion. Even the fear she fought to hide from herself. But, whatever it was, it caused Kaito's expression to soften into one of sympathy.

"I can only assume, then, you came to me for a reason."

"I need a lab, Kaito," said Mel, pleased to be able to concentrate on the practical and leave the emotion out of it. "I need somewhere to work where I can analyze samples from the farms and prove I'm not responsible. I know you have contacts. I'm hoping you can help."

Mel watched her friend's sympathy turn to doubt and then regret. "I'm sorry, Mel. That's going to be a problem."

Mel's hope evaporated.

"If you don't want to be involved, I understand," she said. Even though she didn't.

"It's not that," said Kaito. "I've been asked to lead the scientific team trying to stop the contagion spreading and secure what food supply we have left. I'll be using all my contacts in the operation. More to the point, I'll be under scrutiny. It would be too risky for you."

"You'll be investigating what happened at the farms?" asked Mel.

"That's part of the remit, but it won't be the main focus."

"Then you'll prove I didn't poison the crops?"

"I'm going to try, Mel. But if I'm seen to be diverting too many resources to clear your project – which I supervised – I risk being taken off the team altogether. With the situation as it is, the priority has to be feeding people."

Mel, despondent, stepped back into the street, her mind numb. She had only one plan and that had been taken away from her.

"Why don't you come inside?" said Kaito. "I still have the spare room you can use and I have some food stashed away from before rationing. I'll arrange for a legal team to take on your case and make sure EcoLine supply the best. It's ridiculous to think you had anything to do with this."

Kaito turned to enter her apartment building, but Mel didn't move. She longed for the softness of a bed, the warmth of a meal and the cleansing feel of a shower, but she dared not succumb to the temptation.

"The MSS know we are friends. If they come looking, they will find me."

"There must be something I can do." Kaito looked at what

must have been Mel's disheveled appearance. "At least let's get you a change of clothes."

"OK," said Mel. "Thank you."

Kaito disappeared into her apartment building and re-appeared a few minutes later carrying a battered holdall. "There's a set of my clothes in there, but they might be a bit small for you, so I dug out some of Andrei's old clothes I still had hanging around. I thought, because they're men's clothes, they might work as a disguise."

"Thanks." Mel took the bag from her.

"I've been meaning to get rid of them. As if it wasn't enough him leaving me heartbroken, he had to leave half of his unfashionable wardrobe as well."

Kaito was making light of the situation, but Mel was too wrapped up in her troubles to smile.

Inside the bag, she found a couple of shirts and two pairs of pants. None of them would be a perfect fit, but they would do.

"I've put one of my hats in there from the time I had that hideous haircut," Kaito continued. "And there's some food and water. I wish I could do more."

"These will help."

"Let me transfer some credits to your account as well. I don't want you to run short of money."

Mel shook her head. "I can't access my account, the MSS will be able to trace me."

"Do you really think they'll do that?"

"They invoked special powers to arrest me, placed me in handcuffs and dragged me off to Noctis City because they consider me to be some sort of prime suspect. So, yeah, I really think they'll do that."

"Mel, I'm so sorry. What are you going to do now?"

"I don't know," she said. "Even if I did, it would be safer not to tell you. Then you won't have to lie if you're questioned by the MSS."

Kaito gathered her up in another hug. It was warm, but no longer soothing. Mel was distracted, already thinking about her next move.

"I'll find a way to fix this, I promise," said Kaito. "Then, when food rationing is over, we can have that dinner."

"That would be nice," said Mel.

She turned from her friend's concerned face, gripped the bag tightly and walked down the street. With each step, ideas formed in her mind. Hope renewed itself as she pieced them together, realizing she didn't need Kaito to make a new plan.

CHAPTER EIGHTEEN

The logo of the Helion corporation, with its strong metallic *H* in a circle of bright yellow and its shooting arrow, filled Alex's screen as he waited for the connection to confirm. The symbol represented the ultra-light solar sails on which the corporation had built its reputation – and its fortune. The propulsion system, which used giant mirrors to catch radiation from the sun, like a sailing boat catches the wind, was fitted to some of the early probes that journeyed to the outer solar system and the unmanned cargo ships that brought supplies to the original settlers on Mars.

Alex shuffled on top of the covers of his bed to sit cross-legged as he waited. An endless loop of soothing music confirmed the audio connection to the space station was functional.

The logo blinked off, the music faded, and the smiling face of his father filled the screen. Bobbing gently as he floated in microgravity.

Alex always thought of his dad as bearded and remembered, when he was a small boy, how his bristles tickled his face when he gave him a squeezing hug. But when he was in space, his father kept himself clean shaven and his hair incredibly short.

"Hey, Alex!" said his dad, his voice relayed from tens of kilometers above the planet.

"Hey, Dad. What's it like up there?"

He waited the obligatory fraction of a second while the communication relay sent the audio up to his father, he listened, and his reply came back to Mars.

"Dark," said his father with a chuckle.

It was a family joke. Every time he was asked that question, he always said that space was dark. Because, in the grand scheme of things, even with the bright disc of the sun illuminating the red globe of Mars, most of it was.

"Really, Dad. What's it like? You know, with everything that's going on."

His father's smile lessened a little. "The work is the work, as always," he said. "Preparations for the Soletta project are going well. I should be travelling out to the Lagrange point to help with construction in the next couple of weeks. Not that I'm allowed to say much more about that because of the corporate confidentiality thing. But the boffins are doing their sums, scratching their heads and figuring it out, so everyone's optimistic."

It sounded amazing. Exciting. But so very far away. "So you're OK up there?"

"Sure! We always had to eat what we were given anyway, so the rationing's not making much of a difference out here. Besides, there's usually someone slipping a few credits to the importer folks to get us something special when there's a shipment from Earth. What about you?"

Alex wanted to tell him about everything he'd been doing with Ivan. How they were standing up for the ordinary person on Mars. He wanted his father to be proud of him. But he couldn't be certain no one else was listening. Either out in the space station with his father or eavesdropping on the communication circuit.

So he kept his answer vague. "I wish I knew what was going to happen. Everyone's on edge."

"Is it as bad on the farms as they're saying?"

"No one tells us. We're spending a lot of time sterilizing the fields now in case the crop death is lurking somewhere."

His father nodded sympathetically. "And your mother?"

"She's Mom," said Alex. "You know how Mom is. She always says everything's fine, even when it isn't."

His father chuckled again, but this time both of them understood it wasn't really funny.

"Hey, Alex, I have to keep this short. My shift's about to start."

Alex felt the familiar pang of his father going away. "Will you be coming home soon?"

"Not until things settle down, is what we've been told. They say we're better off out here for a while."

Alex expected the disappointment, but it didn't lessen its impact. "Well… see you soon."

"Bye, Alex. Be good."

His father reached up to touch the screen. The image of his face blinked off and was replaced with cold, white words against a black background: Connection Ended.

CHAPTER NINETEEN

City dust, trapped in the grime left by myriad fingers on the access pad at Isaac's workplace, pressed grit into Mel's fingertip with each digit of Daniel's birth date. After more than a year, she hoped that sentimentality – or, perhaps, laziness – meant that Isaac hadn't thought to change the passcode for the back entrance of the logistics depot. Even though security protocols meant that he should have.

The door clicked open and Mel allowed herself a moment of relief. But gaining access was only the first step.

Lost in the baggy clothes of Kaito's ex-boyfriend, with her hair under the brown beret that had once concealed a misguided haircut, Mel could not hide in Deimos City forever. Even if hiding had been her plan. She needed to be free of skulking in the shadows, she needed access to a lab and she needed help.

Her hopes lay in Pedro Serrano. He worked at an outpost close to the Tharsis mountains where there were ample facilities, few scientists and no MSS officers. It had been a long time since they had been good friends at Mars University. More than good friends. If she was able to reach him, she believed he would help her, despite the intervening years.

Hiring a rover or taking some combination of public transport was too risky, even if she had access to the credits to pay for them. Without knowing anyone rich enough to own their own rover, Isaac's logistics depot offered her another way. She had visited several times in the past, knew her way around and had a plan to stow away on a truck leaving the city. If she could get on board without being caught.

The hum of electric vehicles, hubbub of voices and bustle of moving personnel that drifted through the crack of the open door was a good sign. People came and went every day from the depot and the more there were, the more chance she had to be just one stranger among many. She stepped through.

Parked inside, a giant truck covered in a film of Martian dust blocked her from view of most of the depot. Affording her extra cover for her clandestine entrance.

The anatomy of the building was as she remembered. To her right was the exit to the back service road for internal deliveries or accessing an airlock to leave the dome. To her left, a rack of rad-suits were plugged into replenishing ports. Above and to the side was the glass-fronted corridor of the management offices on the mezzanine floor where Isaac worked.

Her longing drew her to go to him, but logic pulled her back.

Isaac had to be her trump card in case she got caught. A card she did not want to play.

With her beret turned toward the mezzanine floor and any security cameras that might be watching, Mel grabbed a rad-suit, helmet and boots from the rack. Useful accessories to make her inconspicuous among the workers and essential for a journey out of the city.

Turning from the rack, she saw the whole vista of the depot in front of her. A multicultural mix of small, large, dusty, clean, interior and exterior vehicles arranged in five patient lines waiting for their scheduled departure. Among them were the workers. Hurried and leisurely they rushed and meandered between the rows, tired at the end of their shift or fresh and ready to start work.

Above the activity, a status board showed two departures due to leave for the mountain mining regions within the next hour. Mel took note of their numbers: *ROB547* and *ROB981*.

She forced herself to appear relaxed as she wandered the lines of vehicles, searching for the matching serial numbers. Until she found *ROB547*.

She walked casually on for five more nervous seconds before ducking behind the truck. Sandwiched between its rear end and the front of an internal delivery van, she felt for the release button at the base of the cargo door and pressed it with her palm.

Nothing happened.

She hit the button harder. The vehicle did not respond. She was locked out.

Frustrated, she leaned back against the door as an alarm bellowed a warning all around her. Fearing she'd been spotted, she considered running when the truck she was leaning against shifted forward. She stumbled to regain her balance.

Other vehicles in the lines on either side were also moving and she relaxed a little as she realized what was going on.

She had heard the alarm before. It had been on a visit to see Isaac a few years before. It had made her jump while everyone around her had been still and they had laughed at her. It was a siren to alert everyone on the floor of a departing vehicle, which was so commonplace in the depot, people who worked there tended to tune it out.

When one vehicle left, the others moved forward down the lines in an automated waltz to fill the gap at the front of the queue. The only thing that would stop them, other than a manual override, was if the safety systems detected a foreign object in the way. Mel realized she was that foreign object and if she didn't move out of the way quickly, she would draw attention to herself.

She darted out from between the vehicles and the lines glided forward.

Mel resumed her search as the automatic waltz of vehicles came to a halt. A man up ahead of her climbed into the cab of a large truck, swinging the door shut behind him. As he did so, she saw its serial number: *ROB981*.

It was the truck she needed. She reached out to touch the side of the vehicle as she walked along its length, tracing a line in the dust on its exterior.

The cold, inert metal beneath her fingers woke with a sudden tremor. A soft hum and a continual, subtle vibration told her the vehicle was drawing power from its electric engine.

Mel slipped around to the rear and located the control for the cargo door. Willing it to respond, she pressed with the heel of her hand.

The faint whir of a motor replied. The cargo door began

rising, lifting her emotions with it, and revealing a waiting darkness.

She threw in the rad-suit, helmet and boots. Then, when the gap was wide enough, she scrambled in after them.

The light from the depot was enough to confirm that she was the only cargo.

She found another button inside and sealed herself into the dark emptiness.

CHAPTER TWENTY

Mel was jolted awake by the truck suddenly coming to a halt. She must have fallen asleep after putting on her helmet and activating the rad-suit's environmental controls before exiting the airlock at Deimos City. She was thankful she had. The rear compartment of the truck was almost certainly sealed against letting in any dust from the planet's surface and might even have had some provision for heating the container to above zero to stop transported goods from freezing. But it had no separate air supply and wasn't meant to keep humans alive.

Pulling herself from sleep, she checked the locator on the arm controls of the rad-suit and confirmed she was at the destination promised by the departure board: Ceraunius Tholus. The mountain was one of a cluster of volcanos in the Tharsis region which were ripe for mining. When Mars was younger, the volcanic activity would have melted the metals in the rock, creating rich seams of vital resources such as iron and titanium. Which meant it was a prime spot for the Mining Guild to set up operations, pulling in workers from the surrounding cities of Tharsis, Deimos and Noctis. It was also Mel's stop.

She scrambled to the rear and hit the internal switch to open the cargo door. Uncertain what it was opening onto, Mel huddled underneath a dust sheet and left just enough of her visor uncovered to assess her surroundings as light began to bleed through the crack. Checking the controls on her rad-suit again, she watched the temperature and pressure drop until they were what she would expect from the Martian surface in the middle of the day: minus one Celsius with a pressure of 0.1 bar and oxygen levels at around five percent.

The lifting cargo door turned the crack of light into an opening which allowed Mel to see out onto the Martian landscape. The red slope of a dormant volcano rose up to her left, while the gray heaps of loose slag sat to her right, looking almost like a small range of mountains in their own right. The ones nearest to her had probably been there the longest because the sides that caught most of the sunlight were tinged with the yellow of lichen. There were, however, to her relief, no obvious signs of people.

Aware that the white of her rad-suit would make her easily visible to anyone who might look, she kept the dust sheet wrapped around her and crawled along the floor of the truck. At the opening, she hung her legs outside, threw the dust sheet behind her and hopped off onto the ground.

Her boots hit the compacted soil, where truck after truck must have driven, and produced a tiny puff of dust. She peered around the side of the vehicle and saw that it was facing an airlock large enough to accommodate supply vehicles.

Mel turned on the general communications channel to

listen in to any chatter coming from the mine. There was no guarantee that if anyone spotted her, they would use that channel to alert others, but it was the only early warning sign open to her and she would be foolish not to take advantage.

But, as she moved away from the back of the truck, all she heard was the driver requesting clearance to open the airlock and a rather bored-sounding operator complying with the request.

Mel kept herself close to the slag heaps as she pulled up the locator on her arm controls to bring up a route that would take her to the Squyres Research Outpost. The Inventrix-funded station was at least a half hour walk over native terrain which hadn't been fashioned into any sort of road, even a dirt track. But her suit had enough power to last and, even taking into account the exertion required to walk, she had around forty-five minutes of air remaining.

She had the resources to walk to the outpost, but not to make it back. She considered the sobering thought. It was still possible to change her mind, to seek refuge in the mine where there would be enough air and energy to sustain her for much longer.

But, if she did that, she might as well not have escaped from the train.

The truck that had brought her from Deimos City disappeared into the mouth of the airlock and was swallowed up by the mine. Ahead of her, a dumper truck backed up to the newest slag heap at the end of the row of hills and tipped its contents of waste rock alongside. Mel crouched, listening to the silence of no one communicating on the general channel, and hoped that if the dumper was being driven by a human, they would not notice or care that she was doing her best to hide from them.

The dumper truck went on its way. Mel stood and began her walk to seek help from Pedro.

It had been many years since she had walked on the surface of Mars and she had forgotten how hard it was. Not only to carry the extra weight of the suit and the air tank, but also to traverse the uneven ground.

Soon, the buildings of the research station came into view on the horizon. The three semi-circular, translucent domes of their experimental growing facility bubbled up like foam forming on the surface of a liquid.

All the while she listened to the communications, sometimes flicking through the other channels, but never hearing another human voice. Only her own breath and the occasional grunts of exertion.

Rad-suits could not transmit signals far. They were designed for close contact communication, usually among groups such as construction or research crews working on the surface. Even so, she dared not try to make contact with the outpost until she was sure it was the only place that could hear her calls for help.

Eventually, the domes loomed large and the neighboring human habitation zones came into view with their higgledy-piggledy mix of building materials, from reused spaceship hulls to the ubiquitous red bricks made of compressed soil. Mel stopped and opened up communications on the general channel.

"Squyres Research Outpost, respond please."

She waited. There was no answer. Not entirely unexpected.

The skeleton personnel who worked there would not be constantly listening out for messages from random people who happened to wander by. She checked the stats on her suit. She had fifteen minutes of air left – less than she had expected, but more than enough. She resumed her walk.

"Squyres Research Outpost, respond please." Her voice sounded strange and lonely, speaking to itself within the confines of her helmet. She tried to sound more urgent, but not desperate. "Squyres Research Outpost, *please* respond."

An almost imperceptible click from the speaker by her ear gave her hope that someone was listening. "Uh, yeah, this is Squyres," said a disinterested male voice. "Who's this?"

"I'm a friend of Pedro Serrano," said Mel.

"That's nice for you," came the sarcastic reply.

"I need to speak to him."

"Over the comms channel? Can't you use a WristTab or a screen like anyone else?"

"I'm outside."

"Outside?" The responding comms channel clicked off for a moment, like the disinterested man was liaising with someone else or saying something rude they didn't want to broadcast. "This is a research station, you know, not a bar where you can stop by for a few beers when you feel like it."

"I understand that," said Mel, straining her patience. "Can you please tell him I'm here?"

"He's on a rest cycle right now."

"Can you just tell him an old friend from university is here?"

The man let out a groaning sigh and this time he didn't shut off communications to hide it. "I suppose so, if I must."

She wasn't sure how he did it, but the way he turned off his side of the channel sounded like the audio equivalent of slamming a door.

Mel headed for the largest rusty red accommodation block which was likely to be the main entrance. She checked her suit again and watched the gauge showing her remaining air tick below ten minutes. She tried to calm her breathing to preserve the supply, but she was both exerting herself and nervous, so it probably didn't make much difference.

"Hello?" she called out over the channel. "Pedro?"

Reaching the complex, she clenched her hand into a fist and banged it against the airlock door which was big enough to accommodate a rover. It was like hammering on the door of a stone tomb. It didn't feel like her fist made any impact at all.

"Pedro? Squyres Research Outpost? Anyone?"

She checked her stats again. She had less than five minutes. Enough time to contemplate how foolish she had been before she had nothing left to breathe.

The subtle click of the comms channel turned on at her ear. She allowed herself to take in a relieved breath of precious of air.

"Yep, hello, this is Pedro."

She recognized the beautiful, Earth-born accent of the man who had once been her closest friend. "Pedro!"

"Who is this?" he demanded.

She didn't want to say her name over the comms. "You have to let me in."

"There's no sign of a vehicle outside the station."

"I'm not in a vehicle."

"You're *on foot*?" he exclaimed in disbelief.

"Pedro, don't you recognize my voice? I've got less than five minutes of air left."

"Then what are you doing out there? Hold on."

The channel clicked off again. Within seconds, the airlock door began to open.

Mel stood for a long, impatient moment waiting for it to rise to chest height and then ducked her head under the door to enter the airlock.

She stumbled only a few paces before she sat down to save both air and energy and waited for the airlock to close again.

Bathed in brightness from artificial lights much brighter than the Martian sun, she saw that she was in a room big enough to park a rover. Even after the door had closed again, it would take time to repressurize.

Mel stared at the environmental indicators on her arm as the temperature climbed into positive numbers, the percentage of oxygen rose from five to six and then seven percent, and air pressure steadily increased to 0.5 bar.

The claustrophobia of being enclosed in the suit suddenly took hold and she fumbled to tear off her helmet in thick, unwieldy gloves. But she couldn't activate the catches where it attached to the rest of her suit and the harder she tried, the more she panicked.

In her agitated state without the external microphone activated on her suit, she didn't see the inner airlock door open and a man rush in. But suddenly he was kneeling on the floor next to her and helping her off with her helmet.

Mel breathed in a deep lungful of air and looked up into the face of a man who was both familiar and unfamiliar. The deep black hair which he had once worn in a floppy fringe across his forehead had been shaved into a buzz cut and his once-smooth chin was now sporting a neat beard. But there was no mistaking the brightness of the eyes staring down at her.

"Pedro?" she gasped.

"Mel!" The voice, which she hadn't heard for so many years, sounded sweet as he said her name. "What are you doing here?"

"I need your help," she said.

CHAPTER TWENTY-ONE

Deverau opened the small refrigeration unit and stared into the third of a cubic meter of chilled air. He had no food in his apartment.

He slammed the fridge door shut and it reverberated on the countertop. Looking around at the collection of used cups on the side, he counted five of them. Which meant it had been five days since he had had the time or the inclination to clear up the place. Deciding to ignore them for another day, he squatted down and opened the door to the under counter cupboard where he kept food that didn't need to be refrigerated. Or would have kept it if he had actually bought any.

There was only a kitchen towel and an untidy collection of spare packets of vitamins, microbiome supplements and epigenome pills. Everyone on Mars was supposed to take them every day to compensate for the amount of radiation they were exposed to. But, as he rummaged in the cupboard, it was obvious he had too many spares for someone who actually remembered on a daily basis.

In a dark corner at the back, his hand touched something that clearly wasn't a packet of vitamins, but the smooth, cylindrical shape of a half-liter bottle. Pulling it out into the light, he saw it was a bottle of beer. The sort he didn't usually drink because it was brewed with ginger.

Memories of the man who had left it in his cupboard rushed back to him with a tinge of regret. It was almost a year since Jessie had walked out on him and gone back to Earth. Deverau thought he had expunged all traces of him in the apartment they had once shared. It seemed he had not.

But the beer, even though he didn't like it, was calories. After a pressured week at work, both the calories and the alcohol would be welcome.

Deverau took hold of the countertop and pulled himself back up to standing. He made his way to the sofa which was dominated by a screen along the far wall and called for it to turn on.

The latest from ICN appeared in front of him as he flopped to sit. Farah Sharif was giving a news conference as part of her latest attempt to pretend she was in complete control of the situation. He might have immediately turned the screen to something more palatable, but standing next to her at the podium was the scientist recruited to rescue the planet from the crisis.

She was the same woman who had greeted him at the EcoLine labs when he had brought Mel in for questioning. ICN moved to a close-up and the screen was filled with the larger-than-life head and shoulders of Doctor Kaito Tanaka.

"We believe we have isolated the contagion on the farms of

Mars," said the scientist. "This is allowing us to ensure that all fields are safe to resume food production in earnest."

Doctor Tanaka glanced down at her notes, which allowed an unseen journalist behind the camera a chance to interrupt. "What about the suggestion that the fields were sabotaged?"

Deverau watched the scientist squirm under the unexpected scrutiny and chuckled to himself. With a nervous clearing of her throat, she looked directly at the camera, pointedly ignoring the question.

"Agriculture works on a three month average growing cycle for most crops," she said. "With time required on either side for planting, harvesting and processing. However, we are looking at the possibility of harvesting some crops earlier. Although this reduces yield, it will bring food to the table quicker.

"Clearly," she continued. "Shortages will persist and we estimate this will be the case until extra supplies arrive from Earth. But Chair Sharif has been working on a tightening of the ration program to see us through. Farah?"

Doctor Tanaka looked somewhat relieved to be passing the issue back to the politician. ICN cut to a close-up of the chair of the Terraforming Committee.

"Shut up!" Deverau told the screen. The broadcast went mute before Sharif had a chance to say anything. He had no wish to listen to the irritating politician tell him how hungry he was going to be over the next three months.

He twisted the cap on the beer bottle and flung it aside. The cap bounced off the sofa cushion, landed on the floor and rolled to settle somewhere behind him. He decided it would have to stay there until he could be bothered to find it and pick it up. Possibly in a couple of months when work had calmed down a bit. Assuming the whole of Martian society hadn't imploded by then.

Deverau swigged from the bottle and grimaced at the hit of ginger. He never understood why Jessie preferred beer which had been ruined like that. But then, he never understood why Jessie was so keen to come to Mars then decided he hated it so much that he wanted to go home. Or perhaps, Deverau wondered – not for the first time – if *he* were the one who Jessie had learned to hate, and Mars had merely been a convenient excuse.

Either way, Deverau had come to Mars because that's what his partner wanted, and now he was the only one still living here.

He took another mouthful of beer and ignored the taste as he waited for the alcohol to enter his bloodstream.

Deciding it was safer to occupy his mind with work rather than his regretful past, Deverau ordered the screen to bring up some of the MSS files he hadn't had a chance to review while he was in the office. He scrutinized images of the gang who had virtually caused a riot when they handed out food at the transport hub. They had covered their faces with scarves and hats so only their eyes were visible, deliberately preventing the computer from identifying them. The result was a long list of possible suspects that needed an actual human being to wade through.

His WristTab bleeped and the annoyance of being disturbed made him feel tired and stressed all over again. The display on the screen was overlaid with a notification that Superintendent Kim at Noctis City HQ was calling him.

Because it was linked to the wall screen, that also started bleeping to add irritation to his annoyance. Rationalizing that he was off shift and not in a polite enough mood to risk talking to a senior officer, he rejected the call.

He knew Kim was going to put more pressure on him to find Mel. So he compiled a terse reply in text. He told her he would be happy to re-arrest their prime suspect if he wasn't spending all his time dealing with public order issues under instructions from HQ. He added that he would, however, put out a public "wanted" appeal for Mel in the morning.

Finally, he turned off his WristTab, disconnected his screen from calls and messages and went back to trying to relax on the sofa.

He must have fallen asleep after that because the next thing he was aware of was loud knocking on his apartment door.

He stirred in his seat. The bottle that he still held loosely in his hand tipped over and spilled the last dribble of warm, gingery beer over his groin.

He swore as he brushed splashes of liquid off his clothes. With the sound of Jones calling his name from outside, he dragged himself up to standing, took a moment for his head to clear and made it to the door.

He unlocked it to reveal his clean-shaven and neatly dressed, but exasperated, sergeant.

"Did you turn your WristTab off again?" Jones frowned. "I've been calling."

"Uh…" Deverau glanced at his WristTab and tried to focus. "Probably."

Jones looked his boss up and down with disapproval. "Did you sleep in your clothes?"

Deverau regarded his crumpled self and saw the wet patch the spilled beer had left in an unfortunate place. "That's just a… I spilt my drink when *somebody* woke me up. What are you doing here, anyway?"

"Early start this morning – remember? We're supposed to be planning how to divert resources to guarding food supplies and potential trouble spots."

Deverau had a vague memory of making that arrangement. He turned from Jones and went back inside his apartment. "You better come in while I wash and get changed. If I'm going to be late, you might as well be late too."

As he passed the screen, he saw that it was still showing the same list of suspects from the food riot, none of whom he had had a chance to investigate. He ordered the screen to turn off, regretful that the detective work he was supposed to do as part of his job would have to wait. Again.

CHAPTER TWENTY-TWO

Mel told Pedro everything as she lay back in the safety of his sofa, her hands cupped around a mug of hot water infused with mint leaves which he said were plucked from a bush he had grown himself. As she talked, the years fell away and it felt like she was back in his room at Mars University, discussing the merits of engineering Earth plants to grow on Mars versus engineering Mars so it could grow unadulterated Earth plants.

It seemed that becoming older, moving away and starting a career had done nothing to relieve him of his habit of keeping his room a mess. The small living area that he had been allocated at Squyres Research Outpost was crammed with objects that looked like they had been dumped weeks before and forgotten about. From inside out T-shirts that were due a wash, to a tablet which had sat on the little table by the sofa for so long that it had run out of power. There was a separate, cluttered bathroom – which she had gratefully availed herself of – and a closed door which almost certainly led to a messy bedroom.

None of that mattered, as she looked at his face with its strange new beard and short hairstyle and allowed the trauma of the last few days to spill out. He listened, quietly and patiently, focusing on her words as he sat on an office chair beside a desk piled with eclectic detritus including a used breakfast bowl with the spoon still sticking out of it.

Mel finished her story and reached into her near-empty mug to retrieve one of the mint leaves. She placed it in her mouth and sucked the last of the fresh, tingling flavor from its cells.

"So," said Pedro, taking a moment for it all to register. "You got married."

She laughed – his statement was so unexpected. She had given him a complete picture of the horror of her failed experiment, escape and arrest. And yet, that was the detail he picked out. "Yes." She nodded. "I got married."

"Is he a nice guy?"

"Isaac is a great guy." Mentioning his name brought back the memory of his face and the longing to be back home with him and Daniel. She wondered when she would get the chance to see them again. "We have a little boy, he's one."

Pedro gave her a sympathetic smile. "You must miss them."

"Very much."

The tantalizing taste of the mint leaf was spent. Mel pushed it from her mouth with her tongue and dropped it back into the mug. Pushing Pedro's dead tablet out of the way, she cleared a little bit of space on the table beside her to put the mug down.

"What about you?" she said, turning the tables.

Pedro sat back casually in his chair and shrugged like there was nothing to tell. "Still living the single life, as you can tell."

He glanced around his messy room. "There was someone for a while, but… it didn't work out."

"I'm sorry to hear that."

"It was a good thing, really. It gave me the kick up the backside to come out here and sink my teeth into some proper research. When Inventrix recruited me out of Mars University, they promised I would get opportunities to work on some of their big projects. Tharsis Republic wanted to use an Inventrix facility to carry out experiments on growing forests and so I made sure they took me on. I like it here. There's a small team, we get on with it and we don't have to deal with all the craziness you get in the big cities, like the MSS arresting you for no good reason."

Mel slipped her legs off the sofa and sat up properly. "I need to prove that my experiment didn't cause this food plague – or crisis, or shortage or whatever you want to call it."

"I'm sure I can get you access to the research facilities here if I don't mention to the others that you're a wanted fugitive," said Pedro. "But you will need access to your experiment and the affected farm crops to make a comparison and we don't have those here."

"You have contacts, don't you? In the scientific community?"

Pedro scratched his beard in thought. "There are a few people I can approach," he said. "I imagine access to samples of both will be restricted, but I might be able to circumvent that through unofficial channels."

"I'd be grateful for whatever you can get," said Mel.

"I'll give it my best shot," said Pedro.

CHAPTER TWENTY-THREE

The heads of the civilians in the bus nodded in unison with each bump on the road to Noctis City. Alex tried not to be like them. He tried to resist the motion, but it made him feel travel sick and he soon succumbed to the jolts and knocks of the vehicle's ineffective suspension system.

Strangers grumbled about not being able to take the train because of repairs following the "terrorist incident", as Martian Rails described it. Alex waited for them to acknowledge that the attack had liberated food from the greed of the corporations and to be grateful it had been handed out to ordinary people. But no one mentioned it and his acclaim never came. So he listened with increasing anger, glad that Ivan and the others had inconvenienced the grumbling people's day.

If Ivan had shown him anything, it was not to accept what he was given without question. Which was why he was going to Noctis City. In the past, his applications to work in space had been rejected and he had ended up working on the farms. Corporations saw Alex only as some words in a file which were easily dismissed. But he was going to show them, in person, that he had the determination to succeed. Like his father, he deserved to be given a chance away from the stifling gravity of Mars.

So he had skipped his shift at the farm and got on a bus.

The bus let off its passengers at the Noctis Transport Hub and then it was a short tram ride to Corporate Square.

Its domineering buildings faced into the center from all four sides with corporate logos emblazoned across the facades like giant billboards. A pictorial reminder of the organizations that ran Mars.

It had been years since he had last been there on a visit with the school. All the children had been encouraged to point to the corporations that employed their parents. He remembered proudly yelling at the Helion building with its yellow and gray logo and saying that his dad worked for them. Then spinning on his heels and pointing at the Teractor building on the opposite side, with its triple pointed orange logo, and saying that's who his mom worked for. With the naivety of a child, he expected everyone else to be impressed, but they were too engrossed bragging about their own parents to pay any attention.

It was the yellow circle which Alex was drawn to again. As he walked towards it, he remembered how, on that school visit, the center of the square had been bustling with individual food and drinks stalls selling a variety of cuisines from a mix of Earth cultures. The teachers had told them they were very expensive and only for the likes of the busy, highly paid people in charge of the corporations, and the tourists who came to marvel at the headquarters. But the teachers somehow found enough money to treat their pupils to half a dozen buns made with sweetened bread dotted with preserved fruit. Alex, like the other children, was allowed to tear off a piece from one of the buns to eat. He could still remember the heavenly taste. It made him feel hungry just to think of it.

There were no school parties this time, no food stalls and only the occasional person rushing into the buildings on unknown corporate business. Which made the gathering of six Earth tourists in the middle of the square more obvious than they might otherwise have been, standing clustered together with the Martian tour guide towering over their strange, short bodies. The Earth-borns, who had spent considerable sums to travel for months in space to visit Mars, stared in awe as if they had never seen buildings before. A man and a woman were making banal comments in loud, Earth-accented voices, while the rest stood watching as they chewed on snacks half hidden in their hands. Like the food crisis meant nothing to them.

Alex turned away from them in disgust.

The two glass doors at the entrance to the Helion building sensed Alex's approach and slid sideways to allow him into the plush reception area.

Unlike the tired frontage of the building, it was clean, neat and spacious. He had the strange sensation of his feet padding on the almost-spongey covering of a corporate dark gray carpet – a rare imported luxury. To his left, a suite of wide, sprawling sofas covered in Helion yellow fabric offered visitors a space to sit in style. To his right, a collection of plants with dark green fronds, which he understood to be some sort of miniature palm trees, grew from a tiered arrangement of white pots. But it was the massive cinema-style screen hanging from the double height ceiling and angled at forty-five degrees towards him which drew his eye.

The screen, clearly aimed at impressing new arrivals, was showing footage of a Helion space station in orbit. Its blue-tinged solar cells basked in the sunlight around a collection of white, cylindrical habitation pods which appeared bright above the glowing red globe of Mars and against the blackness of space.

Alex couldn't help but stare at the screen. In turn, two of the six security guards placed around the entrance kept a close watch on him. Self-conscious under their gaze, he pulled his attention away.

Three receptionists in pristine, identical uniforms in Helion colors of dark gray jackets and yellow shirts sat waiting behind a crisp, white desk which curved around them in a semi-circle.

That's all they appeared to be doing, sitting and waiting. As if the corporation was so affluent, it could afford to decorate its HQ with idle people.

Alex opted to approach a woman on the far end who had a pale but friendly face and wore her hair pulled back tight into a ponytail. Mars-born and closer to his age than her two male associates, he judged she was more likely to be sympathetic.

He put on his most confident and friendliest smile and walked across to stand, expectantly, in front of her.

She was staring at a screen embedded in the desk and continued to do so without regard for him waiting there. Alex leaned across to see what was on the screen and caught only a glimpse of the wall of text she was reading before she flicked the screen onto a blank standby mode and looked up.

She did not return his smile. "Can I help you?"

"I've come about a job," said Alex.

The woman looked distinctly unimpressed. "Which job?"

"A space job – in orbit." He pointed back at the giant screen and immediately felt foolish because the receptionist presumably knew what "in orbit" meant.

"Do you have a name?"

"Alex," he said. "Alex Pawlikiewicz." Out of habit, he spelled all twelve letters of his surname.

She re-awakened her screen and made a note. "Take a seat," she said, without looking up.

Alex retreated to the yellow sofas where he was made to feel small on his own in the middle of four broad seats. The cushions were a lot harder than they looked and made him sit up straight rather than sink into them. As he waited, his attention was drawn again to the giant screen hanging from the ceiling. It now showed an animation of the Soletta project his father was working on.

An authoritative male voice commentated over rousing music from speakers hidden somewhere behind the sofa.

"The Soletta Project is Helion's most ambitious endeavor yet, set to make the biggest change to the lives of ordinary Martians since the Terraforming Announcement."

On the screen, the animation showed the inner solar system with the small, red dot of Mars the furthest away from the bright yellow sun and dwarfed by the blue globe of Earth.

"Ever since humanity left its birthplace to colonize other worlds, people have dreamed about recreating the conditions of their ancestral home. Helion has been at the forefront of this movement, contributing resources so that Mars can, one day, be a place where forests, oceans and wildlife thrive in a rich environment. But one reality has always prevented us from achieving this goal – Mars is further away from the sun than Earth. We can terraform the planet, introduce greenhouse gases, engineer plants to survive in harsher conditions – even create an artificial magnetic field to protect us from radiation. But the sun will never get closer. Which is why Helion is developing the solution: the Soletta Project."

Virtual cameras on the animation swooped and zoomed into an empty sector of space. As the voiceover spoke, the proposed technological achievement came to life on the screen.

"When the sun shines towards Mars, only a fraction of its valuable light and warmth reaches the planet. Most of the sunlight simply passes by without ever touching the red planet. But what if we could capture that valuable resource and shine it back onto Mars? Helion has already developed prototype mirrors to project light and heat onto small sections of the planet, but Soletta is something much more ambitious.

"At the Lagrange Point, where the gravity of the sun is cancelled out by the gravity of Mars, Helion will construct a giant mirror with unique translucent properties. It will allow the heat and light from the sun to pass directly through. While, at the same time, it will reflect back the sunlight bounced off a whole network of small, specially angled mirrors situated in orbit around Mars. From the point of an observer standing on the surface, it will appear that the sun shines brighter and more powerfully than ever before, increasing the amount of light and much-needed heat reaching the red planet."

With the music building to a crescendo, the animation

changed to imagined scenes of a completely terraformed Mars with ocean waves crashing on a beach of rusty red sand. Children in loose, thin clothing splashed at the water's edge under a sun twice as bright as Alex had seen in real life.

Alex had been so mesmerized by the promotional video that he hadn't seen the woman emerge from behind the reception desk. Suddenly she was standing in front of him, gazing down with an apologetic frown.

"I'm sorry," she said. "I can find no record of you starting a job with us."

Alex felt a flush of embarrassment at being caught out and hoped he wasn't blushing. "No, I'm not starting a job – I've come to see you about a job."

The woman's frown deepened. "Have you applied?"

"Well...," said Alex. "I have in the past."

"Your name didn't come up in a search. Let me check I've spelt it right."

She turned and headed back to the reception desk. Alex took that as a sign to follow, spelling out the twelve letters of his surname all over again. When she sat down, she tapped away at her screen, but her frown remained. "When did you apply, exactly?"

"Exactly?" Alex thought for a moment. He had just left school, so he had to have been about sixteen. "To be honest, it must have been about two years ago."

The woman shut down the screen again with a dismissive flick of her index finger. "That explains why you're not on the system. You will need to apply again."

Alex deflated. He had convinced himself on the long journey that all he needed to do was appear at Helion headquarters and they would re-consider. "They only rejected me because I haven't got the qualifications to enter the training program," he explained. "Which is why I'm here in person, to prove to you that I have the drive and initiative to make a success of it. My father already works in space, so I know what it entails. This job is in my family – it's in my DNA. I'm keen, I'm young and I can learn."

She shook her head. "I'm afraid, it has nothing to do with genetics or your age. It's about taking on the most appropriate applicants."

"I can be appropriate!" said Alex, aware that he was raising his voice and not caring. "Get someone to come here and talk to me. I can tell them. I can *show* them."

"You're welcome to apply again," the woman insisted. "Although, we have recently had a successful recruitment campaign on Earth with employees due to start training when they arrive in the next month or so."

"I can start training now!"

"I don't believe there are any vacancies."

Frustration turned to rage. "You're rejecting people who already live on Mars to train people from Earth?"

He shouted so loud, the other receptionists turned to stare at him and he felt the eyes of at least two of the security guards zeroing into the back of his head.

"Not me personally," said the woman. "Now, I suggest you leave and re-submit an application in case a suitable vacancy comes up."

But Alex was in no mood to leave. Certainly not to be rejected by a receptionist without even being given the opportunity to speak to a real recruiter. "You're Martian –

how can you sit there and defend a policy that gives priority to Earth-borns over people like me?"

"Only Earth-borns with the proper qualifications," she said.

Alex suddenly sensed a presence at his back.

"Sir, I believe you have been asked to leave," said the quiet, but firm voice of an older female at his ear.

"I'm not leaving until I've spoken to someone!"

"I think you've done enough speaking for one day."

The hand of the security guard gripped his upper arm and pulled him back from the reception desk. He tried to shake it free, but she was remarkably strong and didn't let go. He looked into her passive face and saw no emotion whatsoever, like she had hidden her humanity beneath her uniform.

Alex resisted as he was led back towards the entrance. "They're tossing Mars-borns onto the scrap heap," he shouted as the other security guards looked on and two employees who had walked into reception also stopped to stare. "The corporations are keeping food for themselves and pleasing their masters on Earth by giving the best jobs to Earth-borns. We can't let them do that. We're Martians! We're the ones who built this planet!"

The two glass doors opened dutifully as the security guard dragged Alex in front of them. She kept walking until she had deposited him into Corporate Square. Letting go of him with a shove, he stumbled another step before he was able to stand upright. The security guard, without a word, stepped back into Helion headquarters and the glass doors closed behind her.

Alex found himself standing alone surrounded by the powerhouses of all the corporations. Two Earth tourists turned to stare at him with disdain and he felt the heat of rage surging through his body.

The injustice of it all was suddenly perfectly clear. The corporations may have been pulling the strings on Mars, but they were only serving their more powerful masters back on humanity's ancestral planet. If the voices of ordinary Martians were to be listened to, then they shouldn't be fighting people from Mars – they should be fighting people from Earth.

CHAPTER TWENTY-FOUR

Mel spent her first undisturbed night's sleep since her arrest on Pedro's surprisingly comfortable sofa. She had a wash, some breakfast – rationing, it seemed, had yet to bite at the research outpost – and she finally felt human again.

At least the MSS had not publicly revealed that Mel was a wanted fugitive and so Pedro was able to tell his colleagues a version of the truth which avoided them asking too many awkward questions. He said Mel was an old friend who had come to discuss her research, but gave her a false name and claimed she had suffered a rover breakdown, which was why she arrived on foot with no luggage.

She didn't know how long her cover story would hold, but it should keep her safe for a few days. Wearing some clothes borrowed from one of Pedro's female colleagues, she accepted his offer of showing her around. It would look strange, he pointed out, if a visiting scientist didn't get a tour of the facility. So he began by taking her to the smallest of the domes where the scientists had planted a forest.

It was like stepping into another reality. Her whole career

had been spent around plants, but the forest was a living ecosystem like nothing else she had experienced. She hadn't thought it was possible for there to be so many shades of green all huddled together under a translucent sky augmented by artificial lighting. But it was the smell that filled her senses and overwhelmed her with its vibrancy – so strong, she could almost taste it. It was like the hint of mintiness drawn out by the steam of her tea, but magnified a hundred times.

"What do you think?" said Pedro, standing beside her.

"Phenomenal," said Mel, still taking it in. "Impressive… I don't know what to say."

She looked more closely and began to identify the range of species that made up the shades of green. Small pine trees, various types of grasses, the white-capped growths of fungus, the mass of tiny emerald leaves of a ground-hugging bush, the arching fronds of bracken and the yellow of a single brave flower pushing up from a crocus bulb hidden beneath the soil.

"It's a fragile ecosystem," said Pedro. "Ideally, we would like to create a fully populated forest with insects, birds and bacteria, but we're restricted to flora at the moment and some limited soil-bound organisms. There's concern that insects could fly off and infest other plantations or even be the carrier of disease."

"Surely nothing could fly out of here and survive."

"I've made that argument, believe me. But I'm told, despite all of our precautions, something could attach itself to my clothes, hitch a lift with me on a rover and end up in one of the cities. It's annoying because we want to recreate a natural habitat where plants have a symbiotic relationship with their surroundings – insects to pollinate, birds to eat and spread seeds…" He trailed off and smiled to himself. "I'm droning on, I'm sorry. You know all this."

"You're frustrated, I get it," said Mel. "I wouldn't have made it as a botanist if I hadn't faced my own share of dealing with bureaucracy."

"Come on, I want to show you something."

Pedro led her through a path which looked like it had been well trodden by humans, to a section where the trees were taller, the bushes bushier. The plants appeared to be more mature than the ones closest to the entrance, although as Mel looked closely, she could see the diversity was severely restricted. There were only two species in the whole area which, she calculated, amounted to around twenty square meters.

"Was this area planted first?" she asked.

"No," said Pedro with pride. "Second."

She turned to him with a questioning glance. He was grinning and, she could see, still eager to explain.

"This is my experiment," said Pedro. "At some point, Mars is going to need forests all over the planet. When the conditions are right for plants to grow on the surface – not just moss and lichen – we're going to need to create a living ecosystem to maintain the atmosphere by soaking up carbon dioxide and generating oxygen…"

"You're droning on again," said Mel.

"Yes, sorry."

"It's fine." She could see he was excited and it was nice to be reminded that working with plants could sometimes be like that. "I don't mind."

"The point is, we're going to need plants, we're going to need a lot of them and we're going to need them quickly. We can't wait thousands of years for forests to develop naturally like they did on Earth. So I'm engineering forests to grow much quicker. It's just the two species so far, but I'm planning to extend that."

"How did you do it?"

Pedro grinned at the chance to explain his achievement. "By increasing the ability of these plants to fix carbon dioxide from the air."

Mel stared at him as she made sure she had heard him properly. Photosynthesis was a naturally very inefficient process and many eminent scientists had claimed it could be improved upon. But, even though they had tried, no one had actually been able to better millions of years of plant evolution. "I thought that area of research was a dead end."

"I figured, just because no one else had managed to improve how plants harvest light energy, it didn't mean it wasn't possible," said Pedro, his grin becoming wider. "Because this is a Tharsis project in an Inventrix facility, I was lucky to get access to all the previous research done by *both* corporations – including all unpublished data on those apparent dead ends. It was by building on their work that I was able to make the breakthrough."

It was, she had to admit, impressive. "That's amazing, Pedro."

He gave a modest shrug. "The challenge is to ensure that accelerated growth doesn't get passed to the next generation of plants, otherwise we could have runaway forests which might become a problem."

"You need some kind of kill switch," suggested Mel.

"Embedded in the genetic code of the plant, if possible," Pedro agreed. "The Science Board don't want some kind of kill switch released into the environment because of potential unforeseen consequences. Which means I'm a little bit stuck, as I tend to agree with them."

"Once you've let the genie out, you can't put it back in the bottle."

Pedro gave her a puzzled look.

She laughed. "That's one of my father's sayings. It's from an old Earth fable… it doesn't matter."

"Yes, your father." Pedro took on a sudden somber tone. "I thought of you when I heard he'd died."

"It was five years ago," said Mel. The sudden memory brought with it unexpected emotions and heat rose to her face.

"I thought the obituaries were needlessly unkind."

"Some people say my father was unkind."

"He came from a different era on a different planet," said Pedro. "He grew up in a world where the population was paying a universal tax to fund the terraforming of Mars. You can understand why people like him thought the idea of Mars keeping the profits for itself, and even thinking for itself, was a betrayal."

"You're very understanding."

"I try to see both sides, even when I don't agree with one of them."

"Dad could never do that. He fought for Earth to have the final say to his last breath. It tore him up inside. He loved his home planet, but he loved his family too. He couldn't go home without leaving his family and he couldn't be with his family unless he gave up the option to go home. He never fully made peace with his decision to stay on Mars – I think he resented us for it at the end."

"I'm sorry, Mel."

Mel waved away his concern, flapping her hand in front of her face to cool her emotions and dry her threatening tears. "Don't be. Tell me more about your forest."

"There's not much more to tell. Until I perfect that kill switch, I can't move forward."

"Did you want me to take a look?"

"I thought you had your own troubles to deal with."

"Yes," said Mel. "But until the farm samples get here, I could do with the distraction. I think I might be able to apply my viral enhancer technology to your forest."

"I'd appreciate that," said Pedro.

He turned to go, but Mel reached out to take his hand. The gentle touch of another human being was warm and comforting. "Let's stay here a little longer."

He gave her that puzzled look again.

"You don't mind if I sit in your experiment, do you?"

Mel drew Pedro to a tree as tall as a Martian man. She bent her knees slowly, allowing her hand to slip from his fingers, and lowered herself to the forest floor. The ground was hard and dry from where the tree had sucked up all the moisture from the surrounding soil.

"Join me for a moment."

Pedro folded his legs awkwardly to sit next to her. "I've never done this before," he confessed.

Mel rested her back against the tree trunk and looked up at the dome where the hazy disk of the sun was lighting the Martian sky. She had been around plants since university, but they had always been shut away in laboratories, in growing trays or warehouse-like cultivating environments. But Pedro's forest was more like the natural world she had seen in videos or that her father had reminisced about when she was little. There was no birdsong, no insects buzzing around or small mammals running by, but it was still more alive than anything she had experienced on Mars.

Pedro leaned beside her. His reassuring presence brought back memories of when they were students. When she had felt science had all the answers, if only she could unlock them. When the excitement of being with Pedro had made her wonder if she was led by her hormones or if they had shared something deeper.

"Sitting here gives everything a different perspective," said Pedro.

"Yes," said Mel, not knowing if he meant the forest or their relationship.

"It's strange how we think we need to leave the plants alone," he said. "When, in a real forest, animals would be interfering and interacting with them all the time. When Mars gets to a point where we can grow forests outside of a dome, they will inevitably grow alongside people. So, in a way, we're not contaminating the experiment, we're becoming part of it."

"Yes." Mel tilted her head to one side and rested it against Pedro's shoulder.

Her problems drifted away into the simple quiet of the forest. Shaded by its hues of green and masked by its sensual aroma, they existed only at the fringes of her mind. Waiting for her on the other side of the dome.

CHAPTER TWENTY-FIVE

Deverau jumped sideways as a delivery van exited the logistics depot and nearly ran him over. He stopped to watch it enter the service road that lay around the edge of Deimos City. An MSS guard stationed outside watched him intently, but lost interest again as he showed her his credentials.

Reports that a similar depot in Noctis City was distributing food had led to a mob unleashing its anger on the facility. The fact that the van they raided only contained supplies for the sewage processing plant hadn't lessened the possibility that another hub might become the victim of an attack. Hence the extra security and the need to spread MSS resources even thinner than they already were.

Inside, a fleet of vehicles waited their turn to emerge from the depot. One of the members of staff attending to them, an Earth-born woman in casual and grubby work clothes, observed Deverau with a suspicious eye.

"Inspector Deverau of the MSS," he introduced himself. "I'm looking for Isaac Erdan."

Her suspicion turned to curiosity.

"Isaac works in the offices," she said with a strong Earth accent which Deverau recognized as American. "I suppose you want me to show you where his office is."

"That would be kind of you."

She sighed, like it was a great imposition, and escorted him to the back of the building where a staircase led up to a glass-fronted corridor. He paused to look out across the five lines of vehicles below, moving in unison like a segmented snake to take the place of the van that had departed the front of the queue and nearly run him over. A backstage glimpse of the supply network that kept Mars running and which most people had been completely unaware of until the food shortage began to bite.

"It's this way," said the woman impatiently. He turned away from the glass and followed her to the first of a series of office doors set into an opaque wall. The woman knocked and, without waiting for an answer, let herself in.

A pale man with tired eyes sitting behind a desk – who Deverau hoped was Isaac Erdan – looked up at the interruption.

"The cops are here," stated the woman.

Isaac immediately stood and Deverau once again found himself looking up at a Mars-born man.

"Have you found my wife?" he blurted out, confirming that he was Mel's husband.

"No," said Deverau. "I'm afraid not."

Isaac sagged in disappointment. "Then what are you doing here? You should be out there looking for her."

"That's why I'm here. I'm Inspector Deverau."

His name must have resonated with Isaac because his

expression hardened. "You're the incompetent one who took Mel on a train that was attacked by terrorists and then lost her."

Deverau ignored the insult. "Strictly speaking, she escaped lawful custody."

"And what did you do after that? Absolutely nothing as far as I can figure out. I kept fearing the MSS would tell me her body had been found. But I heard nothing and it turned out you'd called off the search team."

"Because we believe she came back to Deimos City," said Deverau. "You've not heard from her?"

"Of course I've not heard from her, for goodness sake! Do you think I'd be going out of my mind with worry if I'd heard from her?"

In the following disquiet, the woman shifted uncomfortably in the doorway. "If you don't mind, Isaac, I'm going to go back down."

"No!" he yelled. "I want you to stay here and witness the continued ineptitude of the MSS. Who, let's face it, are too busy running around arresting the wrong people to actually do their job properly."

Deverau took a moment and hoped it would allow the atmosphere to calm down, but it only served to emphasize the tension around him.

"I will not deny that resources at the MSS are stretched in the current situation," he said, diplomatically. "But I can honestly tell you I am making it my personal mission to find your wife. She ran away from that train deliberately, so it is my belief that she is very much alive. I need you to think, is there anywhere she might have gone?"

"If there is, what makes you think I would tell you?"

"Let me get this straight: you are upset with me for not finding your wife, but you are not prepared to help me find her?"

"That's about the size of it," said Isaac, folding his arms across his chest to show he was resolute.

"You do realize that obstructing the course of justice is a crime?"

"What about selling out your wife to a bumbling security service that are so desperate to pretend they're doing something, they accuse innocent scientists? That's a greater moral crime in my view."

Deverau stood and waited, staring across the desk at Isaac with a patient expression that suggested he would stand in his office all day if he had to. Sometimes, it was the silence and the other person's instinct to fill it that worked best in drawing information out of a suspect, or a reluctant witness.

"I spoke to everyone I could think of," said Isaac. "No one's seen her, no one's heard from her."

"I would still like a list of those people," said Deverau.

"Sure! Waste your time speaking to people with no information. Why should I care?"

"She hasn't contacted you in any way? She hasn't been to your home? She hasn't been here? A logistics depot would be useful if she wanted to go somewhere without using public transport or attempting to hire a rover."

Isaac scoffed at the very idea. "Don't be ridiculous. This place is full of people. She would have been seen."

"Well…" said the woman at the doorway.

Isaac whipped round to glare at her. In the fraction of a second it took Deverau to follow his move, she turned red with embarrassment.

"Well?" questioned Deverau.

The woman glanced at Isaac to get permission to speak. He merely returned her stare.

"Do you remember what I said about obstructing the course of justice?" said Deverau.

She swallowed. "Well, there was that woman the other day."

"What woman?" demanded Isaac before Deverau had a chance to ask the same question.

"A couple of people saw her on the main floor and thought she was a member of staff come in on one of the vehicles."

Isaac folded his arms even tighter. "Why am I only hearing about this now?"

"You were already stressed with … well, with everything… so we thought it was better not to bother you. It's not like she caused any trouble or stole anything."

The possibility of a breakthrough tempted him with excitement. But Deverau pulled back from the temptation, knowing from experience that promising leads could sometimes take him nowhere. "Do you have a description of this person?"

"She was dressed strangely," said the woman. "There should still be a surveillance image on the system."

Isaac, apparently too furious to speak, stood aside and indicated that the woman should use the screen on his desk.

At that moment, Deverau's WristTab buzzed. He wanted to ignore it, but the display told him it was Jones on an urgent call.

"What's up?" he answered. "I'm in the middle of something."

"Sorry, Dev. We've got a bit of a situation."

He frowned at the image of his sergeant. "Define 'situation.'"

"We're getting reports that one of the members of the Terraforming Committee was attacked near Central Plaza."

"Which one?"

"The name hasn't come through yet, but it looks like it was someone important enough to be a target, but not important enough to have a security detail."

"Typical." Deverau pulled up some strength from an inner well which was in danger of running dry. "You go ahead, I'll meet you there."

He hung up the call and walked around to the other side of the desk where Isaac and the woman were looking at the screen. On it was a clear image of what appeared to be a woman in a baggy shirt with her head turned towards the camera so most of her face was hidden by the brown beret she was wearing.

"Is that your wife?" asked Deverau.

"How can I tell? I can't see her face."

But from the way Isaac was staring at the image, it was obvious he was lying.

"I want a copy of that image and the manifest of every vehicle that left the depot after she was seen, with full details of where it was going," said Deverau. "I am, as you can tell, quite busy, so if I don't receive the information by the end of the day, I am happy to come back and arrest everyone in this building until I get some cooperation. Understand?"

Neither of them said anything, but from the frightened expression on the woman's face and the defiant look Isaac was giving him, he was certain his point had been made.

CHAPTER TWENTY-SIX

The potato plant trapped inside the transparent, sealed box decayed in the heat of the laboratory. Already dead, its corpse was food for unseen microbes which broke down its cell membranes to decompose its fibrous body. In the wild, the process would return nutrients to the soil. In the lab, there was no escape from the sample's coffin.

Mel should have returned the specimen to the refrigerator to slow decomposition and preserve it for further tests. But she saw no point. It had already told her its story. She might as well let it rot.

The small lab that Pedro had arranged for her to use was silent. The movement of the automated genome sequencing machines had long ceased. There was nothing left to sequence, nothing left to analyze. The data she had extracted sat on the screen in front of her. Two exact same sequences of DNA, which were as unthinkable as they were undeniable.

Mel lifted her head at the sound of the door. Pedro took a

single step inside and stopped. He regarded her with a somber expression and looked like he was about to speak, but said nothing.

"What is it?" she asked.

"I've ... got some bad news."

She raised her eyebrows at the irony. "It can't possibly be worse than my news."

"I think it might be," said Pedro.

Her anxiety increased as Pedro came over to her screen. He swiped away the data and replaced it with an image of Mel's own face taken from her EcoLine personnel file.

She stared at the unsmiling image of her younger self, captured some ten years before. She remembered the ambition that lay behind her serious expression and wondered if she would have allowed it to drive her career so much if she could have known, back then, where it would lead.

"I'm sorry," said Pedro, and he set the video playing.

The still image was only the opening of a longer piece. Mel watched it crossfade into some surveillance video of her at Isaac's depot. Then some archive footage of her looking nervous as she gave a talk at the Outerbridge Science Conference almost five years before.

A deep, male voice spoke over the images. "*MSS officers investigating farm crop deaths urgently need to talk to Doctor Melanie Erdan. We have reason to believe she has left Deimos City and could be anywhere on Mars. Anyone with any idea of her whereabouts is urged not to approach her, but to notify the MSS immediately.*"

Mel watched with increasing dismay as the video ended on the same still image of her younger self. Alongside of it were listed details of her physical description from her height to her original surname.

"I don't think anyone else at the research station has seen it," said Pedro, looking at her with sorrowful eyes. "But I don't expect it'll be long before they do."

"How did you see it?" asked Mel.

"An old friend of mine remembered I used to know Frank Walker's daughter at university and sent it over. I don't think for a moment she imagined I was the one harboring you."

The image of Mel's own face continued to stare out at her from the past. Like it was accusing her of bringing her youthful ambition crashing down in failure.

"I should turn myself in."

"No!" said Pedro. "Not after you've come this far."

"But I think the MSS is right – the death of my experiment and the farm crops *are* related."

She turned away from him, embarrassed to admit her guilt for the first time.

"You've found something, haven't you?"

She nodded in somber recognition.

"My plan was to look at the samples you were able to get for me in isolation," she said. "I thought it would be easy to show a pathogen was responsible for the farm crop deaths and then I would carry out DNA methylation analysis to identify the epigenetic changes which caused my experiment to fail."

"Sounds reasonable to me," said Pedro.

"I started with the basics and ran DNA sequences on both samples – that's when I saw the impossible."

Mel swiped the picture of herself off the screen and brought back the comparison of the two genomes.

Pedro leaned over. "What am I looking at?"

"Both samples have the same DNA."

Pedro glanced back to Mel. "You mean, they're both potatoes?"

"Not just potatoes – *exactly* the same potatoes. Not like two samples of the same species. More like samples from two brothers. Or twins. Or clones."

Her discovery would have been exciting if it wasn't so horrific.

Pedro stared at her. "You must have got the two samples mixed up."

Mel shook her head. It was the first thing she checked. And double checked.

"I'm absolutely sure. I even looked at the provenance of both samples – one came from my field trial and the other came from a farm outside of Deimos City. Either I clutch at straws and claim that someone screwed up the documentation, or I admit what the evidence is telling me."

"Which is?"

"The DNA of the dead farm crops matches the DNA of my experiment. Including all the genetic changes I introduced. Which means the plants that died on the farms were not ordinary farm crops, they were my virally enhanced potatoes."

Pedro looked at the DNA sequences, then at Mel, then back at the genetic codes. "Someone planted your potatoes in the farms?"

"I believe my experiment has a fatal flaw. I considered that maybe it was introduced while the seed potatoes were in storage, but I think I was simply asking too much of the plants. Producing extra protein, essential fats *and* edible leaves must have overloaded them. I didn't have the chance to carry out an epigenetic investigation before I was arrested, but it's likely it was a weakness which became fatal when they were grown in the vertical farm environment."

Mel avoided Pedro's gaze as she realized she was the one who had brought Mars to the edge of catastrophe. "It's all my fault."

"No," said Pedro. "Don't talk like that."

He came over to comfort her, but she pulled away and walked until she reached the laboratory wall. Turning, she slammed her back against it and allowed the cold, hard surface to radiate through to her skin. It was the only comfort she deserved.

"I can't keep claiming it's a coincidence that my experiment failed at the same time as the crops died," she said. "I need to hand myself in and tell the authorities what I've learned."

"The MSS wouldn't listen to you before, what makes you think they'll listen to you now?"

"I have more evidence."

"You're missing the point," said Pedro. "You followed all the correct scientific procedures. You had a promising experiment which didn't work out when it transitioned to a field trial – that's science. It's why we do field trials. You weren't the one who planted an experimental crop in the farms."

Mel stared at Pedro as his words broke through her mental barrier. She had been so absorbed by the horror of the crop deaths being her fault that she hadn't considered how her potatoes came to be planted in the farms in the first place. "No," she said in contemplation. "It wasn't me."

Mel pushed back against the laboratory wall so she stood up straight again.

She headed back to the screen and tapped her finger on the DNA sequences. The screen zoomed in as the tapping of her nail accompanied her cascading thoughts.

"Which means," she said. "It must have been someone else."

"Why would anyone do that?" said Pedro.

"I don't know," said Mel. "But someone stole my experiment and I have to find out who."

CHAPTER TWENTY-SEVEN

Hunger gnawed at Alex's stomach. There was nothing remaining from the food he had stolen or from what his mother had hoarded. Like almost everyone else, he was living on rations. It kept him alive and it kept him working, but it gave his life no spark.

Alex sat on the ventilation box in the maintenance area with the cold of the metal seeping up through his thighs. Normally, the small space would be full of talking and laughter, but no one had the energy for it. Alex saw his own fatigue reflected in the faces of Pete and Sammi leaning against the wall in front of him. There was not much to say anyway, they were all waiting for Ivan.

They jumped at the confident slam of the maintenance hatch. Heavy footsteps followed and Ivan appeared from around the curve of the hideout's inner wall. He dodged the supports and pipes with the expertise of someone who had memorized the obstacle course. With him, he carried a black carryall which he swung by his side. Elea was behind him, picking her way through more carefully.

It was clear Ivan was enduring along with the rest of the population. His body didn't quite fill out his clothes as it once had and his face was thinner. But he didn't carry the same drawn and gray look like everyone else. Like he was living on an energy burning behind his eyes.

"What's so urgent that you asked all of us here?" asked Pete.

Ivan just grinned, so Pete's gaze naturally fell upon Elea.

"Don't look at me," she said. "He's had something going on for a while, but he won't tell me about it."

Ivan loomed over the ventilation box so Alex – half intimidated and half out of politeness – stood and backed away. Ivan dumped his bag on the box, as if it were too important for the floor, and something metallic clanged inside.

"I have an idea of how we can stand up for Mars," said Ivan. "But it is a proposition that is far more serious than anything we have done before."

"What's in the bag, Ivan?" asked Sammi.

"I want to make sure you are all on board before I discuss it."

Elea nudged him playfully in the ribs. "Come on, Ivan. You said you would show me when we got here."

Ivan turned with a smile before bending down to kiss her firmly on the lips. "OK."

Ivan opened the bag with the hiss of the zipper and pulled out a package as big as his hand and wrapped in a black cloth. He held it out on his palm for all of them to see.

He unwrapped it, lifting the first corner of the fabric to reveal the cross-hatched metal of a sturdy handgrip. He pulled back the second corner and the cylindrical shape of a barrel appeared: so clean that it shone even in the dim light. Ivan unveiled the rest of the parcel by flicking off the final two flaps of cloth, by which time Alex knew that they concealed the trigger of a handgun.

Ivan held the object on the platform of his fabric-covered palm like he was displaying a priceless jewel. Alex stared at the forbidden item with reverie and trepidation. He felt the fear it commanded, but also the power that it offered.

"Ivan," breathed Elea, looking up at him with disbelieving eyes. "Guns are illegal."

"Just as it should be illegal to allow Martians to starve to death."

"But illegal with good reason, Ivan. You shoot one of those things in here or in a bus or anywhere and you're going to breach the environmental seals. You could kill a bunch of people."

"If things go right," said Ivan. "We won't have to shoot anything."

"What if things go wrong?"

"Elea, have a bit of faith." He leaned in to kiss her again.

But she pulled away from his silencing lips. "How do you even get hold of a gun on Mars?"

"With all the shipments coming here from Earth, you can smuggle in anything if you know the right people and can pay the right price."

Alex knew Ivan had his secrets, but he didn't think connections to the criminal underworld was one of them. "You know the right people?"

"I know the people who know the right people."

Alex wasn't sure whether he should be impressed or scared. But he could see the fervor burning within Ivan and it was infectious.

"Does this have something to do with what I said about targeting Earth," said Alex with trepidation.

Ivan nodded.

Alex felt proud that his opinions were being listened to, but the reality of the gun in front of him was terrifying.

"You're right," said Ivan. "Earth should be the target."

"It's millions of kilometers away," Elea pointed out.

"But some of Earth's interests are on Mars," continued Ivan. "The food crisis is going to hit their profit margin already, but soon after it's over, they'll forget about the Martians who died, were malnourished or lived in fear and will return to exploiting us. We need to send a bigger and stronger message back to that dirty, blue green planet that they won't forget."

Ivan took the pistol with his other hand and bounced it up and down to feel the weight. Then he tossed it in the air, caught it by the grip and placed his index finger on the trigger. He thrust his arm out straight so the pistol was an extension to his body and aimed.

"Ivan!" yelled Elea.

His index finger squeezed. Elea's high-pitched scream echoed around them as she clasped her head for protection.

The gun *clicked* and nothing happened. There was no explosion, no speeding bullet, no gunshot.

Alex, who had tensed like a helpless bystander, tried to relax, even though he was still shaking.

Ivan laughed at Elea. "It's not loaded."

Elea, clearly angry at being mocked, but also relieved that someone hadn't been hurt, thumped him hard on the shoulder. "Don't even joke," she said.

Alex stared at the handgun held loosely at Ivan's side. It still scared him. "I don't know how to use a gun," he said. "I've not even seen one in real life before."

"I'll teach you," said Ivan. "Not as if you'll have to use it, just look confident enough that you are prepared to. Besides, I only have two of them and limited ammunition, so not everyone will be armed with these. The others will have shockguns."

"What's your plan?" asked Elea.

Ivan replaced the handgun in its cloth and put it back in the bag. He looked around at them all to make sure he had their attention. Alex, again, saw the burning energy behind his eyes and felt it ignite a passion inside of himself to fight against injustice.

"Alex had the right idea," he said. "We send our message through tourists from Earth. They waste their wealth to come here to stare at us poor little Martians and take the stories back to their rich friends. Well, we'll give them a story to take back like they didn't expect. One that will send a message to the whole of Earth that Mars should be allowed to control its own future."

CHAPTER TWENTY-EIGHT

Mel rushed into Pedro's rooms. She was buzzing with excitement. Or it could have been the coffee.

Unable to sleep, she had been up all night working in the lab.

Pedro emerged from the bathroom, naked from the waist up with a towel covering his lower half. His face wore a not-quite-awake-yet look.

"I've figured it out!" Mel declared.

"Morning," said Pedro, squinting at her as if trying to focus.

Mel didn't have time for pleasantries and launched straight into telling him what she had discovered. "I was taking another look at your forest research."

"There was no need, Mel."

"You're working on accelerated growth to cover Mars with forests when environmental conditions are right – right?"

He gave her a knowing look. "I am aware of that, it being my research."

"Right. Yes, right." Mel's mind was running so fast, it was

tripping over itself. "I thought, what if it could be adapted? Mars will need forests in the future, yes. But right now, it needs food."

Pedro tugged his towel tighter around his waist and perched on the edge of the sofa. "If you're thinking of adapting my accelerated growth to food crops, then I've already considered it," he said. "By the time I could develop it, the farms would be able to harvest ordinary crops. It's a nonstarter."

"Not with viral enhancers," said Mel. "I could introduce genes for accelerated growth into potatoes."

He raised an eyebrow at that.

"It's the crop I've been working with for years, so I wouldn't need to do any preparatory work. I'd make the tuber rich in protein, as I did with my original experiment, but I wouldn't alter the leaves of the plant. That was the last – and hardest – modification I made and I think is what must have overloaded the plants."

Mel stopped speaking, but her adrenaline was still running. She was ready for Pedro to run with her.

But he looked circumspect. Even apologetic.

"How do you know accelerated growth won't overload the plants?"

"Your technology is different. Fixing carbon dioxide from the air is what plants do naturally. This is merely speeding up the process. All my training, all my experience and every instinct I have tells me this can work."

"Even if you're right, Mel, the Science Board is already stalling over approval for my accelerated growth forest. I can't imagine they'll let us do anything with the food supply."

Mel was not ready to have her enthusiasm taken away from

her. "Then we need to show them it's possible. I've made a start. I know it can be done, I just know it."

"Aren't you forgetting something?"

She had run through all the science overnight. She was tired, for sure. And she was less familiar with Pedro's research than her own. But when she was like this, when she was alive with possibilities, she didn't miss anything. "I was thorough, Pedro."

"You're forgetting you're on the run! I'm going to have to tell Gadd the truth about you before he finds out for himself."

Vincent Gadd was Pedro's boss and the owner of the sarcastic voice who had first greeted her when she arrived at the station.

Pedro's rejection stabbed at her vulnerability. "You want me to leave?"

"I don't want you to do anything, but we have to be realistic," he said. "You need to find out who stole your experiment and how it got into the farms to clear your name. You can't do that here and you certainly can't do that if you hang around waiting to be re-arrested."

"I don't know how to do those things."

"You do them in the same way you escaped from the train and in the same way you made it here. You use your intelligence, you use your initiative and you find a way."

The truth of his words hurt. The excitement of the night's furious work in the lab slipped away and the buzz from copious cups of coffee diminished.

With reality intruding in the cold light of morning, she realized she had no choice but to contemplate the inevitable.

CHAPTER TWENTY-NINE

Mel emerged from the bathroom and picked up the small bag with the one set of spare clothes she had borrowed and the few provisions that Pedro had been able to find.

Pedro stood in front of her, fully dressed and ready to work.

It was difficult to say goodbye to the warmth and safety she had rediscovered in his friendship, but it was time.

"All ready?" he asked.

"I would be lying if I said I was," said Mel. "But staying isn't going to change that."

"Are you sure you want to go back to Deimos City?"

"It's where my lab is, it's where my experiment was stolen from. It's the only place I can find the answers."

As she spoke, his WristTab bleeped.

He ignored it. "It's going to be harder now that the public has been alerted that you're a wanted person."

"I'll be careful," she assured him. The WristTab was becoming annoying. "Are you going to answer that?"

He lifted his arm and frowned at the device. "It's Gadd, saying it's urgent. I better get it."

Gadd's voice barked out of the WristTab the moment Pedro answered.

"Do you want to explain why there's a man called Inspector Deverau from the MSS at the airlock wanting to talk to you?"

The name sent a shiver of dread through Mel. She had stayed too long. She should have left the moment she was publicly named as a wanted person.

"Oh really?" said Pedro, adopting a surprised tone.

Mel and Pedro exchanged worried looks over the top of his WristTab.

"He says he's trying to find Doctor Melanie Erdan," came Gadd's voice. "He sent across an image of her. Perhaps you would also like to explain why she looks very much like your visiting friend."

"I'll tell you everything, Vince. Just don't let him in."

"He's MSS! Of course I'm letting him in! He's already negotiating the airlock."

With every turn of the conversation, Mel felt the paths of escape closing around her.

"Send him to my lab, I'll meet him there," said Pedro. "Please don't say anything."

"Fine," said Gadd, begrudgingly. "But we'll discuss this when he's gone."

The call ended without pleasantries and a moment of silence filled the room.

"I'll keep him busy," said Pedro. "Can you get yourself to a rover?"

"Yes." Mel was already thinking about driving herself to Deimos City and how she was going to get past security when she didn't have Pedro's unwanted face to do it for her.

With the moment to leave suddenly upon her, she realized there were many things she wanted to say to him. Not about science, but about how she had been rash to break ties with him after university and what might have been. But she had run out of time.

"Thank you," was all she could say.

He nodded. Whether it was acknowledging her unspoken thoughts or whether it was merely an acceptance of her gratitude, she couldn't tell.

"Good luck," he said.

Mel walked past him without turning back. Entering the corridor outside his rooms, she was already working out a route to reach the rovers without bumping into Inspector Deverau on the way.

After being kept waiting for a suspiciously long time, Deverau was disappointed to discover that the lab he was escorted to at Squyres Research Outpost was much the same as a lab anywhere else. The man he and Jones had come to see, Doctor Pedro Serrano, was oddly welcoming to a pair of MSS officers who had turned up out of the blue.

Even so, all the time he was being polite, he clasped his two hands in front of him with the tension of someone trying to keep their nervousness in check. Deverau had interviewed a lot of people since becoming a police officer and he could tell when someone was lying to him. With Doctor Pedro Serrano, he knew he was going to lie before he even opened his mouth.

"Doctor Serrano," Deverau began.

"Call me, Pedro, please. Everyone does."

"Pedro, you knew Doctor Mel Erdan when you studied together at university, is that right?"

Pedro returned a puzzled look and Deverau had that sinking feeling that he was going to have to put up with a lot of pretense before he actually got anywhere.

Jones reached over with his tablet and showed Pedro a picture of the wanted suspect.

"That's Mel Walker, not Erdan," said Pedro, pointing at the image. "Did she get married or something? Unusual for someone like her to change her name, but then people were always associating her with her father, so I suppose it makes sense."

Deverau maintained his unimpressed expression. Some people became incredibly chatty when they were nervous. He hated the chatty ones. Almost as much as he hated the silent ones. "Have you been in contact with her recently?"

"Should I have?" said Pedro evasively.

"We have reason to believe she stowed away on a truck heading for the mining operation at Ceraunius Tholus."

"Yes, I know it. It's not far from here."

"Which makes me think she might have been heading for this research outpost to look up an old friend."

"Which would be you," said Jones, just to underline the point.

Pedro went silent and his smile became fixed, like he was thinking of a response which wouldn't land him in trouble. Whatever that response was going to be, it was interrupted by his WristTab bleeping loudly. Pedro's smile became apologetic. "Excuse me."

Deverau exchanged irritated glances with Jones while

Pedro answered the call. Arranging to be interrupted was a classic tactic to buy time.

"Pedro," said the voice on the other end of the call. Deverau recognized it as belonging to Doctor Gadd, who had greeted them at the airlock. "Now that the MSS have gone, I think we should have a quiet word, don't you?"

Deverau and Jones exchanged more looks.

"Gone?" said Pedro into the WristTab, looking up at the two officers, who were very much still there.

"Yes," said Gadd. "Their rover's just left the airlock."

"What?" said Deverau. He stepped forward, grabbed Pedro's wrist and yelled at the WristTab. "This is Inspector Deverau – what do you mean my rover's just left the airlock?"

"I... well, I assumed you were on it."

"Didn't you think to check?"

"Well... no."

Deverau let go of Pedro's arm in disgust.

"She's stolen our ride!" said Jones, stating the obvious.

"Looks like it," Deverau said. He glared at Pedro.

The scientist looked uncomfortable but maintained his air of ignorance. "Come to mention it, we did have a botanist visit recently who looked a bit like Mel, but she used a different name."

Furious, Deverau wanted to smash his fist right into the lying man's face. But that was unethical, would risk getting him fired and would do nothing to stop their fugitive getting away.

Jones was already heading for the door. "Dev, if we want to catch her, we need to get a move on."

Deverau pointed an accusatory finger at Pedro. "Don't think I won't come back to deal with you."

It was an empty threat, but if it caused Mel's accomplice a

few sleepless nights, then it was worth it. Deverau waited the second needed for his words to have their desired effect, then followed Jones out of the lab.

The rover Deverau had commandeered from Squyres Research Outpost bounced over the uneven terrain following the tracker on his stolen vehicle. Despite wearing his seatbelt, he held on tight to the internal frame of the vehicle with one hand and onto the dashboard with the other to stop himself being thrown around. Beside him, Jones's driving had reached new levels of recklessness.

"Isn't there a proper road we can take, Jonesy?"

"You want to catch her, don't you?"

"I was thinking I would arrest her, but now I think I'll just throw up over her."

Jones chuckled, but didn't alter his driving one bit.

Deverau tried to focus on the horizon because he'd heard that it could help steady the systems in his brain that were making him feel travel sick. But it didn't help. Not least because his view was obscured by the lorries and machinery of a construction crew not far ahead.

"Oh no," said Jones, staring at the tracker readout on the dashboard.

"Oh no, what?"

"We're closing in on her fast."

"Isn't that what we're supposed to be doing?"

"Too fast," said Jones. "I think she's stopped."

"Again, not seeing the problem."

"In my experience, people on the run keep running."

Jones, much to the relief of Deverau's stomach, slowed as

they approached the construction crew. Close up, he could see they were approaching the parking spot for all their vehicles. He recognized two people transporters, a fleet of five supply lorries and, tucked in on the end, a trio of rovers. Beyond them, a crane reached high up into the Martian sky with a long piece of metal – which was likely a strut or girder of some kind – dangling from a cable at the top. In the distance, it was just possible to see the occasional white figure of a construction worker in a rad-suit.

"It's here," said Jones. He glanced up from the tracking data and drove down the line of vehicles to the rovers at the end. There, between two construction vehicles, was the recognizable shape of their rover with its MSS designation written in distinctive dark blue lettering on the rear and its unique serial number, 621.

Deverau opened the general comms channel and leaned into the microphone to make sure his voice was picked up loud and clear. "This is Inspector Deverau of the MSS, to MSS rover 621, please respond."

"I should be able to connect to the internal systems," said Jones, and began doing something on the dashboard.

Deverau leaned into the microphone again. "Doctor Mel Erdan, this is the MSS. You have nowhere else to go. Respond and we can come to some arrangement."

"Even if she's in there, what makes you think she'll talk to you?" said Jones.

"My charm and my good looks," Deverau retorted.

In truth, he didn't expect her to respond at all. He stood up and took a few paces to the rear of the rover where the scientists kept their rad-suits. If he needed to go out and chase her down, he wanted to be ready.

He had just opened a cabinet to find four fully replenished rad-suits when Jones exclaimed, "I'm in!"

Deverau returned to stand over his sergeant's shoulder. He peered at the data which filled one of the screens on the dashboard, under the heading of *MSS Rover 621*.

"She's gone," said Jones, drawing his finger down the data. "Internal environment shows conditions similar to the surface of Mars and it says the hatch was opened ten minutes ago. I think it's safe to assume she stopped here, suited up and got out."

Deverau closed his eyes against the reality of the data and tried to stop his frustration turning to anger. He needed to think clearly.

"Jones," he said, his police officer's brain firing into action. "Get onto the construction crew, ask if they've seen her and tell them to keep a look out for her. But don't take their word for it – get an MSS team down here to do a thorough search. If they give you any kickback about being busy on crowd control duty, tell them this is a priority. Then I want you to find out the details of every vehicle which has passed through here in the last hour and track its movements. It's possible she figured an MSS rover was too hot and dumped it here to swap it for something else."

"Yes, Dev. What are you going to do?"

"Get suited up and make sure she's not throwing us a double bluff and still hiding in the rover."

"You realize she's got a good half hour head start on us?" said Jones, as Deverau pulled a rad-suit from the cabinet. "She could have gone anywhere."

"Then we haven't got time to sit about stating the obvious."

"Yes, Dev. On it, Dev."

But, as he heard Jones make contact with the construction crew over the comms, he knew his sergeant was right. The scientist had made a fool of him and Mel was, once again, in the wind.

CHAPTER THIRTY

hen Mars was young, it was a violent planet. Volcanos erupted from the pressure of the magma beneath the crust and sent up plumes of gas and rivers of lava. The gas became part of the atmosphere and trapped the heat of the molten rock so it became a warm place cosseted in a blanket of mostly carbon dioxide. But, as the planet aged and cooled, the volcanos began to die. The magnetic field, which had once protected Mars against the ravages of space, dwindled to almost nothing and, over the course of five hundred million years, the solar wind stripped away its atmosphere. By the time humans arrived, Mars was a cold, dead world.

But not all of the heat escaped. Some of it remained hidden in the planet's mantle. It was theorized that digging deep through the boundary between the crust and the mantle, known as the "moho", would release heat and gas once again to allow Mars to remember its youth. The ThorGate corporation won the contract to put the theory to the test and began construction of a series of moholes along Valles Marineris, a valley at the equator where the crust was thinner.

But they had invested in the project with one proviso: that they be allowed to make money from the technology. So it was agreed that the heat from one of the moholes would be diverted to create a tropical paradise where only the rich could afford to spend an indulgent holiday.

Alex sat in the front seat of a rover acquired by Sammi from the mines as it sped down the specially built road toward the Martian Tropics. The resort sat on an outcrop of rock jutting out into Ius Chasma, so the blue-tinted bubble of a dome appeared to be almost floating above the valley.

Ivan glanced behind at where Elea, Pete and Sammi sat on two inward-facing benches running down each side of the rover. "We're about ten minutes away," he said. "Everyone all clear what they're doing?"

"Yes, Ivan," said Elea.

"Clear," said Pete.

"All set," said Sammi.

Ivan looked across to Alex. "What about you, Alex? You're going to be my second in there."

"I'm ready, Ivan," said Alex.

Alex was aware of the weight of the gun resting on his lap. It had grown warm from his body heat in the hour they had been driving, almost like it had become part of him. Ivan had shown him how to use it, but said it was a weapon of fear, not of death, and should never have to be fired. It made Alex feel powerful to run his fingers over its solid surface, knowing that Ivan had entrusted *him* to wield it rather than any of the others.

They drove up to the service entrance of the resort and stopped for one nervous moment.

Silently, the rover communicated with the resort and the resort communicated with the rover. Between them, the automatic systems agreed that they could enter and opened the airlock door.

Where Ivan had procured the security code which gave them access was something he kept to himself. Pete thought he had acquired it from someone who supported their cause. Elea speculated he might have bribed someone for it. Whatever the origin of the information, it had worked.

Running the plan over in his head as they negotiated the airlock, Alex knew he was ready. What scared him, as they entered an arching tunnel built with compressed Martian soil and dimly lit by a strip ceiling light, were the unknowns. He knew how people should react to someone with a loaded gun, but people were unpredictable.

Along the left of the service tunnel were five external supply vans and three rover-type personnel carriers plugged into recharging ports. A space between the final two vehicles was enough for Ivan to slip the mining rover in between them, park up and set it to charge.

"Masks on," said Ivan.

His source hadn't been able to say where security cameras were located, so they couldn't afford their faces to be visible outside the rover. The cameras, they had been assured, were the only things they had to worry about, as the skeleton staff working at that time of day would be safely minding their own business inside the buildings.

Alex pulled a scarf out of his pocket and tied it high across his nose so it covered his face. He put on a thin hat which he pulled down until it reached his brow ridge.

"And remember," added Ivan. "No using names. There's no point in hiding our faces if you tell everyone who we are."

Climbing into the back where Ivan was already opening the hatch, Alex exchanged glances with the others. Their nervous eyes stared back at him from the thin gap in their masks.

All except for Ivan, who exhibited no fear at all as he grabbed the same black carryall which had originally contained the guns and leapt out into the service area.

He led them further along the tunnel to where a narrow-nosed buggy, emblazoned with the logo of a cleaning company, *M&G Cleaning*, was parked. Whether it was the custom for the short range, enclosed vehicle to be parked there unlocked, or whether it had been left for them, Ivan didn't say.

Without hesitation, he climbed into the driver's position and gestured to the others to get into the back. It was a genuine cleaner's vehicle, decked out with all manner of equipment with no provision for passengers. Alex had to step over an automatic vacuum cleaner to find a space to sit.

Ivan drove towards the airtight door at the end of the service corridor and it opened without asking, letting them into the resort itself. Their four heads craned around Ivan's body to see through the only window at the front and catch their first glimpse of the tropical paradise they had all heard about.

The majesty of palm trees as tall as ten meters reached up into the domed sky on either side. Deep brown trunks as wide as the body of a man, and topped with the green hands of many-fingered leaves, dwarfed their small vehicle. Like sentries of the resort, they acted as both a screen to hide the ugliness of the service entrance and to cast shade down on the vehicle.

Gradually, the trees thinned to give way to a breathtaking, open, sandy landscape. A golden carpet of silicon particles reached out in an uninterrupted vista at least four times the size of Central Plaza. At the far edge of the beach, where the blue-tinted sky of the dome arced toward the ground, a cluster of palm trees and dense green vegetation disguised the horizon, creating the illusion that the resort might be much bigger than it actually was.

It was a replica of an idealized part of Earth. Alex might have been in awe if such a stunning achievement hadn't been created to serve only the rich.

The buggy took a turn and it was possible to see the white roofs of tourist accommodations snuggled between two areas of tropical plantlife. Designed with balconies where tourists could relax and look out across the resort without the worry of work, food or life struggles, they were nothing like the rusty red of typical Martian buildings where the reality of life was never far away.

Opposite was the blue of an artificial sea – a calm body of water which reflected the color of the blue-tinted dome just as the vast oceans of Earth reflected the color of the sky.

Between the two areas were the dots of people, made visible by the color of their clothes marking them out as individuals on the sand.

Even at that distance, Alex could tell they were Earth-borns. He seethed at the sight of the tourists they had come for. Privileged and sequestered away from the ordinary Martian, they sat unaware they were easy targets. Alex tightened his grip around the gun.

Ivan brought the buggy to a stop some distance away.

"Quietly," he said.

Elea opened the door to the tropical paradise and a rush of heat, heavy with humidity, blew across their obscured faces. Alex had felt the sudden change in environment many times before, when the door of an embarkation room opened onto a field where crops native to a warmer climate were being grown. The others had spent their lives moving from one precisely controlled environment to another within a city, and he sensed their moment of hesitation.

Alex decided it made sense for him to make the first move. He stepped out of the buggy on the side facing away from the tourists and his booted foot unexpectedly sunk into the sand.

The grains of Martian rock had been stripped of metals and crushed into particles of silicon oxide before being tumbled into smooth granules safe enough for naked human feet. It was hard to walk on and Alex wondered why someone had gone to all the effort to create something so impractical. No doubt, a blinkered view that something native to Earth was superior to anything Mars had to offer.

Elea, Pete and Sammi came out behind him, all ready with their shockguns.

Alex activated the auto-slider of his pistol and listened for the satisfying click of the first bullet of the magazine slotting into place.

Last to emerge was Ivan. He dumped the carryall he had brought with him onto the sand, unzipped it and pried apart the sides. With exposure to the light, four hovercams took to the air like birds released from a cage, their rotors whirring with a gentle hum to lift them above the heads of the gang. Each was programmed to record what was about to happen and relay it back to a central hub in the rover they had left in the service tunnel. After an hour's delay, the footage would be sent in the form of an apparently live-streaming message. It was enough time for the urgency of their voices to be felt, while also giving them time to escape.

Ivan retrieved his semi-automatic pistol from where he had tucked it into his belt at the small of his back and activated the auto-slider. With a nod, he indicated they were ready to move out.

Alex dismissed the flicker of hesitancy as he contemplated what they were about to do. His moment to pull out had been back at the hideout when Ivan had revealed his plan. At that time, his anger at being rejected at Helion HQ in Noctis City was still fresh. He held onto that anger as he stuck close to Ivan.

As they approached, Alex made out five Earth-borns on the beach. A man stood by a small, waist-high black table while the others were lying or sitting on the sand nearby. One of them, a woman, let out a cackle of laughter, oblivious to the armed Martians advancing on their position.

Beyond the tourists, the sea lapped at the sand. The body of water might have sat still, like water in a bowl, if it wasn't manipulated by a hidden wave machine which created swells racing towards the shore as if trying to escape. At the water's edge, each wave lost momentum and collapsed onto the fringes of the land in a white foam of crashing liquid before being pulled back into the body of the sea.

A cooling breeze drifted across from the facsimile of the ocean, probably also artificially created, and ruffled the sleeves of Alex's shirt. A tantalizing smell that stirred his stomach drifted across on the air. He realized, then, it hadn't been a table that he had seen from a distance, but a platform cooking what smelled like real meat.

Any doubts Alex had about striking out against the tourists were wiped away in that moment. He had come from a city where the people feared being forced to struggle through a famine. If they had known that, only a short distance away, a group of Earth-borns sat on a fake beach beside a fake ocean enjoying a barbecue, then they would have been as angry as he was.

One of the women seated on the sand pointed. "Who are those people?"

Ivan continued walking with long, purposeful strides, making light work of the sand which sank with the weight of each footstep. Alex and Pete scampered around the back of him and, with Elea and Sammi taking up their positions at the other side of Ivan, the five of them formed a semicircle.

The sitting tourists scrambled to their feet. The man by the barbecue turned to face them holding a long cooking fork with its prongs pointing into the air. He looked to be in his sixties, while the others were younger. The woman who had called out was probably in her forties, while the second woman was even younger. The two other men were approaching middle age. One, who wore only a pair of shorts, was stocky with slack skin over an otherwise muscular chest which had lost some muscle tone away from Earth gravity. The other one wore a short-sleeved shirt buttoned from the chest to partially hide a slight and unthreatening body. All five of them paled as they stared at the barrels of the guns facing them.

The slight man reached for his WristTab.

"Don't!" yelled Ivan. He swiveled to aim his gun directly at the man's chest.

The Earth-born jolted and froze with his hand in midair.

Alex wrapped his finger around the trigger of his gun to show them he was ready to fire if he had to. But none of the tourists were looking at him, they were all looking at Ivan. It was obvious who was in charge.

"What is this?" said the older woman.

"This," said Ivan, "is Mars telling Earth what we think about being exploited."

CHAPTER THIRTY-ONE

A thin film of Martian dust lay across every surface of the rover taken from the construction site. It was over the controls, across the floor and even clung to the side walls with a mixture of static and moisture in the air.

Deverau sat in the driver's seat where, an hour before, Mel had been sitting. The padding had been cold on his back and his thighs. Not even Mel's body heat had been left behind.

He closed his eyes and tried to get a sense of the scientist. She must have left fingerprints in the dust and carbon dioxide from her breath in the air. But her fleeting presence was lost in the noise of construction workers who had been in and out of the rover countless times before her, bringing particles from the planet's surface on their rad-suits.

It gave Deverau no satisfaction to know he was right when he guessed Mel had dumped the stolen MSS rover at the construction site to swap it for one less traceable.

She could have gone anywhere in that rover, as long as it was in range of the battery, but she had driven it back to Deimos City.

"Why come back here?" he said to himself.

The single syllable word sounded hollow bouncing off the hard surfaces of the otherwise empty cabin.

Of all the places on Mars she could have gone, Mel had come back to the scene of the crime. In his experience, criminals only did that when they had left something behind. A piece of incriminating evidence, perhaps, or an object too valuable to be discarded.

He thought back to their conversation on the train and her plea to be allowed to investigate what had happened on the farms. The answers to her behavior had to lie within that desire, but the further he followed his reasoning down that line, the more lost he became.

"So, Dev…"

Deverau jumped in the driver's seat.

He turned to see Jones's face sticking through the open hatchway.

"Jonesy!" Deverau placed his palm on his chest and felt his heart thumping at the sudden shock. "Don't you knock?"

Jones frowned, as if thinking about it. "Not on an open rover hatch, no."

Deverau relaxed back into the seat and his heart began to slow. "What is it?"

"The airlock operator said the rover came in on credentials from the construction site so raised no red flags. She showed me the security footage. Mel had her face turned away from the cameras all the time, but it was definitely her. She went left, heading towards the center of the city as far as I was able to make out, which means she could be anywhere by now."

Deverau sighed. Left or right, it didn't matter. It was her

destination they needed to know. "Did you find out why they didn't report it? They're supposed to be watching for people on the wanted list."

"She said the rover's credentials checked out, so there was no reason to question the person inside," said Jones. "She also said it wasn't her job to be an agent of the MSS and if we wanted to catch someone, we should do a better job at looking for them."

"Charming," said Deverau. But the airlock operator wasn't wrong.

"So, what now?" said Jones.

"We go back and we interview all her family, all her friends and all her colleagues."

Jones looked tired at the very mention of it. "Again?"

"Yes, again," insisted Deverau.

"I'm supposed to be on duty guarding ration queues this afternoon. I thought you were too."

He was, but Deverau was trying to forget about it. "Then we better get a move on."

Deverau stood from the driver's seat and turned back for a moment to look at where Mel had been sitting only that morning. Dismissing his regret at letting the opportunity to intercept her slip away, he stepped out through the hatch to follow her out into the city.

CHAPTER THIRTY-TWO

The sweat from Alex's body seeped into his clothes in the heat of the resort. It was sweltering under the hat and scarf that hid his face. His blood pumping with the thrill of commanding the group of tourists, he shifted his clammy hands on the grip of the gun.

The Earth-borns focused on Ivan while the four hovercams held a steady, circular pattern above their heads, recording every move and every sound. Only the older man, still holding a barbecue fork after stepping away from his cooking, had anything which could remotely be considered a weapon. Upright like a spear, the prongs trembled in his nervous hand.

Ivan gestured with the barrel of his gun. "Throw the fork over there, away from you and from us."

The man looked at the other tourists. They only stared back at him with stunned faces. He tossed the cooking implement onto the sand a meter from his feet.

"Get rid of it," Ivan told Elea.

Elea reached for the barbecue fork and threw it behind her.

It landed in damp sand where it was lapped by waves from the artificial sea.

"What do you want?" The older woman, who had first pointed them out as they advanced on the beach, stood resolute with her hands on her hips.

"We want to show everyone that privileged Earth-borns are lying around feasting on meat while the rest of Mars is starving."

The smell of cooking was enticing. Left unattended, it had begun to burn, but after weeks of living on rations, even burnt meat smelled good.

Ivan pointed his gun at each of the Earth-borns in turn. "We need to take your WristTabs. Hold out your arms."

Reticent and scared, glancing at each other for confirmation, they each raised an arm to form a line of WristTabs. All except the stocky man.

He looked doubtfully at Ivan's weapon. "You won't use that thing in here. A stray bullet could puncture the dome and kill us all."

Ivan glared at the stocky man and lifted the gun to aim it between his eyes. "So when I shoot you, I'll make sure the bullet rattles around your skull."

Ivan's vitriol was so embedded in each word that Alex almost believed he might do it.

"Don't be stupid, Matt," said the older woman. "Do what he says."

Matt lifted his WristTab arm to join the others and tried to maintain his bravado. But a sheen of sweat on his shirtless, slightly saggy muscular chest suggested he was just as afraid as the others.

Sammi handed his shockgun to Ivan while he relieved the Earth-borns of their devices.

The older woman pulled back her arm after her WristTab was removed. Sammi threw it behind him to join the fork in the sea.

"If you're here to rob us, I can give you money," she said.

"Why am I not surprised you want to tempt us with money. Money is all Earth-borns care about," said Ivan.

"That's not true," she insisted. "We're on the year's tour, here to experience the *real* Mars."

"By being in a pretend version of Earth?" scoffed Ivan. "Not even the waves on the sea are real. There's no wind in a dome to create them and Mars doesn't have a big enough moon to cause a tide."

Matt shook his bare arm resentfully as he watched his WristTab splash into the water. "Tourism from Earth brings in a lot of business for Mars," he said. "You should be grateful we're here."

Matt's sense of superiority sickened Alex and he relished the way Ivan was able to spit his own words back in his face.

"Grateful? That our labor and our sweat is making profits for Earth corporations to enrich their own planet?"

"What do you think pays for most of the things you have on Mars?"

"*Matt!*" warned the older woman.

Her admonishment seemed only to goad him further. "Mars-borns need to understand, they live under domes financed by Earth. Most of them were even built by people from Earth. Our World Government provides the MegaCredits for most of your terraforming projects. Without us–"

Ivan spun, aimed a gun directly at Matt's chest and fired.

Alex juddered, almost as if he himself had been hit. Screams erupted from the tourists.

Matt fell back onto the sand.

Fearing he was dead – that Ivan had betrayed his promise not to hurt anyone – Alex stared at Matt's convulsing body.

A dart stuck out of his flesh, firing electric shocks through his nervous system.

Ivan had triggered Sammi's shockgun. The man was not dead, but unconscious.

Alex smiled under his scarf. Ivan had scared the tourists just as, in that brief moment, he had scared Alex. He should never have doubted Ivan, even for that second. Ivan held them all under his complete control and it was exhilarating.

The power in the dart depleted and Matt lay still.

Above them, the hovercam propellers whirred as they altered their positions to capture the action from all the best angles.

Ivan threw the shockgun back to Sammi, who caught it by reflex.

"Everyone listen!" said Ivan, taking a decisive step forward and pacing between the Earth-borns and the rest of his gang. "Do as I say, be quiet and no one else gets hurt."

The slight man and the younger woman held onto each other. Alex surmised they were likely a couple. The other two stood apart: the barbecue man statue-still and the older woman watching Ivan's every move with unease.

"Mars cannot be seen as the child of Earth any longer," said Ivan, playing up to the cameras, stepping away from the tourists so he was no longer in the line of fire from the weapons held by his gang. "Mars will not be dictated to. We will not be stepped upon. Earth has exploited Mars for too long. We need to be allowed to govern ourselves, to work for *ourselves*! Not through some Terraforming Committee puppet of a blue-green planet three hundred million kilometers away, but proper self-government that doesn't pander to the rich interests of Earth corporations."

Energized by his words, Alex watched intently as Ivan spoke the truth, while the people who needed to hear it were forced to listen.

"When Mars has a problem, when we stare in the face of famine – where is Earth? More than six months away. Mars already has to face the future on its own, why shackle us to our parent like we are some sort of criminal needing to be punished? Meanwhile, Earth-borns lounge on an artificial beach, separated from the rest of us in a rich person's resort, eating food that a starving Mars can only dream of."

He kicked the neglected barbecue to emphasize his point. Pieces of hot metal and charred meat were propelled into the air. The tourist couple jumped out of the way before the burning grate landed on the sand where they had been standing.

"I am prepared to hold these Earth-borns hostage until our demands are met," Ivan told the hovercams. "But I know that what I am asking will not happen today. So, take this as a warning. If nothing is done, there will be worse to come. Mars demands–"

A movement on the sand caused Alex to turn. Matt – silently recovered from the shockdart while Ivan had held everyone's attention – was on his feet.

"Watch out!" yelled Alex.

Matt dived at Ivan.

He struck him in the stomach before Ivan had time to react. Alex saw the brief moment of surprise in his eyes before he was knocked backwards. A shot exploded from his gun before he hit the sand, sending a bullet directly above him.

"The dome!" cried the older woman. The other tourists looked up at where a stray bullet could have punctured the resort's protective membrane. But Alex kept his gaze fixed on Ivan as he crashed onto the sand with Matt on top of him.

"Ivan!" shouted Elea, forgetting their directive not to use each other's names.

The Earth-born, naturally stronger than even Ivan's muscular frame, easily resisted Ivan's attempts to break free. Tugging his scarf down, Matt revealed Ivan's panicked face.

Pete fired his shockgun at them. But in the screaming and confusion, his aim was off and the dart landed uselessly on the beach.

Alex's sweaty finger slipped on the trigger as he turned to face the grappling men. But their two bodies were intertwined. He couldn't shoot the Earth-born attacker without risking hitting Ivan.

Matt reached for the gun in Ivan's right hand. Ivan countered with his left fist, striking the Earth-born's jaw and knocking his head backwards. Ivan turned to get to his feet.

The men parted for a moment and Alex took his shot.

The blast rang out across the resort, like the dome was cracking in two, with a force so great the recoil forced Alex's hands to flick up as the bullet left the barrel. Elea screamed.

Alex waited for the Earth-born to collapse like shooting victims fell to the ground in films.

But it was Elea who fell.

She had stepped too close to the firing zone and Alex's wayward aim had sent the bullet into her shoulder.

"Ivan!" she yelled as she lay on the ground, screaming in pain with blood seeping into her shirt.

Alex lowered his weapon in horror. He stared, unblinking, at Elea clutching at her wound. Her hands were unable to stop the bleeding and red oozed between the gaps in her fingers.

In that moment of distraction, Matt launched himself at Ivan a second time and the pair went sprawling. Ivan's back struck the sand and Matt grabbed a wrist with each hand to pin him to the beach. Straddling him, Matt pressed the full force of his weight upon Ivan's body. Ivan kicked and struggled, but he was outmatched.

"Drop the gun!" demanded the Earth-born.

"No!"

"You want to shoot more of your friends?"

Ivan glanced over to where Elea lay. She had pulled down her scarf to aid her labored breathing and it had revealed her face contorted in pain.

Ivan writhed in the sand, but Matt remained in control. He stamped one knee on Ivan's left forearm. Ivan cried out as he realized his arm was still pinned down while the Earth-born had freed up his hand to reach for the gun.

Squeezing Ivan's wrist so his finger couldn't activate the trigger, Matt grabbed the barrel with his free hand and twisted the gun away from his opponent's grasp.

With a victorious grin, Matt jumped clear and pointed Ivan's own gun directly at him. Ivan was scrabbling to his feet.

"Stay down!" ordered Matt.

Ivan froze. Still kneeling on one knee, he looked up at the barrel. Matt's finger curled around the trigger, ready to fire.

Pete and Sammi stood with their shockguns out in front of them, pointing them at the Earth-born with an uncertain aim.

"Put your weapons down!" ordered Matt.

Alex's gun hung loosely at his side in trembling fingers. He had lowered it after shooting Elea. Or he assumed he must have, he didn't remember. Time continued around him while shock left him paralyzed. Glancing at Elea, as she lay alone and terrified bleeding out onto the sand, only made it worse. Even without looking, he heard the panic in her breaths which became shorter and more rapid with each minute.

The gun Alex thought had given him power had actually left him powerless. He let the deadly weapon slip from his grasp and it thumped to the sand at his feet.

Fear and uncertainty in Pete and Sammi's eyes stared out from their disguises. They hesitated. Neither firing, nor giving up their weapons.

"Think you can incapacitate me before I kill your friend?" asked Matt.

Alex knew they could not. A bullet might have stopped the Earth-born, if it could have been fired quickly and accurately enough, but the dart from a shockgun, even if it hit before Matt could fire, would still give him valuable fractions of a second before it seized up his muscles.

Sammi threw his shockgun aside.

Pete looked at Ivan as if asking for help.

Ivan didn't move. It was the first time Alex had ever seen him scared of anything. "Do it," said Ivan.

Pete tossed away the shockgun.

Matt grinned again in satisfaction. The rest of the Earth tourists relaxed. The legs of the younger woman collapsed from under her and she sank to the sand.

The wailing sound of an alarm blared out from the accommodation buildings.

"What's that?" said the barbecue man.

"It's a breach warning," said Matt. "The first bullet must have shot a hole in the dome. Reduced air pressure will set off the alarm."

Alex was breathing hard and fast. He assumed it was because he was terrified, not because the air was thinning. A bullet hole, even in a dome as small as the resort, would take a long time to cause critical oxygen and heat loss. He hoped.

"Anton, go call the Mars Security Service," said Matt.

The barbecue man scuttled off down the beach to the shoreline where Sammi had thrown the tourists' WristTabs.

The older woman went over to Elea and knelt beside her. "It's OK," she said soothingly, her voice barely audible above the wail of the alarm. "I'm a doctor, you're going to be OK."

"We can't wait for the MSS to get here!" said Ivan, looking up at his own gun still aimed at him. "Half the atmosphere could have vented by then. It'll kill you as well as us."

Two Mars-born members of resort staff had run out of the accommodation buildings at the sound of the alarm and closed in on the beach party. "Everyone back to the safety room!" shouted one, a young and slender woman in a white tunic suit. "This is not a drill!"

She stopped when she saw the standoff. Her colleague, dressed in the same white uniform, and only two paces behind her, skidded to a halt in the sand.

"Let them go," said the doctor, still kneeling beside Elea. She had her palms flat on Elea's shoulder, one on top of the other, putting pressure on the wound which seemed to be stemming the bleeding. "What else are you going to do? Drag them back inside?"

Matt's eyes narrowed as he glared at Ivan. "Stand up," he ordered.

Ivan slowly got to his feet. He splayed out his hands to show he offered no threat.

"Ivan!" yelled Elea.

Where she lay on the sand, a patch of golden grains had turned crimson with her blood. Ivan said nothing. The regret on his face said everything.

"Let me up!" said Elea. She lifted her chest against the pressure from the doctor's palms.

The doctor pushed her back down again. "You can't get up, you'll bleed out."

"Ivan, don't leave me here to die!" Elea's eyes filled with tears of pain and fear.

"You're not going to die," said the doctor. "I'll look after you."

The searing wail of the alarm was breaking through the defenses of Alex's ears. Screaming for attention and pulling him out of shock.

Matt gestured with Ivan's confiscated gun. "Go on, leave. Before I change my mind."

Ivan looked down at Elea with regret.

"Don't worry," said the doctor. "I'll look after her. If you try to move her, you could kill her."

Whether Ivan believed her or whether he preferred to save

himself, it wasn't clear. "I'm sorry, Elea." He looked to the others. "Let's go."

"*Ivan!*" Elea's scream turned to sobbing.

Ivan had already turned away from her and was running the best he could across the sand. Pete and Sammi ran after him.

Alex paused as he neared Elea. He wanted to say sorry, but fear and shame had stolen his voice.

The resort staff hustled for the tourists to get back into the building.

"I need a med evac pod!" the doctor called out to the woman in the white tunic.

As he turned to follow his friends, it seemed to Alex that the Earth-born was really helping her. Even though, above her head, the atmosphere was leaking out of a bullet hole in the dome. He tried to understand why she would do that, moments after Elea had been pointing a shockgun at her. But he didn't have the mental capacity to reconcile the contradiction. He needed to escape and turned to run, struggling to catch up with the others as the sand shifted under his boots with each step.

CHAPTER THIRTY-THREE

Doctor Kaito Tanaka was a difficult woman to track down. Deverau's messages went unanswered and everyone he spoke to said she was too busy dealing with the food crisis to talk to him. But, like most of the population, he was aware of the one place and time where she would be – in front of an ICN camera giving a daily news briefing.

The briefings were held in Hunter House, the administrative hub for Deimos City which took up one whole side of Central Plaza. The building was guarded by MSS officers, so he gained access by simply showing his credentials.

The media room, which had seemed to embody so much gravitas when he had seen officials broadcasting from it, had a strange deadness to it. Black, absorbing curtains hung from all four walls which dampened his footsteps and swallowed up any extraneous light. At the head of the room, Kaito stood at one of two lecterns facing an audience of empty chairs, a camera and three members of an ICN crew.

A woman with an ICN ID badge turned to him with a

disapproving glare. "Excuse me, you're not allowed in here."

"It's OK," said Kaito. "This man is an inspector with the MSS."

She seemed unhappy, but stepped aside to let him pass. "We go live in ten minutes."

Deverau continued down the aisle between the two rows of empty chairs and past the camera.

"I've been trying to get hold of you," he said pointedly.

"I have a member of my staff filter my messages," she said. "I'm sorry they didn't realize it was important. Do you have news about Mel?"

He stopped beside the lectern. "Not exactly."

She frowned. "Then why are you here, *exactly*?"

"We have reason to believe Doctor Erdan is back in Deimos City."

Deverau watched her surprised reaction and judged it most likely to be genuine.

"Do you know where she might go in Deimos City or who she might contact?"

"I already gave a list to the MSS."

"I'm trying to narrow it down," said Deverau. "Perhaps you could start by telling me when you last saw her."

She dropped her gaze to the tablet she had placed on the lectern. But her stare suggested she was thinking rather than reading through her notes.

"OK," she said, raising her head to look directly at him. "If you must know, I saw her shortly after that business with the train."

Deverau was taken aback. "She came to you after she escaped from the train?"

Kaito frowned again. "I haven't got time to answer the same question twice, inspector. I have a news briefing to prepare for."

"What I meant was, you should have reported it."

"I know I should have, but she was my friend."

"*Was*?" Deverau clarified.

"*Is* my friend. Anyway, there was nothing to report. I gave her some clothes, some food and then she left."

"I find it hard to believe that's all she came for."

"She wanted access to a lab, but I couldn't give that to her because of my new job."

Deverau thought back to his conversation with Mel on the train and her insistence that she should be the one investigating what went wrong on the farms. It was consistent with what Kaito was telling him.

"Have you seen her since?" he asked.

"No." Her response was instant and definitive. "If she came back to Deimos City, I imagine it's for something important. Have you asked her colleagues at the lab?"

"My sergeant is there now."

"Then there's nothing else I can say."

But the conversation on the train was still on his mind. "Do you think she did it?"

Kaito looked surprised at the question. "Deliberately destroyed all those crops? It's difficult to think anyone would do such a thing. If I wasn't busy trying to feed Mars, I would devote resources to finding out."

It was hardly a resounding expression of support for her friend.

The ICN woman approached. "Excuse me, but we need to carry out checks before we go live. Which is in a few minutes."

"Of course," said Kaito. She took up position behind the lectern on the right, smoothed down her jacket and faced the camera.

Deverau could feel the gaze of the ICN woman on him and knew he was in her way, but there was something Mel had asked him on the train which he hadn't been able to answer. "Are all the crops potatoes?"

"I beg your pardon?" said Kaito.

A less experienced interviewer might have taken Kaito's discomfort as a reaction to the subject coming out of the blue. But Deverau saw something deeper. Like she was embarrassed or uncomfortable about the nature of his question.

"That was the crop Mel was working with," he reminded her. "She told me all the images she saw of dead crops were of potatoes. I'm having a hard time understanding how the failure of one type of food crop could cause such a widespread problem. Surely Mars grows lots of different things."

"Potatoes can feed a lot of people, Inspector. On Mars, we have a lot of people to feed."

The ICN woman ran out of patience. "Are you going to move, or do I have to call security?"

Deverau backed away. He had no desire to be dragged out by his own officers. Especially not in front of a soon-to-be-live camera.

The ICN woman followed him to the door. As he turned to leave, he glanced back at the empty lectern on the left where he would have expected to see the chair of the Terraforming Committee.

"Isn't Farah Sharif supposed to be here?" he asked the ICN woman.

"She's doing her bit from Noctis City," she said. "The pair of them are so busy, it's getting harder to get them together in the same room."

"No big announcements today, then?" asked Deverau.

"We think there will be. The word is, some staple foods are getting low and the ration is going to be tightened."

Deverau's stomach grumbled at the news.

"If you promise to be quiet, you can stay and watch," the ICN woman offered.

"Thank you, but she's not the only one who is busy."

He turned to go. Hearing the headline was bad enough. He didn't need to sit there and torture himself with all the unpleasant details.

CHAPTER THIRTY-FOUR

Alex sat in the front seat of the rover speeding along the road leading away from the Martian Tropics resort. He had no memory of running across the sand, escaping in the cleaning buggy and getting back to the rover parked in the service area. The only image in his mind was Elea's panicked face as she clutched her red-stained shirt with blood trickling out through her fingers.

"This is not good," said Ivan.

Alex's attention was pulled to the present. "What?"

Ivan nodded toward the windshield. "MSS."

Up ahead, a vehicle was heading straight towards them. Most likely another rover, by the size of the dust cloud created in its wake.

"You don't know that," said Alex, looking at the vehicle which was far enough away that it was impossible to tell. "It could be anyone."

The rover's control systems spoke as if responding to their conversation. *"Communication request from Mars Security Services rover."*

Ivan flashed Alex a knowing look. "Hang on, everyone."

Without giving Pete and Sammi in the back a chance to respond, Ivan pushed the control stick hard left and the rover swung off the road. Alex was almost thrown out of his seat as the rover hit the bumpy Martian surface.

"Urgent communication request from Mars Security Services rover."

"No, I don't want to talk to them, you fatuous machine!" Ivan shut down communications. They could now no longer receive calls demanding their surrender, or call out for help.

The rover struck the edge of a boulder the size of a rover wheel and Alex was thrown forward. He reached out to stop himself being catapulted through the windshield and his hands slapped on the dashboard. Pushing himself back into the seat, he fumbled for the seatbelt.

Grinning, Ivan swerved hard past another boulder almost as large as he clung onto the control stick like a rider on an unruly horse.

On the dashboard's left display, the image from the rearview camera showed the MSS rover in pursuit. Ivan kept driving one handed while he put on his seatbelt.

"Can we outrun them?" said Pete.

"Maybe," said Ivan. "I'm more concerned with them figuring out where we're going and sending another rover to cut us off. Lucky for us, I know the mining works around here – almost certainly better than they do."

The rover lurched a second time and Alex was thrown against his secured seatbelt.

Sammi had also strapped in at the back, but Pete was more cavalier and staggered forward, ducking to avoid hitting his head while the rover struggled to smooth the ride over the rough terrain. He leaned between the two front seats. "Are you sure you should be doing this? If you hit the wrong rock, you'll turn us over and get us killed."

"You want to get caught?" Ivan barked at him.

"Well... no."

"You want to go to jail?"

"No, but I don't want to die either."

"Then trust me and sit down."

Alex watched with increasing unease as the MSS rover grew larger in the rearview screen. A threat confirmed by the distance counting down on the readout. "Ivan, they're gaining on us."

Ivan frowned at the view screen. "Everyone suit up!"

"What are you going to do?" said Alex.

"A little trick I learned from some mining pals of mine. But I'm going to need you to drive."

"Me?"

Alex looked doubtfully at the unfamiliar controls. He'd driven a rover in a simulator, but never for real.

"I'll set us on course for the old Sinai mines," said Ivan.

Through the windscreen, Alex saw a disused mine works building and its piles of waste discarded on the surface of the plain.

"You need to drive as close as you can to the slag heaps," continued Ivan. "But don't let your wheels go too far up the slopes. With the increasing temperature on Mars, they're becoming unstable. At least, that's what I'm banking on."

Pete's warning about getting them all killed replayed in his head as Alex tried to remember his lessons in the simulator. "I'm not sure I can."

"I have faith in you, Alex. But you'll need to suit up first." He glanced around and shouted at Pete and Sammi. "That goes for you too – suit up! For this to work, I'm going to have to open the hatch."

"The hatch?" Alex feared that venting their breathable atmosphere, by effectively opening a hole in the vehicle, could potentially make the rover unstable and even more difficult to drive.

"*Quickly!*"

Ivan's orders shocked Alex into moving. He unfastened his belt and slipped between the two front seats to get into the back, banging his head against the hull as the rover lurched to one side.

Sammi pulled out all five rad-suits from the compartment near the hatch. Enough for all of them, including Elea. They each grabbed one, leaving Elea's suit abandoned and alone on the bench.

Alex suited up and, as he needed to be ready first, Pete helped him.

Pete stood ready with his helmet as Alex waited for him to finish. "I hope we're doing the right thing," he said.

Alex was about to reassure him that Ivan had always got them through in the past, but Pete slipped the helmet over his head and secured the seal, cutting off his chance to reply.

Locked into his own individual environment, Alex felt suddenly alone. Ivan had told them not to use the suit comms unless absolutely necessary in case the MSS were monitoring and so all he could hear were the suit's life support systems, the rapid beat of his heart and his own nervous breath echoing back at him.

Walking awkwardly in the cumbersome suit, Alex returned to the front. The slag heaps Ivan had talked about were up ahead. The trackway, mostly cleared of major obstacles after years of mining vehicles operating in that area, was relatively smooth. The readout alongside the image of the pursuing MMS rover showed it had closed in a little, but Ivan's wild driving had sustained a reasonable distance.

Ivan unfastened his seatbelt and slipped out of the chair while maintaining his grip on the control. Alex took it from him and felt the resistance of the vehicle as Ivan let go to jump into the back of the rover. Once seated, with a few testing moves, Alex was able to judge the sensitivity of the controls, even through the thickness of his gloves. Keeping up the speed, he headed for the slag heaps.

Piles of mining waste, like a range of mountains stretching around the base of the dead volcano, towered off to the side, some almost as high as a city dome. Lichen had colonized the far side of the peaks where they would have caught the sun and enough warmth for the primitive organism to creep its tiny, leafless branches across the surface.

The rover's right wheels slipped on the loose slag at the bottom of the first heap. Alex swerved to compensate, sending the rover too high up the mound and tipping it sideways by almost twenty degrees.

Alex yanked the controls back the other way and the rover sped down the waste, showering a scatter of slag out behind it as it bumped down to the track. He watched the dust and debris fly away on the rear viewscreen. As it cleared, he saw the MSS rover getting closer by running a tight, straight and far less chaotic path next to the heaps.

Ivan's helmeted face appeared beside him. Alex thought he might be there to re-take the helm, but Ivan was only interested in the dashboard. He punched up the fail-safes and entered overrides to allow the hatch to open while on the move.

Ivan gave Alex a last look through his visor as if to tell him to get ready, then selected the option to open the hatch.

Even in the thin air, the slight change in aerodynamics caused the rover to waver. But Alex had quickly learned how the vehicle responded to his hand on the control stick and compensated without straying too much from the path. High on the thrill of self-satisfaction and pumping adrenalin, Alex also knew that it might take only one miscalculation to crash the rover. He hoped that, whatever Ivan was planning, he did it soon.

He snatched a moment to glance behind and saw Ivan holding an explosive charge, similar to the ones they had used to derail the train, but without the magnetic attachment.

Alex returned focus to his driving. A collapsed part of the slag heap rapidly approached with an unassailably large mound of debris blocking their path. Alex swung around it. The rover tipped dangerously and the near side wheels bumped over the edges.

The MSS rover took a straighter, more direct path and gained a little ground. Alex sped up as much as he dared.

Something too big to be a piece of loose slag bounced across the view relayed by the rear camera and came to a stop at the bottom of the heap behind them. Ivan had thrown the bomb into the path of the MSS rover from the open hatch.

With no time to avoid it, the MSS rover drove right over it. Alex willed the rover's destruction.

A second later, a flash erupted behind the MSS and a blink of flame silhouetted their pursuers. The MSS rover rocked with the force of the explosion, but emerged intact from the cloud of dust and debris. The explosive had gone off a split second too late.

Meanwhile, Alex had gained ground. Filled with the excitement and confidence that they could actually beat the MSS, he concentrated on driving. Ivan tossed another charge out of the open hatch.

It struck something on the track behind them and flew off at an angle. Alex watched the view screen with disappointment as it spun away out of view and exploded to the side. He saw no flash, but felt the rumble permeate through the ground. The MSS rover was still in pursuit.

Soon, there would be no more slag heaps. There were only two more hills and then the open plain. Alex decelerated to give them more time to make a final attempt, taking a risk that it wouldn't allow the MSS to catch them.

Glancing over his shoulder, Alex saw Ivan grab at the handle by the hatch with one hand and swing his body out of the vehicle. He launched a third explosive charge.

It came into view on the rear screen, bouncing once on the track and embedding itself in the slag.

Ivan pulled himself back inside, turned from the hatch and crouched to brace himself.

The MSS rover approached the bomb. It was, Alex anticipated, a second before detonation.

But the explosion didn't wait. A bright flash ripped into the mound, scattering a shower of rubble into the air.

Caught in the blast zone, Alex was thrown sideways as

their whole rover swerved towards the hill. It careened up the slope, the wheels struggling to grip on the loose rubble.

The MSS rover still hurtled, untouched, towards the site of the explosion.

Then the side of the hill collapsed. The entire mound slid into the gap blown out from underneath, pieces of slag tumbling down onto the trackway to block it completely.

The MSS rover was obscured behind it. Alex could only see the roof of the pursuing vehicle as it turned sideways – too late to avoid the obstacle – and crashed right into it, coming to a complete halt.

"*Yes!*" Alex yelled.

In the rear viewscreen, the roof of the MSS rover peering over the collapsed slag heap became smaller as they raced away.

Laughing to himself – his whole body alive with the elation of victory – Alex allowed the rover to slow. He sat back in the driver's seat and felt his sweat cool in the breeze from the rad-suit's regulated environment.

Ivan was suddenly at his side, his grin visible through his visor. He accessed the controls on the dashboard to close the hatch and re-pressurize the vehicle. It would be a few minutes before they would be able to take off their rad-suits and speak freely.

Ivan tapped on Alex's helmet with a gloved finger to gain his attention. "We're going home!" he mouthed.

Relief almost made Alex want to cry, even while he was still laughing.

He looked out of the windscreen as they left the mining area to enter out onto the plain. Then he checked all external cameras and confirmed there were no more MSS vehicles in sight.

Ivan took over to punch in a course back to Deimos City.

Alex was grateful to be going home. It was only the thought of what he was going to do when he got there that scared him.

CHAPTER THIRTY-FIVE

Hot from having to wear body armor in the perfectly controlled temperature of Deimos City, Deverau felt the material of his sweaty MSS uniform damp against his skin.

At least, the uniform from the MSS store which he had been mandated to wear. He understood crowd control duties required him to appear distinct from members of the public, but it still felt like a demotion. He hadn't worn a uniform since his graduation ceremony on Earth when he was a young man starting out in his career. His parents had been proud to see him dressed like that, while he had felt embarrassed at being turned into a clone of every other graduate in the hall.

The armor he didn't mind so much. With tensions running high among the population, the stab vest and helmet were necessary precautions. There had been multiple scuffles among people in ration queues and several more serious outbreaks of violence. One officer at the station, Cinquetti, had to have one of his fingers sewn back on after he stepped in to quell an argument and someone had pulled a knife.

Deverau's shift on one of the ration queues had been less eventful, like the mood in the city had changed. He merely stood as people shuffled past to collect their allocation of food, their faces blank with acceptance. In some ways, he would have preferred them to have fought and argued, at least it would have shown they were alive. Stunned by Sharif's announcement that rations were to be tightened, the people appeared to have lost their fighting spirit. Or they were keeping it bottled up inside which, should it spill out all at once, threatened to be even more dangerous.

Relieved to get back to the locker room at the station, Deverau placed the helmet on one of the benches and sat beside it to remove his stab vest.

He saw from his WristTab that Jones had been trying to contact him. He considered waiting to speak to him until after he had peeled off his sweaty uniform, but decided if there was something he needed to know, he was better off knowing it sooner than later.

He returned Jones' call. "What do you want, Jonesy?"

"Dev, thanks for getting back to me. We got a call about a serious firearms incident in the Martian Tropics resort."

"Firearms?"

Deverau sat up straight, suddenly alert.

"As in illegal gun," confirmed Jones. "As in actual bullets."

Deverau thought of the layers of security personnel who had failed to do their job properly in allowing bullet-firing weapons to be smuggled to Mars. Their incompetence angered him. He remembered reading a report which said ninety percent of lethal contraband was seized before it reached Mars, as if that was some sort of victory. The authors of the report didn't have to deal with the ten percent that was missed.

"At a holiday resort of all places," said Deverau. "Do we even have jurisdiction there?"

"The MSS does, but which branch has responsibility is… debatable. Deimos claimed it because one of our operatives took the call and we're nearest. Sort of. The shooters got away, but if we went to the crime scene now, we could claim the investigation ahead of Noctis…"

Deverau tapped his fingers on the top of the helmet beside him. The idea was tempting. "You do realize how busy we are?"

"Yes, but I thought you would want the option."

Deverau pulled at the fastenings of his stab vest as he considered adding to his workload. If ten percent of lethal contraband was going to end up on Mars, the least they could do was make sure it was dealt with by one of their more experienced officers.

"If we took the case," said Deverau, thinking aloud, "it would annoy the heck out of those smug, over-resourced charlatans at Noctis City."

"That's what I thought," said Jones.

Then they were agreed.

"Book a rover," said Deverau. "I'll get changed, then I'll join you."

CHAPTER THIRTY-SIX

Darkness hung in the cafe like the ghost of a happier time. Only a short walk from the Tall Greenhouse, it had once been a pleasant place to take a lunch break or hold an informal meeting. But it had been forced to close by the food crisis and all Mel could see inside, as she cowered in the porchway set back from the glass frontage, were the upturned chairs stacked on top of tables. She flashed back to the time she sat with Kaito, soon after she came back from maternity leave, and talked about her ambition for the viral enhancing project.

Mel huddled with her back to the stream of people walking by at the end of the day, pretending to be checking her reflection in the glass. But all the while she was wiping an imaginary smudge of dirt off her cheek, tucking a piece of loose hair behind her ear or straightening her blouse, she was actually watching the reflections of people behind her. Waiting for someone she could trust.

She heard Raj before she saw him, his voice emerging

mid-discussion as he came closer. "… I'm telling you, they're overrated."

"So says the loser backing Deimos City," said a second voice which she was sure was Ben's.

The glass reflected the unmistakable images of her two colleagues approaching her position. She needed to speak to one of them and, out of the two, Raj was her preferred choice. He was both cleverer than Ben and less likely to turn her in to further his own career. But she needed to speak to him alone and away from the stream of other people.

Mel tugged at the button on the bottom of her blouse until the thread broke and she was able to roll it loose between her thumb and forefinger.

"You only support Tharsis City because they're winning," said Raj.

"Picking the winners is always the best strategy," Ben was saying. "And not only in basketball."

Their faces moved out of the reflection zone which meant they were passing by her. Mel turned and located the back of their heads receding down the path. She twirled the button in her fingers, found her aim and flicked it the short distance.

The button struck Raj on the back of the neck. He turned back to see where it had come from.

Mel peered out from the porch and his eyes widened in surprise as he saw her. He opened his mouth to speak, but she shook her head. She turned and walked back the other way, keeping her head down to avoid being recognized in the crowd, all the while desperately hoping that Raj would follow.

"I forgot something back at the lab," she heard Raj say.

"Don't change the subject just because you know I'm right about Tharsis City," replied Ben.

"No, seriously. You go on, I'll see you tomorrow…"

If they said any more to each other, their voices were lost in the surrounding footsteps and chatter.

Mel approached a side street which served as a back entrance to the cafe and nearby buildings, knowing that it would be quiet. As she did so, she risked a glance back and was relieved to see Raj hurrying to catch up with her. Pausing just enough to make sure he had also seen her, she turned.

The narrow passageway, only wide enough for a single supply vehicle, was bordered by two lines of three-story red brick buildings with rear entry doors. A little further down, someone had left out a cluster of recycling bins. Mel ducked behind them.

Raj appeared from around the bins and turned to face her. "Mel! What are you doing here?"

Mel reached forward and grabbed hold of his sleeve. "Don't stand in the middle of the street, you'll draw attention." She pulled him closer.

"Do you know everyone's been told to report if they see you?"

"Why do you think I brought you back here?" she said in an urgent whisper.

"They're saying you sabotaged the farms – did you?"

The sting of the accusation, coming from a friend, was painful and unexpected. "You don't seriously believe that?"

"No, but…"

"I don't want to explain here – even I don't have all the details – but I think someone stole my experiment."

"Are you serious?"

"It's why the authorities think I'm to blame. I need to find out who it was and why they did it, and the only way I can do that is to get back into my lab."

"You can't go in there," said Raj. "The MSS have been back asking questions about you. People will report you. And, anyway, facial recognition will flag you as soon as you're in the building."

"That's why I need your help, Raj."

"Mel…"

Tears were forming in her eyes. She couldn't help it. She was so tired, so hungry, so scared… If she couldn't trust Raj, then she had no one else to turn to. "Please."

He must have seen her desperation because his posture softened. He gave her a reassuring smile and she saw, in his expression, the trusted colleague she remembered from the days before she had been arrested and her life had been turned upside down.

"OK, if you're certain. What do you want me to do?"

CHAPTER THIRTY-SEVEN

The black rectangular blot in the sky lay like a geometric sunspot on the dome of the Martian Tropics resort. Deverau squinted to try to see the bullet hole that had been fired into it. But he saw only the silhouettes of people in rad-suits and harnesses climbing over the exterior of the dome checking for more damage.

He had been told the hole had been patched and the resort's environment restored to optimum conditions, but the fact that there were still people up there made him suspect he was being given a sugar-coated version of the truth.

"Dev!"

Deverau turned away from the dome and looked out across the sand where, as his pupils grew wider to compensate for the lower light levels, he saw the figure of Sergeant Jones walking towards him. He recognized the crumpled blue suit he was wearing as the same one he had on the week before. Most likely hung up after it had been worn and dusted off again that morning to pretend he was organized enough to put on clean clothes.

Jones was holding something that looked remarkably like a hovercam.

"What's that?" said Deverau.

"It's a hovercam," said Jones.

Deverau frowned. "I can see that. I meant, what are you doing with it?"

"The attackers brought it. Actually, they brought four of them. The whole incident was captured on camera."

"That was very considerate of them to record all the evidence for us," said Deverau sarcastically.

"That's the good news," said Jones.

"Which suggests there is also some bad news."

"They rigged the hovercams – or, at least, they rigged the receiver – to broadcast the footage with an hour's delay. So the whole thing has now been released and is publicly available. I've asked the tech crew to get it pulled down, but they're almost as busy as we are, so we're going to have to resign ourselves to it being out there and staying out there."

Deverau considered the balance of good and bad news and decided they were still on top. "Anything good on the recording?"

"One thing stood out." Jones fiddled with his WristTab and brought up the footage of the attackers which he showed Deverau. "The leader's face scarf slipped in the scuffle. Facial recognition should have no trouble identifying him."

Deverau looked at the screen on Jones's wrist. The footage, expertly captured by several hovercams and cut together automatically, showed two men fighting each other on the sand. Despite them being from different planets, they seemed evenly matched. Deverau didn't know who the Mars-born man was from his face, but there was still something familiar about him.

"I think this could be the same lot who caused that near-riot handing out food in the transport terminal," he said. "What do you think?"

Jones turned his WristTab back to face him. "Could be. Difficult to tell."

The more Deverau thought about it, the more he was sure. Four young Mars-born men and one woman. It had to be.

He let out a puff of air as he realized he was sweating. "Is it stupidly hot in here, or is it me?"

He took off his jacket which, he realized, was the same one he had been wearing all last week and was even more crumpled than Jones' suit.

"It's stupidly hot in here," said Jones. "Which is, I believe, the point."

"Lovely, though." Deverau looked out to the fake sea, which was oddly calm after the wave machine had been turned off for the duration of the repairs. "How much does it cost to stay here?"

"You'd have to save up for a long time on an inspector's salary."

"Hmm." As he contemplated, not for the first time, his choice of occupation, which involved long hours and not the greatest remuneration, he saw someone walking towards them from the direction of the accommodation buildings.

As she came closer, he could see she was Earth-born and in her forties. She wore a short-sleeved blue shirt and a pair of khaki shorts both stained with blood. By the way she was walking with confidence and purpose, he assumed it was somebody else's blood.

"I understand you wanted a word with me?" she asked.

Deverau nodded. "I'm Inspector Deverau and this is Sergeant Jones."

"I'm Doctor Toplovski," she said. "I believe you're the one who's stopping me from having a shower and getting changed."

Deverau ignored her thinly veiled rebuke. "I wanted to ask you about the woman who got shot."

"She was alive and conscious when the medics got here," said the woman. "As far as I could tell, the bullet missed her organs. My worry was it might have punctured the top of her lung. Patients can go downhill rapidly with that sort of injury."

"You're a medical doctor, then?" asked Deverau.

"Twenty years in hospitals on the southern coast of Europe where I saw too many gunshot wounds. I wasn't expecting to see one on Mars."

"I'm sorry you had to, doctor."

"She called him Ivan."

"What?" said Deverau.

"The injured woman. She called their leader Ivan. I don't know if that helps you catch those terrorists. We were lucky it wasn't one of us who was shot."

"It helps, yes. Thank you."

"Can I wash the terrorist's blood off me now?"

Deverau was taken aback by the use of the word terrorist, but nodded. "Yes. Thank you, doctor."

She turned and marched back the way she had come.

"I also saw too many gunshot wounds on Earth," reflected Deverau. "I used to carry a gun myself back then. I didn't think I would have to contemplate carrying one on Mars."

"That's the problem with people," said Jones. "You can

begin a new civilization on a new world, but you still have to populate it with the same old human beings."

Deverau turned away from the accommodation buildings to gaze back out across the fake sea to the oddly close horizon, where the arching dome marked the edge of the resort. To the side, in the direction of the service tunnel where he had parked the MSS rover, his attention was taken by a group of four people striding across the sand towards them.

"Talking of people being a problem..." he said.

Jones turned to look.

"... what's the betting that they're investigators from Noctis City?"

"It's a strong bet," said Jones.

Deverau took another deep breath. And, this time, not because of the heat. "Wish me luck."

"Luck with what?"

"Telling them this is my case because we have reason to believe the attackers are from Deimos City. Then demanding more resources be put towards crowd control to free me up to do the proper investigation I should have been doing to start with. An investigation, I will have to point out, that might have prevented this entire incident from happening if I'd been allowed to get on with it."

Jones let out a whistle. "Good luck, Dev."

Deverau walked towards the delegation from Noctis City and offered them a friendly wave, knowing that he was going to need more than luck.

CHAPTER THIRTY-EIGHT

Mel had once used what she called the "coffee trick" to smuggle a boy into student accommodation after hours when she was at university. The boy had turned out to be a mistake and had she sent him packing, but she had kept the knowledge of the trick because she had the feeling she might need to use it again.

The university rooms had unsophisticated security compared to the measures installed by EcoLine at the Tall Greenhouse. But they still relied on the inflexibility of automated face recognition and the over-flexibility of the human mind.

She needed to avoid bumping into any other workers who might recognize her, so the plan was to go in after everyone, apart from workaholics and security guards, had left. But not so late that it would arouse suspicion. Mel settled on eight o'clock as the optimum time and had to wait around for Raj to return.

Several anxious hours followed in which she hid in the

shadows and walked through under-populated streets. All the time she looked at her feet to avoid eye contact with other pedestrians or any cameras that might be watching.

Mel had been shielded from the effects of food shortages during her time with Pedro. Returning to the city, she was exposed to its gloomy and foreboding atmosphere. People walked with their heads down, their faces gaunt from living on rations and troubled from the stress of potential starvation. There was no sense of joy or laughter in the streets. They merely shuffled their feet as they moved from one place to another.

As close to eight o'clock as she could estimate, Mel headed back to the side street to return to her hiding place and wait for Raj. She was shivering, not because she was cold, but because she was frightened he wouldn't return. She wished she had a WristTab so she could check how early she was and how long she dared to hang around if eight o'clock came and went.

While she waited, she thought back to that moment six months before when she had arrived at work to find both the door to the cold storage area and the refrigerator containing her nuclear stock had been left ajar. All that time that she had admonished herself for being careless and had neglected to consider an alternative possibility – that she wasn't the one who left them open.

The appearance of Raj's unmistakable figure strolling towards her warmed her like a rush of hot air. He brought with him, as arranged, two lidded cups of coffee.

"Raj!" she greeted him, stepping out from her hiding place. "You came."

He gave her a quizzical look. "You thought I wouldn't?"

"I never doubted you." It was a lie, but only because of her own insecurities, not because of his reliability.

Mel took one of the cups from his hand.

"I had to bring these from home," he said. "All the cafes are closed because of rationing. Are you sure this is going to work?"

"It has to," said Mel.

She took a sip through the mouthpiece in the lid of the cup and contorted her face at the shock of cold coffee.

"Sorry it's cold," said Raj. "It's a long way from my apartment."

"It doesn't matter." Mel adjusted the lid to make sure it was loose. "Let's go."

Raj put out his arm and Mel placed herself underneath it. With his hand on her far shoulder, she nuzzled herself into his chest. Just as she, as a student, had cuddled the boy in close to her body.

They took the short walk to the Tall Greenhouse.

At the entrance, which was closed after hours, they stood and waited for facial recognition to accept Raj as an employee. Mel kept her face turned away and her body close to Raj to trick the system into seeing only one person.

The swish of the door sliding open told her the first part of the plan was working. Carefully, she moved with Raj to step inside.

She wanted to relax, but fooling a computer without artificial intelligence was the easy bit. Dealing with people was more difficult.

Inside, two guards were stationed in the atrium and took it in turns to make occasional patrols of the rest of the building overnight. Timing their entry with only one guard out front was difficult, but also ran the risk of unexpectedly running into the second one further inside. So it was better that, as she walked in with her face close to Raj, she sensed two people. One, a woman to the left of her, and on the other side of Raj, a male guard at the monitoring station.

If the computer recognized one face entering, but the guard saw two bodies, their ruse would be discovered. Which was where the coffee came in.

Extricating herself from Raj, Mel lifted the coffee cup to pretend to drink while also obscuring her face from the guard. As they approached the internal scanner, she caught a glimpse of the guard from behind the coffee cup. He was slumped in his seat looking bored and tired. Just as she had expected and just as she would have been if she were forced to do his job.

"Good evening," said Raj to the guard.

"Evening," replied the man, his voice saturated with boredom.

Silently and invisibly, the scanner recognized Raj's face.

Mel tipped the coffee cup further and knocked the loose lid free with her teeth.

A cascade of cold coffee tipped down her front. Shivering at the sudden dankness on her blouse, she jumped back and dropped the cup. The rest of its contents splashed across the floor in a pool of black.

"What are you doing?" yelled Raj in feigned, if convincing, annoyance.

"I'm *so* sorry! The silly lid wasn't on properly." Mel looked down at the mess she had created, which kept her face turned away from both the guards and the scanner. "Let me clear it up."

Mel bent down to pick up the cup, deliberately stepping

into the coffee, so her shoes traipsed black footprints with each step away from the spillage.

The male guard let out an irritated sigh. "No, don't bother. It's fine. We'll deal with it."

Mel sensed the female guard approaching, now aware that she had to keep her face turned away from two people.

"Stella!" called the male guard. "Do you know where the cleaners keep their machines?"

"Yeah," came his colleague's reply. "I'll get one."

Stella turned to walk in the other direction. Mel allowed herself a moment of relief as she counted down one guard out of the way and only one more to sneak past.

"Let's leave them to it," said Raj. "We need to get to the lab for you to review my data ready for the morning."

Raj returned to her side and scooped her up under his arm again.

Stella's voice called out from behind them. "Give me a hand with this, will you?"

The male guard grumbled and left the monitoring station.

Mel pressed herself into Raj's side and they walked past where she knew the scanner was working silently and invisibly.

Nothing happened.

No one was there to notice the security system had seen only one face enter the building when, in reality, there were two people.

Mel gave Raj a thankful squeeze. They were in.

CHAPTER THIRTY-NINE

The ominous quiet of the lab at night made Mel feel like an intruder in her own workspace. Lights triggered to spotlight her and Raj as they entered, making their surreptitious presence more conspicuous. The rows of empty benches would not be occupied for many hours, but it was still a finite amount of time which meant they had to act quickly.

Mel tried accessing the lab's systems on the off chance, but as she suspected, she was locked out. She had to rely on Raj to do everything for her.

Raj sat at his usual spot on the central bench and placed his undrunk and unspilled cup of coffee beside him. Mel pulled up a stool.

"When do you think someone got into the cold store?" he asked.

"Six months ago," she said. "Possibly a bit more than that."

"I should be able to access those logs. If I can remember how. I don't usually do this sort of thing, you know."

"I know. Thanks, Raj."

Raj tried several approaches before he was able to bring up a list of times and dates when people had entered the cold store. The data filled the screen and kept filling it as Raj scrolled down. A lot of people used that cold store.

"What about this?" said Raj, peering closer at the screen. "Twenty-fifth of June, 02:34."

"2:34 AM?"

"Yeah." He pointed at the data.

Mel suppressed her excitement at the rogue time, *02:34*, hidden within the rows of ordinary workday times. It wasn't yet proof that someone had stolen her experiment, only that someone had accessed the cold store in the middle of the night. But next to the time was an employee number, *301224G*.

"Can we find out who that is?" she said, tapping the screen.

"It's definitely not me," said Raj. "My number's *402189G*."

Mel glanced at him sideways. "You remember your own employee number?"

"Doesn't everyone?"

She raised her eyebrows at the concept. "No."

Raj brought up the internal personnel record for employee *301224G* and Mel felt the blood drain from her face. It was her own personnel file. She stared at the same image of herself that the MSS had used in its wanted alert – the expressionless, unsmiling picture which made her look like a criminal.

"It can't be," she whispered.

"Are you sure you weren't working late and accessed the store?" said Raj. "Or came back in the middle of the night for some reason?"

"No. And definitely not six months ago."

It had been a long time since she had stayed up all night working. Six months ago, Daniel had been going through a phase of not sleeping, so if he wasn't keeping her up, she would have been asleep herself.

Mel ran her fingers through her hair, trying to think of an explanation. "Someone else must have used my code," she said.

"Why would they?" said Raj.

"To make people think it was me," she said, irritated that he wasn't seeing what she thought was obvious. "There's a security camera on the cold store – can you access it?"

Raj shrugged. "From here?"

"Try."

Mel leaned forward on her stool, willing Raj to find a way, but after several minutes of trying, he sat back in defeat. "The lab systems aren't connected to the security systems. Even if we could get in, we don't know if they've kept footage from six months ago."

Mel tapped her fingers on the bench. "There must be a way of finding out."

"The security personnel will know."

"How are we supposed to get them to help us?" said Mel. "Throw more coffee until they give in?"

Raj frowned at her defeatist attitude. "We could try asking."

"I doubt they'll be very receptive after we made them clean up all that mess in the atrium."

"When I say asking," Raj began. "I was thinking more of bribing. They might do it in return for a ration token."

"I thought the tokens were non-transferable."

"Officially, but you can't set up a system as quickly as they did and make it hack-proof. I'm told there's an increasing black market in the things."

"I can't ask you to give up your own food for this, Raj."

"If what you've told me is true, you could be giving up your own future. Missing one meal is nothing compared to that."

Touched by his offer, she agreed.

He left and, after the swish of the closing door faded away, she was left in the silence of the lab. The smell of stale coffee drifted up from where she had spilled it on her blouse.

Mel tried to access her files from Raj's screen, but they – like her access to the systems – had been locked. There was nothing to do but sit with her own thoughts and remember how life had been in the time when she could relax in the lab without having to worry about someone finding her. When frustration was an emotion triggered by the unpredictability of plants and when her only fear was that her experiment would not be a success.

To calm her nerves, she reached for Raj's abandoned coffee cup. She removed the lid and drank directly from the side, taking mouthfuls of cold, black liquid. She shivered at its bitterness, but kept drinking until she had drained the cup to the dregs. She waited for the caffeine hit to help her find the strength to keep going.

Raj had to have been gone for around half an hour before he rushed back in with a smile on his face and an eagerness in his eye.

"Well?" said Mel, standing as if that would help her get the information sooner.

"Got it," said Raj.

He rushed over to the screen. "The guard sent everything from this part of the building over the past year to my account.

We should be able to see who entered the cold store on the twenty-fifth of June at 2:34 AM."

"You haven't looked already?"

"I thought you'd want to see for yourself."

Perhaps it was the effects of the coffee, but after half an hour of patient waiting, the few moments it took Raj to pull the video footage from his account and figure out how to play it felt frustratingly long.

"OK," said Raj and sat back.

Mel, too energized to sit back down again, leaned into the screen.

The image was almost entirely black apart from the glow of green lights from the refrigeration units along the far wall. Even in that macabre glow, it was possible to tell the camera was positioned high up above the door.

A shaft of light spilled from the adjoining corridor with the opening of the door. Then the sudden flash of lights turning on with movement in the room. The camera quickly adjusted to the new light source and it was possible to see a figure enter.

The time code at the bottom right-hand corner read 02:34.

"That's it!" Mel's cry of vindication was out of her mouth before she could stop herself.

Right in front of her, on the screen, was the person who had destroyed her life. And was in the process of destroying everyone else's life on the face of Mars.

By the body shape, it was a man both taller and wider than her, suggesting he was muscular and Mars-born. He carried a black cloth bag across his shoulder and wore a flat cap-style hat which obscured his face from the camera's angle above him.

"That's definitely not you," said Raj.

So relieved to see the footage proved it wasn't her, Mel hadn't had time to think who else it was. "Do you recognize him?"

"No," said Raj, after a moment's consideration. "I'm fairly sure it's not someone from the lab."

Mel studied the figure a second time and mentally ticked off everyone in their small team. None of them walked like the man on the footage or were as muscular as him.

Mel continued to watch as the man opened the first fridge and pulled out a rack of sealed jars. Mel felt a sting of dread as she realized he was tampering with her microplants, even though the events she was witnessing happened six months ago and she was powerless to stop them.

"What's he doing?" said Raj.

The man put the rack on the floor and leaned over the specimens so his body shielded his actions from the camera. He reached into the bag and pulled out a silver-colored vacuum flask.

He pulled a specimen jar out of the flask. As far as it was possible to tell from the angle of the camera, it was almost identical to the ones Mel used. Then he picked up a jar from the rack containing Mel's microplants.

For a moment, she thought he was going to switch the two jars. But, instead, he opened them both. Reaching into his pocket, he pulled out a small metal tool which briefly flashed at the camera as it caught the light. He leaned forward and the next few vital moments were concealed by his body.

"What's he doing?" Raj asked again.

Mel didn't need to see. She already knew. "He's taking a sample."

It sickened her to think how easily she had been fooled. She watched the image of the man's back as she imagined him using a scalpel or a pair of tweezers to snip off part of one of her valuable plants and take it away in his own vacuum-sealed container.

It was as clever as it was simple. Take a piece from one or two jars in the middle of the collection and leave behind apparently intact specimens. That way, the thief could take away enough of the plants to be useful, while the legitimate owner would never suspect anything had been stolen.

"You couldn't grow enough from one small sample to plant half the farms on Mars with enhanced potatoes so quickly," said Raj.

"No," said Mel, wondering the same.

The man stood, put the flask in his bag and turned to the back wall. The static camera remained focused on the rack laying abandoned in the center of the room while only the man's back was visible at the edge of frame.

Mel's defeat was complete.

She didn't need to see him to know that he was taking seed potatoes from the bins. If he had scooped up a little from each bin, it would have been enough to fill his bag, but not enough to noticeably deplete the three storage units.

The timing was horribly perfect. Six months ago gave the thief roughly three months to propagate enough seed potatoes from the original tubers to populate the farms, using the cutting from the nuclear stock as backup. Another three months allowed time to distribute and grow them on the farms, only for them to fail a little more than sixty days later.

Something must have spooked the man, because he started

moving quickly. He grabbed the rack from the floor, shoved it back in the refrigerator and pushed the door closed with not quite enough force to seal it shut.

He turned to exit with the heavy bag bulging on his shoulder. His face was hidden under his hat to the last moment.

Anger and humiliation had burned all of Mel's energy to leave her empty.

"You were right," said Raj.

"Yes," she said. Suddenly being right wasn't enough. "I need to know who he is."

"He was clever, he hid his face. But the camera's at a bad angle in the storeroom. If we're lucky, we might get a better angle on one of the other cameras."

"You've got footage from other cameras?" Mel asked.

"I told you, I've been sent everything from this part of the building from the past year."

It took a while, and a certain amount of swearing, but Raj eventually pulled up footage from a camera facing the elevator on the fifth floor.

They watched an empty corridor and the closed elevator doors while the time code in the corner ticked from 02:32 to 02:33.

Before it reached 02:34, the doors opened and the figure emerged wearing exactly the same hat placed at exactly the right angle to conceal his face.

"I don't believe it!" said Mel. "Is he doing it on purpose or something?"

It was a rhetorical question, but Raj answered it in any case. "If he used your code to get into the cold store, it's possible he had inside information about where the cameras were."

The unpleasant thought lingered as Mel watched the man leave the view of the camera without once giving away his identity.

"Maybe we'll get lucky when he leaves," said Raj.

Raj skipped through the footage to 02:35. At 02:28, the figure returned. This time facing the other way so they saw only the back of his head.

"You're right," said Mel. "He knows exactly where the cameras are."

"Wait," said Raj.

The elevator doors opened and the man stepped inside.

Then he did what all people do when they get into the elevator. He turned around to wait for the doors to close.

The camera caught a brief, but clear, image of the man's face.

"I told you!" said Raj.

A shiver of recognition passed through her.

"Let me see it again," said Mel. She had to be sure.

Raj re-played the moment and she watched the man turn to reveal his identity a second time.

The man in his early twenties had the same face she had seen inside the helmet of one of the people throwing food boxes out of the train. It was the same face she had glimpsed as she hid behind the boxes in the back of the thieves' truck and heard them discussing their plans.

"I know who that is," said Mel with cold certainty. "He's the leader of a gang of criminals."

CHAPTER FORTY

Contradiction lived in Ivan Volkov's apartment.

For everything about it that was ordinary, there was something extraordinary.

Deverau walked into Ivan's bedroom where rumpled sheets and discarded clothing suggested an ordinary, untidy working man who had no time or inclination to clear up after himself. Much like, Deverau hated to admit, his own apartment. Opening the flimsy and cheap closet, he ran his fingers along the fine material of some of the clothes hanging up inside. They were expensive. Including several jackets which Deverau would have loved to be able to afford.

The living area was just as small and cluttered. In itself, not unusual for a standard apartment allocated to a mine worker. What *was* unusual was all the clutter had been pushed to one end to make room for a holographic simulation unit. An exclusive gadget which was in reach of few salaries on Mars. The technology was simple enough, but some of the components contained imported elements which were in high demand and prioritized for use in industry.

Deverau switched on the unit to see what environment Ivan had last simulated. He imagined a young man like him might have chosen something exotic such as one of the moons of Jupiter or one of the environments on Earth. At first, that's exactly what he thought he had found. But he soon realized the facsimile of waves lapping on a beach was in an environment with a domed sky and was, in fact, a simulation of the Martian Tropics resort. A useful tool for someone planning a raid on the place and a damning piece of evidence pointing towards Ivan's guilt, if any more were needed.

He walked into the image and the light bent around his body so the beach surrounded him. But without the sand under his feet, the hint of a breeze brushing at his cheek and the heat, it was no more real to him than an image on a screen.

Deverau turned it off and the reality of the small, cluttered room returned.

The hint of an unpleasant smell drew Deverau to the attached kitchenette. He traced the culprit to a ration pack which had been opened, half eaten and left on the side to go moldy. A shocking waste of what was rapidly becoming Mars' most valuable commodity.

The kitchenette was the only room in the whole apartment to include a window. Like much of the Martian housing in that area close to the center of the city, the block only had windows at the front to look out onto the main street. It was one of the things that Deverau found strange about Martian society, that people there had little appetite for looking out at the back streets. He imagined it was because, unlike Earth, there was not really any "outside" to look at when the whole city was enclosed in a dome.

Deverau, however, liked the way a window allowed him to feel connected with the world and took the opportunity to gaze out at the street. Ivan's apartment was on the top floor and so the people down below were indistinct moving figures with the different colors of their clothing standing out against the backdrop of the city's rusty red tiles. Watching them, he drifted into a daze and thought about the man who lived in the apartment.

Facial recognition had easily identified Ivan Volkov as the leader of the gang whose scarf had been pulled off in the fight with a tourist. Analysis of the footage taken from the transport hub during the handout of stolen food proved he was also there. That, in turn, implicated Ivan and his gang in the train robbery.

MSS officers had been to his work and his home, but of course he never showed up at either. Ivan may have been over-confident in recording himself committing a crime, but he hadn't compounded that mistake by going to where the MSS could easily arrest him. Which meant, along with Mel Erdan and several unnamed members of the gang, Deverau was chasing multiple fugitives.

At least he now had the authority to spend all of his resources on locating them, after his superiors at Noctis City had finally excused him from crowd control duty. It only took a near-fatal shooting for them to see reason. But that put the onus on him to make arrests, and make them quickly. Otherwise he might find himself placed back on crowd control duty permanently.

"Dev." It was Jones' voice behind him.

Deverau turned to see Jones looking as tired as he felt after a long day chasing down leads on Ivan Volkov across the city and getting nowhere. "Anything?" he asked.

"Only a few people in neighboring apartments opened the door and even fewer admitted to knowing Ivan by sight," said Jones. "They weren't aware of any gang or gang members meeting here."

Deverau frowned. It wasn't surprising, but it wasn't helpful either. "Any useful information at all?"

"A couple of people seemed to think he has a girlfriend. By their description, it sounds like the woman who got shot. What about you?"

"I want to check his financial records," said Deverau. "It looks like he came into some money recently."

"You think somebody paid him?"

Deverau had spent the morning interviewing Ivan's colleagues at the mine and all seemed to think he had a genuine grievance about the life of ordinary Mars workers. So his speech at the resort hadn't been an act. He also had no criminal record, which meant he would have made an effective patsy for someone wealthy who wanted to keep their nose clean.

"I think it's a possibility," he said.

CHAPTER FORTY-ONE

In the back of the thieves' truck, hidden behind the boxes of stolen food, Mel had listened to the criminals' conversation. At the time, their words had been incidental, a noise that meant it wasn't quite yet safe to creep out of the truck and escape into the city.

Seeing the leader of the gang on the security footage gave their discussion new significance.

She thought back and tried to remember. They had talked about a hideout where they met. From what she had been able to discern, it was in a maintenance area at the edge of the dome in the west of the city. Not exactly an address, but a place to start.

Raj had offered to help her in any way he could. The only thing she asked for was his WristTab with a copy of the footage from the Tall Greenhouse stored on it. Most people felt lost without their WristTab if they ever misplaced it, had it stolen or managed to break it, so she understood why he was reluctant. She knew too well the feeling of that bare patch on her arm leaving her unconnected to the rest of the planet. However, after securing a promise from her that she wouldn't look at anything private, and consoling himself that he could always get another one, Raj handed it over.

A city as large as Deimos meant the west side encompassed a sizable area. According to the maps she was able to study on Raj's WristTab, for most of the district, buildings nudged up against the perimeter wall. In others, it was simply too busy for a gang of criminals to gather in secret. Which limited the possibilities to a single housing district where there was a narrow walkway between the accommodation blocks and where the city came to an end.

By the time she reached it, the evening was closing in. Rays from the sinking sun shone down through the arching glass only a couple of meters above her head. It was a quiet and out of the way place with the only discernible sound the distant laughter of playing children.

Mel stood at the far end of the space and looked along the red curving perimeter wall until her view was obscured by a housing block. If there was a way to get to the other side, then it was well hidden. She put her hand on the cool, smooth surface and allowed her fingers to run along the gentle curve. Looking for imperfections which might indicate some sort of entrance.

The touch of her fingertips detected the split in the wall before she saw it. Standing back, she could see the shape of the hatchway cut almost imperceptibly into the fabric of the curve. It was a door with no handle, no access pad and no visible way of being opened. Most likely, it was operated by some kind of key carried by maintenance technicians or robots. If that was the case and the gang had somehow got hold of a key, then she was locked out.

Not to be deterred by one locked door, she kept walking.

Mel stopped at the sound of small, running footsteps. Amplified by the echo in the close confines at the back of the housing blocks, they were getting closer.

A little boy, probably no older than eight, ran out from between two buildings about five meters in front of her. He turned to keep running, but saw Mel and stopped dead. He stared down the passageway with the uninhibitedness of a child who hadn't yet learned that it was rude to stare.

A squeal of laughter spilled out from the same gap, followed by a little girl of about ten years old. She stopped short of the boy and turned to see what he was looking at.

"Hello," said Mel, not sure what else to do.

The pair of them kept staring. By the look of their similar features, Mel suspected they were brother and sister.

"Are you the one what killed all the food?" said the little girl.

Mel flushed. She had been sneaking around Deimos City worried about being recognized by all the adults around her and never thought she would be accosted by a ten year-old.

"Don't be silly," she said. "If I was her and she was me, why would I be here?"

The girl frowned as she tried to untangle the riddle.

Mel remembered when she was that age. She wasn't allowed to run around in the streets, but her brother was older and given more leeway. She would often annoy him by following him around. Hours of exploring meant they had known every square meter in the vicinity of their apartment. Perhaps the children were the key she needed.

"You could help me, actually," said Mel in a bright and breezy tone. "I'm looking for some people who come down here. I thought they might be behind this door, but it doesn't open."

The boy looked decidedly unimpressed at the door Mel was pointing at.

"That one's stuck," he said.

His sister thumped him on the arm like he should have kept his mouth shut. "*I* know which door you mean," she declared. She strode around her brother with an air of superiority and proceeded to march down the walkway for several minutes with the little boy tagging along behind.

The girl eventually stopped and pointed at the wall. "This door."

Mel approached. It seemed exactly the same as the first door, except there were scratches down one side where it looked like someone had been attempting to pry it open. Mel tried to get her fingernails underneath it, but she could only scrape at the crack.

"Not like that!" said the boy, as if she should have known better.

Mel watched as he took off his WristTab and held it above his head to where an adult's waist might be and where the scratches were. Then he slipped the strap into the gap between the wall and the door, twisted it in some way that Mel couldn't see and the lock released with a gentle click. The boy grinned with pride and pushed the door open into the darkness beyond.

"Thank you," said Mel.

"I know the people you mean," he said. "But they're not in there now."

"I don't mind," said Mel. "I can wait. But you won't tell anyone I was here, will you?"

"OK," said the boy.

The two children, their superior knowledge proven, seemed to lose interest.

The little girl looked at her WristTab just as an adult might in a similar situation. "We need to go home," she said. She thumped her brother on the arm again and ran off.

Mel listened to their disappearing footsteps until they were lost to the quiet. She ducked her head down into the hatch and entered.

CHAPTER FORTY-TWO

Alex sat on the ventilation box in the gang's hideout, exhausted, confused and upset.

He had barely slept. Thoughts of Elea's terrified face and the sounds of her pained cries intertwined themselves with his nightmares of being captured by the MSS and accused of crimes he never meant to commit. He had only ever wanted to do the best for Mars, which was, in turn, best for him and for everyone he cared about. But it had all turned to disaster.

Ivan stood in his usual spot, leaning against one of the supporting struts. He looked tired and stressed, but not defeated by their ordeal. The fact that they had evaded capture by the MSS was a victory in his eyes, even though it had come at a terrible cost.

Pete and Sammi skulked opposite, squatting down near to where the edge of the dome was embedded in the ground. Their confidence had been stripped away and they huddled more like frightened children than the carefree young men he remembered sitting with on the side of the lake in Central Plaza.

"What do we do now?" said Pete.

"Go back to our lives," said Sammi. "Forget this ever happened. Forget we ever knew each other."

"They've seen my face," said Ivan. "They'll come for me at my home, they'll come for me at my job. There's no going back."

"For you, maybe," said Sammi.

"They know there were five of us," said Ivan. "There's no guarantee any of us are safe."

Alex stood. "We trusted you. *Elea* trusted you."

"Yes, and *you* were the one who shot her," said Ivan.

Enraged that he dared dump the blame on him, Alex pulled back his fist and charged.

Ivan leapt out of his way and doubled back behind him. Alex swiveled to see Ivan dominating the center of the maintenance area with his broad, muscular body. Physically, Alex was no match for him, but Alex didn't care if he got beaten up as long as Ivan felt the full force of his anger.

"You gave me a loaded gun!" Alex yelled. "What did you think would happen?"

"I thought you would be sensible enough not to put a bullet into one of your friends."

Furious that Ivan was trying to use his feelings of guilt against him, Alex launched himself a second time.

Pete jumped into his way. Alex's attack was already primed and his fist lashed out to strike. Pete dodged the blow and caught Alex around the waist to hold him back.

Thrashing against him, Alex screamed, "Let me go!"

"Everyone calm down!" Sammi pleaded.

Not that Alex was going to take any notice of him. Ivan

deserved to be beaten until he was left bleeding and in pain on the floor. Just like he had left Elea.

Sammi's hands grabbed Alex's arms from behind. He squirmed, wriggled and cried out in frustration, but Pete and Sammi's combined strength was more than he could overcome.

Ivan stood watching it all.

"Fighting gets us nowhere," said Pete, releasing his grip on Alex, but still standing in his way.

"You can't let Ivan get away with what he did!" insisted Alex.

Alex was angry at Ivan, angry at Pete and Sammi for holding him back, and most of all, angry at himself for being so easily led.

"We're here to decide what to do," said Pete. "If you two want to fight, you can do it afterwards. Understand?"

"If you say so," said Alex. He felt Sammi's hold on his arms lessen and he shook himself free. "But I want Ivan to admit what he's done."

"Ivan?" Pete turned to him.

Ivan shrugged like he didn't care one way or the other. "I may have been the one who came up with the plan, but we all agreed to it."

"Don't try to put the blame on us!" Alex jabbed an accusing finger at him.

"Enough!" yelled Sammi. He joined Pete to strengthen the barrier between Alex and Ivan.

"We're here to decide what we do next and that's all we're here to do," said Sammi. "We make our plans and then we go our separate ways, OK? I'm not ever going through what I went through these last couple of days ever again. *OK?*"

Ivan nodded. "OK, Sammi."

"OK," said Pete.

Alex felt sorry for Sammi. Like the rest of them, he had been drawn in by Ivan's rhetoric and led into a battle that was bigger than all of them and more dangerous than they had imagined. "OK," he said.

Mel watched the four young men argue from a corner of the maintenance area where the light sensors could not detect her presence. It was the same gang she remembered from the truck, but the woman was missing. Apparently shot in an operation that had gone seriously wrong. The gang were falling apart and their leader, who the others called Ivan, was on the run. It meant this could be the only chance she would have to confront him.

Seeing him only a few meters away, surrounded by other members of the gang, made that prospect scarier than she had imagined.

She silently accessed the controls on Raj's WristTab and sent the security footage from the lab over to the MSS for the attention of Inspector Deverau. She knew that the very act of sending it would alert him to her location, but she didn't care. Ivan would have to explain what he did and, if she couldn't get the information out of him, the MSS would have to.

"Does anyone know what happened to Elea?" asked Pete.

Renewed guilt and regret at what he had done sent a shiver through Alex's body. He looked hopefully at the others for answers. Pete obviously knew nothing and Sammi stared out ahead like a frightened child.

"She's OK," said Ivan.

He had sat down on the ventilation box with his head mostly bowed down towards his shoes. Perhaps to avoid showing his own guilt, or perhaps to avoid starting another fight.

"How do you know?" said Alex. He wasn't sure whether to believe Ivan anymore.

"I asked someone who knows someone," said Ivan.

"What's that supposed to mean?" said Alex. It was the same evasive answer he had given when Alex and Elea had questioned him about the illegal guns.

"She's in hospital," Ivan added. "I'm told it could have been worse if the woman on the beach hadn't given her medical attention."

"That means she'll be in police custody," said Pete. "Will she talk?"

"Elea's loyal and brave, but we can't rule it out," said Ivan.

Sammi slumped back against the wall. Alex maintained his outward countenance of composure, but inside he felt control over his own life slipping away.

In the contemplative silence that followed, Alex heard a noise. He tensed. It sounded like someone shuffling in the dirt. "Did you hear that?"

"Hear what?" said Sammi.

"Listen," Alex urged them.

"It's probably one of the pipes," said Ivan.

"No." Alex was sure. "I know the sound of the pipes. I think someone's in here with us."

All their WristTabs suddenly bleeped an alert. Alex glanced at his. It was an incoming video message sent to all devices in close proximity.

"Who's doing that?" said Sammi.

"Not me," said Pete.

Ivan held out his arms to show he had no WristTab. "I had to ditch mine, didn't I? It's like wearing a mobile tracking device."

Alex looked around nervously. Proximity messages could only be sent by someone very close by. If none of them had sent it, it must have come from the intruder he had heard shuffling in the dirt.

"It was me," came a woman's voice from behind.

Movement further down the maintenance area triggered lights to turn on. They illuminated a Mars-born woman walking towards them. Twice his age with a face haggard by stress and fatigue, Alex sensed something familiar about her.

Ivan leapt off the ventilation box and pulled out a shockgun which he had concealed inside his jacket.

Caught off-guard, the woman stopped mid-stride and held up her hands to show she was unarmed.

Alex stared warily at Ivan's weapon. He thought they had left all the guns back at the resort. "What are you doing with that?"

"I saved it in case it was needed," said Ivan. "Turns out, I was right."

"I don't want any trouble," said the woman. "I just want to talk."

Sammi, who had been the only one to accept the incoming message, was staring at it, open-mouthed. "Ivan, this is you!" he said.

Ivan, irritated at the interruption, scowled at Sammi. "What do you mean, it's me?"

Pete, like Alex, had ignored the message. He was staring at the woman.

"I know who you are," said Pete. "You're the one wanted by the MSS for sabotaging the farms."

A flinch on her face suggested she resented the allegation. "I'm Doctor Mel Erdan. My work was stolen to make it look like I was the one who sabotaged the farms, but it wasn't me."

"So why do we care?" said Ivan.

"Because you were the one who stole it," said Mel. "The footage I've sent to you proves it."

Ivan turned to Sammi. "Give me that!" He grabbed hold of Sammi's arm and twisted it so the screen of the WristTab was facing him.

Alex finally accepted the message on his own WristTab and saw it was some sort of security footage. It showed a Mars-born man who looked to be Ivan's height and build, but he couldn't be certain it was him until the footage cut to a different view. The man entered an elevator, then turned so the camera caught his face for a brief moment before the doors closed.

There was no doubt – it was Ivan.

Alex wondered if this was another secret Ivan had concealed from them.

Ivan laughed and let go of Sammi's arm. "That's absurd. I don't know what that footage is, but it certainly doesn't show me sabotaging any farms. I'm a mine worker – what would I want with some science experiment?"

"It's the reason the farm crops died," she said.

Alex might not have believed it if he hadn't seen the fear in Ivan's eyes. His exterior cool was cracking.

"Is this true?" said Pete.

"Pete!" Ivan played innocent, but the footage had unnerved him and it was an unconvincing performance. "You're going to believe *her* over *me*?"

Alex didn't want to. If he accepted Mel's word, then he had to accept his own foolishness in following Ivan.

"It depends," Alex told Ivan. "What's your explanation?"

"It's nonsense," said Ivan. "I shouldn't have to tell you that. You know I believe in the future of Mars and Mars-borns – I wouldn't plunge the whole planet into a food crisis."

"Then why steal my experiment?" said Mel. "Were you working for someone else?"

Ivan re-aimed the shockgun at her, but it was with an unsteady arm. "No one! That footage is a lie. You can't pin this disaster on me to save yourself."

Ivan and Mel faced each other. Neither backing down. Mel, unarmed and vulnerable. Ivan pointing a shockgun at her, but losing the confidence of the gang around him.

No one moved. And yet, in the tense silence, Alex heard movement.

By the uneasy expressions on the faces of the others, he knew they'd heard it too.

A male voice spoke from their WristTabs. It was another proximity message, but one that didn't have to be accepted to be received.

"This is Inspector Deverau of the MSS," the voice declared from all four WristTabs, surrounding them with the sound of his authority like speakers surrounding an audience. "Raise your hands and prepare to surrender."

Automatic lights banished the darkness at either side of

their meeting place, meaning the MSS were advancing on their position from their only two escape routes. The narrow corridor of the maintenance area, which had been their space for so long, had become a trap.

An Earth-born, plainclothes MSS officer with thick body armor strapped to his chest, but no helmet, emerged from around the curve of the wall with a slow and steady pace. He had a shockgun aimed at Ivan with the surety of someone trained to handle firearms.

Ivan spun to face him, his own shockgun wavering in shaky hands.

"Put the shockgun down," ordered the officer. His voice, spoken in their presence, was the same as the one that had spoken from their WristTabs, confirming that he was Inspector Deverau. "There's nowhere to go."

Ivan spun back the other way as a Mars-born officer, also in armor and armed, paced slowly and steadily from the opposite direction. "Raise your hands!"

Other officers emerged from the corridor and flanked them with their weapons drawn.

Helplessness drained the last of Alex's fighting spirit. Reluctantly, he raised his hands in surrender.

Pete and Sammi avoided eye contact as they did the same.

Ivan hesitated. But even he had to accept the inevitable. He lifted both his hands slowly above his head, still holding the shockgun in his right hand.

"Drop it!" The Mars-born officer advanced, backed up by two others in uniform.

The first stopped when she reached Pete, who was the unfortunate person to be closest. She ordered him to turn round and he was pushed hard, face first, against the wall while she pulled a set of handcuffs from her belt.

Ivan, finally accepting defeat, turned the shockgun in his fingers to let go.

Then he spun. Strengthening his grip on the gun, he found the trigger with his finger.

Deverau returned fire. The dart sailed through the air where Ivan had been before he spun. Alex jolted as it pinged off a supporting strut next to him.

Ivan aimed his gun at the ceiling and fired. The dart whizzed into the air and embedded itself in the oxygen pipe overhead.

A blue spark of discharging energy erupted like an ignition. The oxygen pipe exploded in a cloud of orange, yellow and red flame. Deverau ducked as the fireball – lashing out like an angry solar flare – billowed over him.

But the officers next to Deverau didn't duck in time. The one in front lifted his arm to shield his face and fire ignited his sleeve. Screaming in terror, he batted at it with his other hand, fanning the flames rather than putting them out. His colleague rushed to help.

The smell of burnt human flesh was so sickening Alex could taste it. Not knowing what else to do, he watched the horror unfold around him.

But Ivan seized his chance for freedom and leapt forward.

He kicked Deverau aside and ran past the officers trying to extinguish the man's arm.

Above, safety mechanisms in the pipe shut off the oxygen feed. Sprinklers activated and water rained from the ceiling. Spots of cold landed on Alex's head and shoulders and soaked through his hair and into his clothes.

"Dev!" yelled the Mars-born officer. He fired a poorly aimed dart after Ivan's fleeing figure and ran to the inspector.

Another dart flew past Alex's nose. It struck Sammi, whose hands were still raised in surrender, and the dart discharged shocks into his body.

"No darts in the water! You'll shock us all!" yelled one of the officers.

Sammi, unable to control his muscles, splashed face-first into the stream accumulating on the floor.

Pete, his hands in cuffs behind him, staggered away. "Help him! You have to help him! He'll drown."

The officers didn't move, but discussed whether they dare step into the water while the dart was still firing. Pete kept screaming at them to do something.

Alex had only a moment to take advantage of the chaos. He looked across at Mel, standing with water running off her hair and down her face, and wondered what she knew about Ivan.

Their eyes connected and it was like an understanding passed between them. If what she said about the security footage was true, she was as much Ivan's victim as he was.

He took a bet that Mel didn't want to be arrested any more than he did. So Alex grabbed hold of her hand and they ran.

CHAPTER FORTY-THREE

Ivan's boot kicked pain into Deverau's ribs. Crying out, he fell sideways and struck his head on the wall of the maintenance area. Struggling to right himself, he saw through blurred vision the fleeing figure of Ivan Volkov.

Deverau lifted his shockgun to fire and saw the blood-red burns on the back of his hands where the fireball had torched him. Ignoring it, he pulled the trigger. But his hands were shaking and the dart veered to the right where it hit the edge of the dome and dropped uselessly to the ground.

It started to rain.

Deverau was confused.

He didn't think it rained on Mars.

"Dev?" Jones was suddenly leaning over him. "Are you all right?"

Deverau – winded – nodded.

"Are you sure?"

"Go after him," Deverau managed.

He watched Jones run after the suspect who had already disappeared around the curve of the wall.

Deverau stood and the pain worsened in his side. Wincing and holding onto his ribs, he saw that the fire was out, but one of the uniformed officers held a red-raw arm under the sprinklers to douse it with cooling water, while the remnants of a burnt sleeve dangled beneath it.

One of Ivan's gang stood with his hands cuffed behind him under the charge of a uniformed officer. The gang member looked distressed, but unharmed. Another was unconscious after being hit by a shockdart and had been propped up against the wall, still handcuffed, and sitting in a flopped over position.

Mel was nowhere to be seen.

The water made a gurgling sound at his feet as pipes hidden in the floor sucked back the valuable resource to be recycled.

Deverau selected his WristTab to contact all MSS officers in the area. "This is Inspector Deverau. Suspect Mel Erdan seen at my current location within the last few minutes. Believed to be on the run and heading in…" He looked at the other officers who responded with either shrugs or blank looks. "… heading in an unknown direction. Urgent response needed. Also believed on the run is suspect Ivan Volkov, with Sergeant Jones in pursuit – use his location to coordinate urgent response."

Deverau also pinpointed Jones' location and headed down the maintenance corridor in that direction. Clutching his aching side while ignoring the pain in the back of his hands, he tried to break into a run. But the exertion was too much and it soon became more of an uneven jog.

He emerged through the inspection hatch feeling a little woozy. He rested against the perimeter wall while he checked Jones' position on his WristTab. It showed the shortest route to reach him was down between two housing blocks. Deverau pushed himself off the wall and resumed his jog.

After five minutes, Jones appeared to have stopped. Deverau hoped that meant he had the suspect in custody and not that the suspect had shot him or something worse had happened.

Deverau picked up speed, wincing again at the pain in his ribs, and jogged down a residential street. A passing man stared at him like he was a monster that had crawled out of a lake and it was only then that he realized he was still soaking wet from being under the sprinklers. It would be many minutes before he dried off in the ambient temperature of the city and automatic systems were able to reclaim the water vapor.

Up ahead, he saw what appeared to be Jones' leg sticking out of a doorway as he stood half in and half out of one of the residential blocks. Fierce yelling was coming from inside. By the sound of it, it was the sort of yelling officers used when demanding a suspect obey them.

"He's inside," said Jones when Deverau approached, answering the unspoken question. "Two officers have gone in after him. He's locked himself in somewhere up on the third floor. We think he's got someone in there with him."

"A hostage?"

"Unclear."

Deverau sighed and ran through the ramifications in his head. None of them were pleasant. Hostage situations generally had two outcomes. Either a long, protracted negotiation in which the criminal realized he was never going to get out and surrendered. Or exactly the same process with a more gruesome ending.

He looked up and down the street to get his bearings. It had a strange familiarity about it which took him a moment to place. He had considered moving out that way after Jessie had left, before eventually deciding he would be better off staying near the center of the city where he was closer to the office.

It had been a hard decision because the apartments were larger and generally nicer than the one he lived in. He had theorized they had been designed by either an Earth architect or by one heavily influenced by Earth architecture because they included details that reminded him of the homes where he grew up. Most notable was the provision of back windows.

"How many officers have you got covering the back?" said Deverau.

"Back?" said Jones, like the question made no sense.

Deverau swore and started running again. "You really need to do a sabbatical on Earth, Jones!" he called back to his sergeant.

The blocks were long and it took him too many minutes to find a pathway that led to the rear. He turned to look down the long line of red bricks peppered with back windows. Three stories up, a man's body dangled out of one of them.

Deverau closed in.

He raised his shockgun and gripped it tighter. His hands stung at the cracking of the scabs which had begun to form across his burns.

"Stop! MSS!"

Ivan could not stop. His entire body was hanging, feet first, out of the building with his hands gripping onto the edge of the window frame. Unless he had some kind of super strength, or someone helped him, he wasn't going to be able to haul himself back inside. The only thing he could do was drop to the ground. Even for a tall Mars-born, it was a nine-meter drop.

Ivan let go of the window. Deverau heard the nauseating crack of bone as his feet hit the ground, coupled with a pained yell. But it didn't stop him. Fueled by the fear of capture, Ivan was on his feet and hobbling away.

"Stop! MSS!" Deverau raised his shockgun, stopped to ensure his aim was true, and fired.

The dart struck Ivan square in the back. In the quiet behind the residential building, it was possible to hear the shocks discharging into his body. His muscles contracted and he collapsed to his knees. The weight of his torso tipped him forward and he fell onto his front.

Deverau walked up to him and waited for the dart to fully discharge. Savoring his moment of victory, he grinned as he imagined the expression on the faces of his bosses at Noctis City when he informed them he had captured the man behind both the train raid and the incident at the tropical resort. Possibly even involved in the crop deaths.

Deverau cuffed him with two satisfying clicks so his hands were secure behind his back. Ivan was unconscious, but Deverau didn't want to take any risks when he awoke.

One of the officers who had gone inside the building peered out of the window and paused at the sight of Ivan under Deverau's control. "All clear in here," she shouted down. "The resident's shaken up, but he didn't hurt her."

Jones arrived just as Deverau ensured Ivan was safely laying in the recovery position.

"You see," Deverau explained to him. "On Earth, a lot

of criminals try escaping through back windows. This is something police officers on Mars often forget."

Jones looked down at Ivan. "Is that really the man who caused all the crops to die?"

"You can ask him when you get him back to the station," said Deverau.

He expected Jones to arrange to take the suspect away, but instead he stood there giving Deverau a very strange look. "Are you OK, Dev?"

"Of course I'm OK," he said. As he was thinking that, the image of Jones went blurry and he felt dizzy. He was suddenly aware of Jones catching him. He must have blacked out for a second because he didn't remember falling.

"You're not OK," said Jones. "Let's get you to the hospital."

"No hospital."

"Yes, hospital. Sergeant's orders."

CHAPTER FORTY-FOUR

The young gang member let go of Mel's hand as he led her down the maintenance corridor until they found an inspection hatch which they hoped was far enough away from where the MSS had ambushed them. The door was stiff, it hadn't been used for a long time and although safety measures meant it didn't need a key to open from the inside, they virtually had to batter it down.

Breaking their way out hadn't been exactly quiet.

Mel imagined they would emerge to find a team of MSS officers waiting for them with their shockguns drawn. But there was no one. Only a narrow gap between two buildings barely wider than the hatch itself.

"The MSS must have followed Ivan and not us," said the young man she had escaped with.

"Or are waiting for us outside a different door," she added.

They walked gingerly, and in single file, to the front of the buildings to find themselves in a commercial district. It was night-time and, if anyone was around, they were busy inside their offices. Mel took off the WristTab Raj had given her, dropped it to the ground and attempted to crush it under her heel. She didn't think Raj would mind. He was going to have to buy another one for himself anyway.

The device was tough and she had to stamp on it several times before it smashed into several pieces.

"What are you doing?" said the young man.

"They could be tracking it."

He took off his WristTab and dropped it beside hers. It broke with one hard stamp from his heavy boot.

"My name's Alex, by the way."

"I'm Mel."

They shook hands. It was a very formal and strange thing to do after holding hands for the first few seconds as they escaped from the MSS, but social norms meant it felt like the right thing to do.

"Why did you help me get out of there?" said Mel.

"You know stuff about Ivan. If he was hiding something from me, I want to know what it is."

Mel wanted to know too, but they were too exposed so close to the maintenance area. If the MSS hadn't already tracked the signal from Raj's WristTab, they would soon be working out its last known location.

"We need to go," she said.

"Go where?"

"I know a place."

Alex watched Mel type a code into the pad next to the back entrance of where her husband worked. She was tense, having warned him that there was a possibility the code might have been changed since she had last used it. But, with the input of the last digit, the locks disengaged and she smiled with relief.

No one would be working there overnight, she had told him, but she pushed open the door a tentative crack and listened just in case. When they had satisfied themselves the building was empty, Alex followed her inside.

The large hangar had rows of vehicles parked up on charge, many of them freight trucks with the ability to go out across the Martian surface. Alex eyed them with thoughts of escaping the city, but Mel took no notice and headed straight to the back stairs which led up to a glass-fronted corridor looking down onto the depot. It was an impressive view, but she didn't even turn to look.

She tried the handle of the first office door on the opposite side of the glass. "It's open," she said, and went in.

It was a normal, unremarkable office with a desk, a personal screen and a couple of chairs. At the back was a larger screen taking up half a wall with a list of code numbers, times, dates and places. It seemed to be a tally of freight deliveries and collections across Mars.

"What are we doing?" asked Alex. He thought they were going somewhere where they could hide from the MSS. "We can't stay here, people will be coming to work in the morning."

"I need to access the screen," said Mel.

"If you wanted to look up information, you could have used your WristTab before you smashed it."

"This information," said Mel, going around the back of the desk, "is specific to Isaac's logistics business. You can't look it up on a WristTab."

"Be quick," said Alex.

Adrenaline pumped through his body, telling him to run, but he decided he would give her ten minutes. If she hadn't finished by then, he would try to break into one of the trucks and leave.

"Unbelievable," she said, glaring at the screen.

"What is?" said Alex.

"It requires a registered user to gain access."

"Can't you use your husband's credentials?"

"If I knew them. It seems Isaac takes the security of his company's data more seriously than he does access to the back door."

She kept trying, but got nowhere and sat back in the chair, defeated.

"What's so important? We need to go."

"The plants Ivan stole had to have been propagated to produce seed potatoes to be sent out to the farms. Isaac's business is one of the ones making those deliveries. If I could find a record, I might be able to figure out who propagated them."

Alex studied the chart on the wall behind her. As far as he could tell, it displayed the details of freight deliveries across the course of a week. The data was too current to be useful for what she wanted. Alex remembered planting some of the potatoes that had succumbed to the crop death and it must have been three months ago.

"When we came out of the maintenance area," said Mel. "You said Ivan was hiding something from you. What did you mean?"

Alex shrugged. He wasn't really sure himself. "Recently, he's been evasive when we ask him things, like where he got the guns from and how he knew what had happened to Elea."

"Elea? That was the woman who got shot?"

Alex was surprised. "You know about that?"

"I heard you arguing."

Her explanation made sense – unlike many of Ivan's. "Ivan had all these great ideas about how Mars-borns need to stand up for ourselves. They sounded so exciting and possible when he talked about them. He made me so angry about what it's like to be born on Mars, that I wanted to fight back. Then Elea got shot…"

Emotion that he hadn't realized he'd been holding back was suddenly at the surface. He struggled not to cry in front of a woman he hardly knew.

Mel's face became alert. "Quiet. I heard something."

Alex listened. Someone was moving around in the depot. "What time do people arrive for work?"

"Early," said Mel. "But not this early."

He had been a fool to wait even ten minutes with her in the office. "Is there another way out?"

"Out the front, but we still need to get down the stairs into the main depot." She got off the chair and down onto her hands and knees. "Get under the desk. Maybe they won't come up to the offices."

Alex got down to the floor and crawled under the desk with her. As soon as he did it, he realized his mistake. This left him nowhere to run. If they were found in the office, they were trapped. The lights were still on around them and there was no way of knowing if they would sense a lack of movement and turn off before whoever had entered the building saw them and came to investigate.

Alex thought about making a break for it anyway when he heard footsteps coming up the stairs and knew his decision had come too late. He pulled his knees up against his chest and huddled close to the leg of the desk, staring across at Mel who was doing the same.

The door to the office was hurled open. Alex readied himself to run.

"Is someone in here?" demanded a male voice.

Mel's staring eyes turned to recognition. "Isaac?"

"Mel?" he questioned in surprise.

Delight filled her face and she scrambled out from under the desk.

Alex, bewildered and not quite sure what was going on, crawled out to watch.

Mel virtually skipped the distance between her and the man in the doorway. She flung her arms around him and he caught her and held her tight.

Embarrassed at the emotional reunion happening in front of him, Alex turned away, irritated that they were wasting time.

CHAPTER FORTY-FIVE

Ivan Valkov sat across the interrogation table from Deverau. Seeing as he was about to be charged with everything from resisting arrest to hostage taking, he appeared remarkably relaxed. Which was more than could be said for his legal representative, who sat alongside him nervously fiddling with her suit or looking at notes on the tablet in front of her. She was either a newly appointed duty lawyer or someone with little experience of serious criminals.

Deverau liked to interview his suspects as soon as they were in custody. It gave them little time to think through their situation and decide what pathetic story they were going to trot out in their defense. But Ivan had broken his leg jumping from the window and had spent an hour in hospital getting his right fibula re-set.

Deverau had been in the same hospital getting his own injuries attended to. Ivan's sharp kick to his side hadn't broken any of Deverau's ribs, fortunately, but they were severely bruised. It was his hands that Deverau was more worried about.

Third degree burns had stripped the skin off the backs around the knuckles and he'd had to have artificial skin grafts on both of them. Bandages had been placed over the wounds which made his injuries look more dramatic than they actually were.

Jones had warned it would make him look weak in front of Ivan and allow their suspect to gloat at the damage he had done to his accuser. But Deverau didn't care. Let him gloat. Ivan already hated him for being Earth-born. If displaying his injuries made his suspect feel superior to him, then it only gave him further to fall.

"I would like to thank you for making my job easier," Deverau began.

He matched Ivan's glare across the table. He was trying to play it cool, but Deverau suspected it wouldn't take much to break that facade.

"I wish all my suspects recorded themselves committing the crime and released the footage to the public. It would save everyone so much time. Sergeant Jones, if you would."

Jones responded by pulling up the footage and turning the tablet so it faced Ivan and his lawyer.

The footage showed Ivan pacing in front of the hovercams, ranting with zeal while innocent tourists watched, terrified, in the background. *"Mars will not be dictated to. We will not be stepped upon. Earth has exploited Mars for too long. We need to be allowed to govern ourselves, to work for ourselves!"*

Ivan adjusted himself in his chair in a seated version of a swagger. He seemed proud of himself, even in custody.

His lawyer sat prim in her seat. "My client does not deny that it is him in the footage. He was expressing a legitimate grievance."

Deverau held up his hand for her to stop. "Save your mitigating arguments for the courtroom, counsellor."

He resumed focus on Ivan. "Who paid you?"

A flicker of unease moved across Ivan's face. Only for a split second and almost imperceptible, but it was enough for Deverau to know he was onto something.

"Getting hold of bullet-firing guns smuggled from Earth isn't cheap," continued Deverau. "As for getting into the Martian Tropics resort undetected without bribing anybody... well, let's just say it's highly unlikely. Not something you would expect from someone on a miner's salary."

"You underestimate how many people want to send a defiant message back to Earth," Ivan replied.

"Really?" said Deverau. "What about the nice clothes hanging in your closet or the very expensive holographic unit in your apartment?"

"I saved up," he said.

Deverau leaned forward and tried not to wince at the pain in his ribs. "Perhaps you don't understand what you're facing. As well as your actions at the Martian Tropics resort, you were seen handing out stolen food at the transport hub, which links you directly to the attack on Martian Rails. You even used mining explosives taken from your job, Ivan. I have run out of fingers and toes to count up how many years you are going to spend in jail."

He paused to let the reality of it sink into Ivan's mind. "Tell me who paid you," Deverau demanded. "It'll look good for you when the time comes for sentencing."

Ivan sat defiantly in his chair and said nothing.

Deverau didn't expect him to confess everything in the first interrogation. It was enough to plant the idea in his mind. A few more nights in a cell should give him time to think. Perhaps his nervous lawyer might persuade him to talk.

After the silence had become uncomfortable, Deverau waited a little longer for the discomfort to become palpable.

Then he changed tack.

"I have another piece of interesting footage to show you," he said. "Sergeant Jones?"

Jones showed his tablet to Ivan and his lawyer a second time.

"It's security footage from the twenty-fifth of June," Jones explained. "It shows *you* taking something from an EcoLine research facility in Deimos City."

As the footage played, Ivan leaned forward to take a closer look. Which was difficult because his leg was unable to bend in the cast under the table. He shook his head at the image of the man taking a rack of plants from a refrigeration unit.

"That's the room where the experiment alleged to have caused the food crisis was kept," said Deverau.

"That's not me," said Ivan.

"Really? Keep watching."

Deverau scrutinized the real and present face of Ivan Volkov across the table as he watched the thief turning in the elevator to reveal his identity. When Ivan saw himself, his arrogance evaporated.

"That's fake!" Ivan declared and jumped up from his chair so quickly the chair tipped over backwards. Hopping on his good leg, he pointed an accusing finger at Deverau.

"You're not going to pin that on me!"

Jones called for backup on his WristTab.

The lawyer desperately failed to get her client to sit back down.

Deverau sat still, watching his suspect's reactions unfold and made a mental note of every single one.

"I did the other stuff," Ivan ranted. He returned to the table and jabbed his finger on the tablet. "Show the other stuff. I'm proud to have stood up for the rights of Mars-borns. But *that*?"

He tossed the tablet into the air and Jones had to duck to avoid being hit on the head before it clattered to the floor.

"You can't pin the food crisis on me. I didn't do it!"

Two uniformed officers rushed in and grabbed Ivan's arms. Hobbled by the cast on his broken leg, he didn't resist them physically, but kept shouting his innocence.

Deverau terminated the interview and turned away to hide his smile of satisfaction.

The stinging pain in Deverau's arms was getting worse and he would soon have to succumb to doctor's orders and take the painkillers he had been prescribed. He willed himself to hold out a little longer. He needed to keep his mind sharp.

Sitting in the viewing room adjoining the interview suite, he again watched the footage Mel had sent him. He was so engrossed that he didn't even look up when Jones came in.

"I thought you'd like to know," said Jones. "Uniform found two smashed WristTabs near one of the hatches that leads into the maintenance area on the west side. The assumption is, they belonged to Mel Erdan and the gang member who ran off."

"They ran off together?" said Deverau in surprise. "Any indication where they went?"

"By the time uniform got there, it was impossible to tell," said Jones. "But they managed to get one of the WristTabs working – it's linked to the account of a farm worker called Alex Pawlikiewicz."

"If a farm worker was part of the gang, could that be how Ivan got the stolen experiment into the fields?" said Deverau.

"He's only a general worker, but I suppose it's possible," said Jones. "I've put out an alert for his arrest."

"Good."

Deverau should have been pleased at the development, but he hadn't stopped thinking about the footage which was still running on the screen. He watched, for the umpteenth time, the perpetrator turn to reveal Ivan's face.

"Why would he deny it's him?" said Deverau.

Jones leaned over to take a closer look. "Suspects deny crimes they obviously committed all the time."

"I know that, but he admits everything else."

"Maybe the footage really is fake."

"Computer analysis says not," said Deverau. "Even if we accept the possibility that Mel is clever enough to fake it so it fools the computer, how did she know to point the finger at the one man responsible for two of the biggest crimes on Mars over the last year?"

Jones thought about it for a moment. "It seems unlikely, I agree."

Deverau watched the security footage reach the end of the loop and return to the point where Ivan entered the room with an empty bag. When he had interrogated Mel and later spoken to her on the train, he didn't get the sense she was capable of a conspiracy of such magnitude. But if she hired

Ivan to steal her experiment and use his contacts to get it into the farms, it wasn't so much of a stretch to think she was behind the train raid as well.

He stopped the footage and brought up the text message which had accompanied it:

> *I didn't cause the crops to die. This is proof someone stole my experiment. His name is Ivan. He is here.*
> *– Dr Melanie Erdan*

Deverau turned back to his sergeant. "She sent this message from a WristTab knowing we could trace it, then stayed around until we showed up. If Ivan hadn't fired that shockdart, we would have arrested her. She must have known that."

"I'm not saying I have all the answers, Dev."

"Mmm." Deverau parked that question in the corner of his mind.

"How are we getting on with tracing the money?" he asked.

"I found nothing untoward on Ivan's account," said Jones. "If he was getting paid, then it was through unofficial channels."

"Keep looking," said Deverau. "While you're at it, check Mel's financials."

"Will do. It seems an unlikely pairing, though – a respected botanist and a mine worker more than ten years younger than her."

"You're backtracking on your own theory now?" Deverau teased.

"Well, I…"

Deverau smiled. "No, you're right. None of this makes sense. Yet."

He was still missing a key piece. Deverau knew, until he found that piece, the answers to all of his questions would remain elusive.

CHAPTER FORTY-SIX

It hurt to pull back from Isaac, after they had been apart for so long, but Mel's logical mind knew she couldn't hold on to him forever. The emotions surging inside were a distraction, and so she gathered them up as best she could and pushed them away.

When they parted and the cool air brushed at her skin, she was embarrassed to realize her face was damp from shedding silent tears.

"Mel, what are you doing here?" said Isaac.

"She wanted to gain access to your screen," said Alex.

Mel turned to see the young man standing beside Isaac's desk having crawled out from underneath it. She had forgotten he was there.

"Who are you?" said Isaac.

"Isaac, this is Alex. He's..." She tried to think of a way to describe him which didn't make him sound too much like a criminal. "He's also hiding from the MSS. Alex, this is my husband."

"I'd sort of gathered," said Alex.

"You shouldn't have come," said Isaac. "The MSS have been here. They knew you stowed away on one of my trucks. They could even be watching me now."

"I didn't want to get you involved, Isaac. I didn't think you would be here so early."

"You triggered the silent alarm."

"Silent alarm?" She cursed herself for not considering that. It had been naive to think the only security on the building was the entry keypad.

"You're lucky I was the one on call. What if it had been someone else? What if we had linked it up to the MSS?"

Isaac reached out a hand to steady himself on the back of a nearby chair, suddenly overcome by the shock of it all.

"Isaac! Are you all right?" Mel helped him to sit down.

"Mel, I've been so worried." He bowed his head and rubbed at his temple like he was trying to erase an unseen mark on his skin. "I didn't know what had happened to you. I was scared you might be dead."

Mel crouched down in front of him. Seeing him like that, she realized what pain she must have inflicted on her family. "I'm sorry, Isaac."

He stared back at her. There was fresh doubt in his eyes. "Tell me, Mel. Honestly. Did you do it? Did you sabotage the farms?"

The accusation stabbed at her heart. Of all the people who might doubt her, she never thought Isaac would be one of them. "No, of course not."

"I knew you couldn't have. But everyone was saying it was you. Because you'd gone on the run, everyone said you were guilty. You weren't there to ask and..."

"I'm sorry, I couldn't risk contacting you," she said. "How is Daniel?"

Being away from her son ached so much that she tried not to think about him most of the time. It was hard knowing that he must be missing her and wondering why she had left without even saying goodbye.

"He's too little to understand," said Isaac. "Which I suppose I should be grateful for. Children are resilient. He's coping better than me, to be honest."

The guilt of leaving her child was worse than even the fear of jail. But it was the thought of being locked up away from him – more than even her own safety – which kept her going during her darkest moments.

"Look," said Alex. "Are you going to get this information or what? Because if you're not, I'm going."

"What information?" said Isaac.

"I came to find some logistics data," said Mel. "But I can't get access to your screen."

The mention of something work-related pulled Isaac out of his melancholy. "What logistics data?"

"Do you remember before anyone admitted the food crisis was real, you were complaining about delays coming from the farms?"

"How can I forget? It caused havoc with my schedule."

"If your company was scheduled to collect food from farms, then it makes sense that it also delivered the seed potatoes which caused the problem. If we can trace back those deliveries–"

"You could see where they came from!" said Isaac. He got to his feet and went round to the other side of the desk where he accessed the screen with ease.

Mel and Alex joined him to look over his shoulder.

"Right!" said Isaac. "I need to know which farms suffered crop deaths."

"I know that!" said Alex, suddenly excited. "Well, some of them anyway."

"I can extrapolate others from when they requested delaying collection," Isaac added.

Isaac pulled up document after document of data that Mel didn't understand and, by the look on Alex's face, he didn't either.

"We need to work back to before the crops died," said Isaac. "How long are we talking about?"

"Two to three months," said Mel.

"Got it!" said Isaac.

He continued to work through a lot of confusing data with the lightning speed of someone who knew what they were looking at.

One name kept coming up: Teractor.

Isaac sat back in his chair. "There's your link."

The information was so easy to find, it was difficult to believe. "Are you sure?" she said.

"There are other logistics hubs, of course, and we don't have details of all the farms affected," said Isaac. "But, if your timescales are right, then it seems all the deliveries came from Teractor."

All three looked at the screen. It had been a simple deduction. One, surely, that any investigation would have easily uncovered.

"Do you think Kaito knows about this?" said Mel.

"If she does," said Isaac, "she's not made it public."

Mel turned to Alex. "What about Ivan? What links did he have with Teractor?"

Alex shrugged. "None, as far as I know. He works for the Mining Guild, and when he's not doing that, he's hanging out with us or Elea."

"I have to tell Kaito," said Mel. "She'll have the power to investigate further and clear my name."

"I thought we came here to find a way out," said Alex.

"He's right," said Isaac. "It's too dangerous for you to stay in Deimos City."

Mel knew it. She felt the danger inside of her with every breath, but it would always be with her unless she proved her innocence. "I have to act, Isaac. Besides, I don't have anywhere else to go."

"I might know somewhere," said Isaac, his eyes brightening. "I received a message from one of your old university friends."

Alex chipped in. "Is this relevant?"

"I think so." Isaac lifted his WristTab. "His name was Doctor Serrano."

"Pedro?" said Mel in surprise.

"I think that was his name." Isaac found what he was looking for and streamed it to his work screen.

Pedro's bearded face stared out from a recording made in one of the labs at Squyres Research Outpost. "Hi Mel. I don't know if this will reach you, but I'm sending it to your husband in the hope you'll be able to see it soon. I've got something to show you."

Pedro moved aside and a mass of green behind him came into focus. Hundreds of tiny plants, around ten centimeters high, reached up from planting trays. On the ones nearest the camera it was possible to see the distinctive oval, pointed shape of the leaves.

"Potato plants!" said Mel and Alex together.

"You were right, Mel." Pedro moved back in front of the camera and it re-focused on his face. "Enhanced potatoes with accelerated growth can work. When you left, I took what you had started and began propagating. Any day now, there'll be enough microtubers to grow seed potatoes in one of the domes. I wish you could come here and see for yourself."

Pedro smiled and the message ended.

"That sounds like an invitation to me," said Isaac.

Mel was uncertain. "But Inspector Deverau knows Pedro and I are friends. He already tried to find me there."

"Then maybe he won't try looking there again."

The thought of returning to Pedro and using their combined scientific knowledge to feed Mars was tempting. But going there would only bring her the illusion of safety.

Handing Ivan to Deverau was supposed to have been her last move. Mel had expected to be arrested and for the MSS to figure out the truth using the evidence she had given them. The decision to run with Alex had been on the spur of the moment and bought her some unexpected freedom. She had to use it wisely because she didn't know how much longer it would last.

"I can't," she said.

"What?" said Alex. He pointed at the blank screen where Pedro's face had been. "He's offering you sanctuary and you're going to turn it down? I came with you because I thought it would be safe. Now I've wasted all this time when I could have been getting away."

Mel looked at the teenager. He was too young to be embroiled in such a mess. She had only known him a few hours, which was not enough time to really get to know anyone. But he had grabbed her hand and helped her escape when she had been ready to give up and let the MSS take her. She had a sense that, whatever he might have done, he was not a bad person at heart. And he was right that she had brought him with her when he could have been getting a head start. She owed him something.

"Go to Squyres Research Outpost without me," Mel told Alex, hoping her friend wouldn't mind. "Explain to Pedro what we've found out and tell him I'll follow when I can."

The joy that had filled Isaac's face when he had first seen her had all but seeped away, to be replaced by sadness and worry. "Mel, are you sure this is a good idea? Kaito is famous now. I'm not even sure you'll get near her."

"She's my friend, Isaac. I'll find a way to see her. Then I'll come back, take one of the rovers and go to Pedro's."

Tears were forming in Isaac's eyes. "If you're sure," he said. "I'll remember to accidentally leave one unlocked for you."

"Then you'll let me take a rover now?" said Alex.

"If that's what Mel wants," said Isaac. "I can hide its disappearance in the company records for a while."

He stood and pulled Mel close. She allowed herself to be engulfed in his arms. "Stay safe," he whispered into her ear.

The comfort of him was almost too much. Part of her wanted to stay in his arms for as many hours as she could before the MSS found her and took her away. But she now had information that had the potential to buy her freedom forever. If she could find a way to use it.

"Give my love to Daniel," she said and pulled away.

Mel headed for the door. She didn't want to experience the pain of stopping to look back at what she was leaving behind. So she kept walking. Out the door, into the corridor, down the steps and back out into the city.

CHAPTER FORTY-SEVEN

Mel leaned against the corner of Kaito's apartment building and tiredness sank into her body. Taking public transport wouldn't have been safe, so she had walked through the night. By the time she arrived, she had burned through the adrenaline which had fueled her escape from the gang's meeting place and the excitement of seeing Isaac had passed into memory.

The lights of the dome, brightening to augment the rising sun of a Martian morning, meant Kaito was most likely awake. Mel considered taking a risk to openly call for her through the building's intercom, but she was wary of the security cameras that scanned the entrance and of alerting others to her presence. So she elected to wait, tucked around the side of the building, away from the main thoroughfare of the street, where she could watch and listen for signs of Kaito leaving for work.

Fatigue begged her to rest. Even standing put strain on her aching body after such a long walk. Mel allowed her back to slide down the wall until her buttocks touched the cold, hard tiles of the street. Her feet tingled with relief and her eyes momentarily closed. Feeling sleep trying to take her, she blinked herself awake. But soon, without realizing, the tempting bliss of darkness lulled her into a doze.

Mel was woken by a shout.

Her heart thumped a fast and frantic rhythm as she pulled herself to her feet. Scared she had been recognized, she glanced around the corner of the building. With relief, she saw Kaito was emerging from the entrance and walking towards her.

The shout came again. "Doctor Tanaka!"

Running across the street towards Kaito was a man with two hovercams buzzing around his head. "Just a few questions for ICN, Doctor Tanaka. What's the latest on the food crisis?"

Mel ducked back behind the wall and tried to quieten her alarmed breaths. She had come too close to putting her face back on the news.

Her pounding heart told her to run, but she daren't risk drawing attention to herself.

"I have no comment to make," Kaito told the journalist. "You know that all information is provided in our daily news briefings."

"What about Doctor Mel Erdan? Can you comment about her?"

Mel tensed at the mention of her name. She pressed her back closer to the wall and listened.

Kaito's footsteps stopped. Like she had turned to address the journalist. "I'm sorry?"

"You're a friend of Doctor Erdan, aren't you? Did you know she was the one who sabotaged the crops?"

"We don't know that for sure."

"But isn't it a conflict of interest for you to be the one investigating what happened?"

"Not at all. First of all, Doctor Erdan is *not* my friend. I was her supervisor at EcoLine, nothing more. In fact, we barely saw each other."

Kaito's easy dismissal of their friendship cut deep.

Mel thought back to all the happy times of their friendship. From trying to find their way around their first jobs at EcoLine, to the many nights Mel had consoled her after the painful breakup with her old boyfriend, to the way Kaito had encouraged everyone to party at Mel and Isaac's wedding. Kaito had turned her back on it as if it were nothing.

"Secondly," Kaito continued, "if she was the one who sabotaged the farms, then she did well to hide it from me. I have no doubt that she had the capability to do it, but whether or not she did is something the MSS will have to determine. They have my entire backing in their search for Doctor Erdan and in bringing her to justice. My priority is to feed Mars. So, if you'll excuse me, I have a lot of work to do."

Kaito's footsteps resumed. With her words still burning, Mel turned away.

CHAPTER FORTY-EIGHT

The itching in Deverau's arms was ever present. Like a devil was on his shoulder, whispering: *scratch, scratch, scratch.*

Deverau even hovered his hand over the bandages and clawed at the air to try to pacify the constant irritation. It made no difference and he had taken to scratching at the exposed skin above the bandages until he had two tell-tale red marks on each arm. After a while, the patches of skin started to hurt, but at least it quelled the devil for a while.

The nurse who had changed his dressings at the hospital had scolded him for his childish behavior. The itching was a good sign, he said, as it showed the skin was healing and he should be grateful for it.

The nurse had been gentle and caring, but there was a weariness about him. Deverau sensed the same fatigue and anxiety among all of the staff and patients when he walked through the hospital. A population living on rations without knowing when or how the crisis was going to end created a tension which rumbled under everything and everyone.

Deverau had combined his appointment with a visit to Elea Kyllo, who was almost ready to be discharged into MSS custody after being treated for her gunshot wound. He had formally charged her with offenses related to the events at Martian Tropics and the transport hub, and had watched the regret deepen within her eyes with his every word.

He also questioned her about Ivan and received the same response as he had from other people who knew him. She believed Ivan's pro Mars-born zeal was genuine and the food crisis, along with an inheritance from a recently deceased uncle, had given him an opportunity to do something about it.

Deverau knew there had been no inheritance because Ivan had only one uncle and he was still living in Tharsis City on an average mine worker's wage. The timing of the supposed bequest, however, was interesting. Elea's memory suggested he came into the money around the same time as security footage had caught him breaking into Mel's lab.

Deverau found himself scratching the already-raw patch of skin above his freshly applied bandages on his left hand as he emerged from the hospital. He kept his gaze fixed on the street and the way back to the station so he could ignore the tired, anxious and sick people who hung around the entrance.

So he didn't notice the man walking straight towards him. Until he spoke.

"Inspector?"

The man looked familiar, but he couldn't think where from.

"Have you found my wife yet?" he asked.

Instantly, Deverau realized it was Isaac Erdan, Mel's husband. But his question was odd. A relative of a missing person who had gone to the trouble to track down the MSS officer assigned to her case should have been frantic. Instead, he was matter-of-fact. He asked his question in the same way someone might if they were inquiring how long to wait until the next tram.

"I haven't found her," said Deverau. "But something tells me you already know that."

"Me?" said Isaac. "I don't know anything. But I have some information which helps prove my wife's innocence."

Isaac beckoned Deverau away from the people at the entrance and hugged in close to the wall of the hospital.

Deverau, curious, followed.

Isaac spoke quietly, leaning in close to Deverau to ensure no one else heard. "You should be looking into Teractor," he said.

"Teractor?" said Deverau in surprise. The name was as familiar as any big corporation on Mars, but it had nothing to do with his case. "A corporation full of lawyers?"

Deverau had not kept his voice low and Isaac looked uncomfortable that someone might have overheard. As if to compensate, he spoke even quieter. "They made their MegaCredits drawing up legal contracts, but they've been expanding into other projects for years. Including farming. I have information you might find interesting. Let me send it to your WristTab."

Deverau brought up his bandaged hand with the device strapped loosely over the top. He granted permission and Isaac sent across the data.

With his message delivered, Isaac turned to go.

Deverau called after him. "If you'd seen or heard from your wife you would tell me, wouldn't you?"

Isaac looked back over his shoulder. "Of course," he said, then hurried off down the street.

Deverau knew he was lying. But, as he watched his departing figure he realized Isaac must have known Deverau might come to that conclusion. Which meant, whatever data he had given him, it was important enough for him to take the risk.

CHAPTER FORTY-NINE

Mel stepped out of the rover to find Pedro waiting for her in the echoey chamber of the vehicle airlock. His beard had grown out since she had last seen him and she guessed he had been too distracted to keep it trimmed.

"Sorry to impose on you again, Pedro."

"Nonsense. If I had wanted you to stay away, I wouldn't have sent that message to your husband."

"Then I'm grateful."

"Although," he grinned, "Gadd is starting to wonder if we're operating some sort of underground refuge for fugitives."

Mel thought of Alex. She had wondered if he really would go to Squyres Research Outpost as they had discussed, or take Isaac's rover off somewhere else, never to be seen again. "Alex is here?"

"Yes. In fact, he's keen to show you what he's been helping us with."

Mel went weak at the thought of it. Her knees buckled and Pedro had to grip her arm to steady her. "Hey, are you OK?"

She shook her head. After her rejection from Kaito, she had had to hide until night came before she could access Isaac's depot and take the rover he had left unlocked for her. There had been some food and water on board which she had been able to take advantage of, but she had had only snatches of sleep at best across the past forty-eight hours.

"I'm tired, that's all. I could use a lie down."

She expected him to accede to her request, but he hesitated.

Mel felt nervous. All manner of possibilities tumbled through her head, from Deverau being there waiting to arrest her, to being told to get back into the rover and leave.

"It will only take a few minutes," said Pedro. "I promised Alex."

"What's so important?"

"To be honest, we're concerned about him. He seems normal during the day, but people have heard him screaming in his sleep. I tried asking, but he won't say what happened to him."

Mel considered, for the first time, the trauma he must have gone through. Up until that point, she had been too absorbed in her own problems. "From what I understand, he accidentally shot a friend of his," said Mel. "She nearly died."

Pedro exhaled at the thought. "That's enough to give anyone nightmares."

"Yes," she said, contemplating.

"We can swing by the dome on the way to my rooms. It won't take long," he said. "I have to confess, I'm rather excited to show you myself."

The forest was gone.

All that was left of the trees and plants were the brown stumps of chopped down trunks and the occasional green of a discarded leaf resting on the reddish-brown dirt.

"What happened?" said Mel, stepping inside and breathing in the earthy smell of freshly turned soil.

"We had no choice," explained Pedro. "We needed a large planting area and had to utilize one of the domes."

"But your experiment…"

"Can be re-grown. I have samples in cold storage."

Looking out across the flat circle of nothing under the arch of the dome, it seemed so destructive.

A movement caught her eye. People in dark clothing, who she hadn't seen at first because they were camouflaged against the dirt, were standing near the outer edge. One of them waved at her and came over.

As he jogged closer, she saw that it was Alex. He was dressed in what had to be borrowed clothing, because it hung loosely over his skinny body, and he appeared full of energy.

"Did you tell her?" he said.

"No," said Pedro. "I promised I wouldn't."

Alex, his eyes bright with optimism, dashed off again to a line of ceramic pots which stood at mid-calf height near the entrance. Mel had walked right past them without even noticing.

What he brought back was a pot half filled with the distinctive white, pebble-sized globes of microtubers. "They're mini seed potatoes," Alex explained.

Before she could stop him, he had put his hand into the pot and pulled out one to show her. She was so used to being careful not to contaminate plants in the lab, that her instinct was to pull back. But Alex had already touched it and so she allowed him to place it into her hand, where it rolled around her palm like a marble.

Mel looked from the microtuber to Pedro. "You did it."

"*You* did it, Mel," he replied. "I only completed what you had started. If we plant these today, we'll soon have actual plants ready to harvest."

"Hey, Alex!" called someone from across the dome. Mel thought it was Gadd. "Are you helping or what?"

"If you help us too," Alex told Mel, "we could get the dome planted today." Then he turned and called back, "Coming!", before he ran back to join the others.

Mel was proud at the thought of her potatoes finally doing the job she had engineered them to do. But she was also worried. "What happens when the plants are grown?"

"That's where we run into problems," said Pedro. "A dome this size isn't going to produce enough food to feed Mars. We need to get the crop into commercial farms. But Gadd can't get our proposals past the Science Board. I'm hoping you could help with that."

"Me?" Mel laughed. "I'm discredited."

"You are friends with Kaito Tanaka. As the scientific lead on the crisis, she has a lot of power and the ear of Chair Sharif."

It might have been the lack of sleep, but Mel actually felt sick when she thought about the woman she had once considered a friend. "Believe me, Pedro, you are better off without me."

"What do you mean?"

She wanted to tell him what had happened, but she hadn't the strength to face it. "I'll fill you in later. After I have slept."

•••

Alex was exhausted. But it was the good type of exhaustion that comes with working hard to achieve something. He had spent all day in the dome planting the little potatoes with the scientists from the research outpost. He was amazed at how little they knew about the practicalities of farming, despite all of their collective experience and education. They were used to raising small clutches of experimental plants in the laboratory, whereas he had spent his working life planting crops on an industrial scale.

He told them how they planted seed potatoes in the farms. Although the scientists had assistance from robots, he knew at what depth and at what distance apart the tubers needed to be. They listened to him as their equal and took his suggestions on board.

He felt important, proud, valued.

But once the dome had been planted, the scientists went their own separate ways and left Alex to the quiet, where thoughts of his situation inevitably returned.

Gadd had made it clear that he was welcome to stay for a while because Pedro had vouched for Mel and Mel had vouched for him. But he knew it was a temporary cocoon of safety from which he would soon have to emerge.

Pedro allowed him to come back to his rooms for the evening where Mel was joining him after spending the entire day asleep. The two of them took either end of the sofa while Alex was left to sit on Pedro's office chair. As the two old friends became engrossed in their conversation, Alex felt as if they had forgotten he was there.

But he preferred it to being alone. And so, he stayed and listened.

"You have to remember," Pedro was saying. "Kaito was speaking in front of ICN cameras when you saw her. She might not have meant what she said."

Mel, her feet tucked up casually under her thighs, didn't look like she believed him. "Kaito has her position to maintain with the Terraforming Committee and I've been branded a criminal – she can't be seen to be helping me. I was foolish to think I could even ask."

Pedro looked down at his hands clasped in front of him. "Revealing what you know to ICN isn't such a bad idea, you know."

Mel seemed amused by the concept. "What do you suggest? I offer them an exclusive interview?"

"You could," Pedro considered. "I was more thinking of getting into one of Kaito's news briefings and asking some pertinent questions. They're live, so whatever you say can't be censored."

"How am I supposed to do that?"

"Infiltrate the ICN crew?" Pedro suggested with a shrug.

"You're forgetting, ever since the MSS put out a public alert, my face couldn't infiltrate anywhere."

"I didn't say I had a fully formed plan."

"What about the plants you're growing in the dome?" said Mel. "If the Science Board won't listen, do you have a fully formed plan for that?"

Pedro sat back in his chair and let out a long, contemplative sigh. "We haven't even got a half-baked plan. We expect the microtubers to produce a sizable crop which can be used as both seed potatoes and for testing as a food source. Gadd has worked out how to go through the necessary regulatory procedures in parallel to fast track everything. With accelerated growth, we could be feeding people within weeks. But, even with his contacts, he's coming up against solid barriers at the Science Board."

"I'm so sorry I can't help," said Mel.

Pedro shook his head. "Don't be. It's just so frustrating. If only we could plant them in *one* commercial farm, we could prove the viability of the science."

Alex listened to them talk, waiting for them to draw the obvious conclusion. But they did not. Older people were so intransigent when it came to the accepted way of doing things.

"Why do you think you need permission?" asked Alex.

Pedro turned round and gave him a doubtful look. "We can't just walk into a commercial farm and start planting whatever we like."

"I could," said Alex.

Mel also turned, and Alex enjoyed the thought of knowing more than they did.

"I mean," he said, "why go to all the trouble of getting someone to agree to tell the farm workers to plant them, when you can ask the farm workers direct?"

"They would do that?" said Pedro.

"If I got my friend Kurt to help and they knew it was to feed to people on Mars, then yes. They would do it. Absolutely."

CHAPTER FIFTY

The *I told you so* moment when Deverau personally delivered his report on the raid on Martian Rails and the incident at the Martian Tropics resort gave him immense satisfaction. He had arrested all of the gang, bar one, and, although they had revealed little in interrogation, he had more than enough evidence to prove their guilt in court.

He didn't mention to the charlatans at Noctis City that, had they given him the resources to do his job properly in the first place, the unpleasant business with the Earth tourists could have been avoided. He let them work out that bit for themselves.

As gratifying as it was to gloat in front of his superiors – still wearing the bandages on his hands to gain that extra bit of sympathy – he had an ulterior motive for coming to Noctis City: the information Isaac Erdan had given him about Teractor.

The Head of Teractor's Martian operations, Meike Fischer, had agreed to meet with him for an "informal chat" while he "happened to be" in the city. Which meant taking a detour to Corporate Square.

Teractor, unlike other corporations, had no claims to fame of its own. It was effectively a law firm which had grown so big it had become a corporation. So it celebrated the achievements of humanity as a whole with holographic recreations of key moments in Mars' history in the foyer of its headquarters.

Years were compressed into minutes on either side of him as Deverau walked to the reception desk. Buildings rose out of a barren rusty red landscape to his left. Politicians gathered to form the first Terraforming Committee to his right. Fiery asteroids rained from the sky above him and rad-suited holograms planted the first adapted lichens into dry dirt near his feet.

It was impressive.

The display looped back to the beginning as Meike Fischer's assistant came to collect him. He left the holograms to rebuild cities and replant lichen while he and his chaperone took the elevator to the top floor.

He was led into an executive office twice as big – and twice as equipped – as his apartment. Complete with kitchenette, sofa area and a 180-degree curved window which looked out across the whole city in front of him.

The expression "breathtaking" could almost have been invented for that window. Attached to the underside of the dome for support, it had a God's eye view of human life below. Lines of streets snaked across the disc of the city. Buildings short and tall rose up on either side of the pathways, while trams moved along them like toy cars. Arching over it all was the translucent membrane of the dome with the hazy circle of the sun approaching the apex.

"Inspector," said a woman in a light gray tailored suit, who had to be Meike Fischer. She stood from behind a sprawling corporate desk big enough to serve five officers back at the station. "I see you've noticed my window."

Deverau pulled his eyes away from the view to look at her properly. She was Mars-born and a few years younger than him, with the confidence of someone completely in charge. "It's a little difficult to miss," he said.

She offered him a chair and he sat on the opposite side of her corporate desk where he was forced to squint against the brightness behind her. An excellent way to stop him noticing any nuances in her expression as she answered his questions.

"I was also admiring your holograms in the entrance," said Deverau. "Are you trying to take credit for all the achievements on Mars?"

"We may not have been the headline act," she said. "But without Teractor working behind the scenes to ensure all legal considerations were met, some of those achievements would have had a rocky road to success."

"I see," said Deverau. He glanced down at his lap to gather his thoughts and to rest his eyes from the light.

"If you don't mind me asking," she said. "What happened to your hands?"

Deverau turned them over as if he had forgotten they were bandaged. "I had an encounter with a suspect that had unintended consequences."

"I'm sorry to hear that."

He shrugged it off and hoped he had gained a little of her sympathy.

"I have to say, inspector, I was intrigued when your message said you were investigating the woman who caused the food crisis – 'Erdan', is it? I'm told she was employed by EcoLine, not Teractor."

A woman like Meike Fischer, as the head of a corporation of lawyers whose very job it was to worry about the details, would have done her homework before meeting with him. The fact that she pretended she hadn't, was a cause for suspicion in itself.

"At the moment, I'm more interested in Teractor's involvement with farming," he said.

Meike leaned back on her chair. "Teractor, like almost every other corporation, has diversified into many areas since the Terraforming Announcement," she said. "But, unlike other corporations, we understand that colonizing this planet isn't only about chasing MegaCredits handed out by the World Government. No matter how worthy the terraforming project might be. We know we must invest in infrastructure to keep pace with development."

"And farming?" Deverau prompted.

"Agriculture is one of our more recent endeavors. Teractor understands that you can't bring ship after ship of Earth-borns to work on Mars without the capacity to feed them."

"Except it all went wrong," he suggested.

"Which is why I am fully supportive of your attempt to catch this Erdan woman. Although, as I understand it, the MSS already caught her once and managed to lose her."

It was a cheap shot to try to anger him, but Deverau had heard much worse from suspects in the interrogation room.

"The data I've received suggests it was Teractor who supplied the farms that suffered crop deaths."

She sat up straight again and glared across the table. "What data?"

He ignored her attempt to throw the interrogation back on him. "Why would Teractor want crops to die?"

"I thought you were here to ask questions, not make accusations."

Deverau squinted against the brightness of the window, but still couldn't see her face clearly.

He said nothing, waiting for her to fill the silence.

"Commercial farms on Mars have many individual fields and not all of them failed, so it's impossible to make that link, even if it existed. You should know, inspector, that data can be misinterpreted if you don't have the complete facts. Why don't you let my office send over a *complete* set of data? I'm sure that will dispel any misunderstandings."

Deverau was sure it would. After the data had been censored.

However, he kept that suspicion to himself. "I would appreciate that," he said.

Deverau continued his questioning, but the Teractor executive was the product of expensive legal training and gave nothing else away.

He left her office, escorted by her assistant to make sure he didn't go wandering around the building, and returned to the impressive holograms in reception.

It was as he turned to leave that, stepping through the ghosts of rad-suited figures, came someone he recognized. Out of context, it took a moment to place the Earth-born woman in a dark blue suit as she walked past and headed to the elevator.

"Doctor Tanaka!" he called after her.

She turned. The brief moment of alarm in her expression was swiftly covered with a smile, but not before Deverau had made a mental note.

"Inspector! What are you doing here?"

"I was about to ask you the same," he said.

She approached. A man, who Deverau had taken to be a Teractor employee who happened to have walked in at the same time as her, followed. He was also Earth-born, but a little older and with a thin, gaunt face.

"I was visiting my partner," said Kaito. "Felix, this is Inspector Deverau of the MSS."

Deverau offered his hand to the gaunt-faced man. Felix, somewhat bemused by the encounter, shook it perfunctorily. "Nice to meet you, inspector."

He spoke with a strong Earth accent which Deverau placed somewhere in Europe. "Been on Mars long?"

"Almost five years," he said. "Teractor offered me a position as head of personnel, which I never would have achieved if I'd stayed on Earth."

"Of course you would have, Felix," said Kaito. "It might have taken a little longer, that's all."

Deverau nodded. It was a familiar story among migrant workers. "How do you know Kaito?"

"We met when she was doing some consulting work here," he said.

"I didn't know you had connections to Teractor," said Deverau.

"I'm sure the inspector doesn't want to hear all the details," said Kaito, making a play of glancing at her WristTab like she had some urgent business to attend to. "It was nice seeing you again."

She bustled off towards the elevator with Felix, still looking bemused, following behind.

Deverau stayed in the foyer, reflecting on the coincidence of bumping into Kaito at Teractor of all places. Unless, of course, it was no coincidence at all.

CHAPTER FIFTY-ONE

Alex drove the Squyres rover into Isaac's logistics depot. It was night-time and Isaac was the only member of staff on duty.

"Squyres rover," came Isaac's perfunctory voice over the comms. "Park up at the end of row D and release your controls to the automatic systems."

Mel's heart warmed to the sound of her husband, but she couldn't respond. They had come into Deimos City under the premise of being a science rover and they couldn't risk anyone overhearing their conversation. So she stayed quiet and sat nervously in the back of the vehicle while Alex and Pedro sat up front in control.

It had been a week since Alex had rushed up to Mel in the smallest of the outpost's experimental domes and showed her the microtubers they were due to plant. Over the following days, she had watched them grow into a miracle.

Every morning she would wake earlier than anyone else in the complex and creep into the dome expecting to see the black, withering leaves of a failed experiment. But every morning, she was greeted by a burgeoning mass of healthy plants. By the time they had matured, each had produced an average of ten tubers to use as food or seed.

Their plan was for Alex to persuade the farm workers to plant them in one of the commercial farms with Pedro overseeing the operation. Mel, meanwhile, had business with Kaito.

"Depot, this is Squyres rover," said Alex. "I'm parked and controls are yours. Comms off."

Pedro turned to face Mel. "Are you sure you don't want me to come with you?"

She shook her head. "Planting the crop is more important. Besides, I have a better chance of getting to Kaito on my own."

As Pedro had suggested, she would reveal what she knew about Teractor during one of Kaito's news briefings. If the woman she had known for years refused to listen, at least she would have her say in front of the ICN cameras.

Getting access, especially with her recognizable face, would be the difficult part. But the public's increasing frustration with tightening rations had presented her with an opportunity. Underground chatter suggested there would be a mass demonstration outside Hunter House the following day, giving her the cover she needed to get in.

Automatic systems moved the rover into line with the other vehicles in the depot, like a computerized valet system. Pedro stepped into the back, leaving Alex to operate the hatch.

"Good luck, Mel." He held out his hand for her to shake.

She stepped past his hand to give him a hug. Their embrace was short, but heartening. "You too, Pedro."

"Good luck, Alex," Mel called up to the front.

"I don't have to hug you, do I?" said Alex. "It'd be like hugging my parents."

Mel laughed, even though it made her feel suddenly old. "No, you don't have to hug us."

"I'll just say good luck, then." Alex looked to the controls. "Opening the hatch now."

The seals released with a hiss and the hatch swung open.

"Thanks, Alex," said Pedro. "You're really good at this, you know – and with everything you did back at the dome. I'm sure your actual parents would be proud of you."

"They might have been if I hadn't got involved with Ivan Volkov," he said with regret.

The name sent a chill of recognition through Mel's body. She reached out her hand to steady herself, even though the rover was perfectly still.

"Volkov?" she questioned.

"Ivan," said Alex. "He's the one you said stole from your lab."

She turned from the hatch. "But, *Volkov*? His name is Ivan *Volkov*?"

Alex blinked, confused. "Yeah. Didn't you know?"

Memories resurfaced from years ago, of talking to Kaito long into the night. "Is Andrei Volkov Ivan's father?"

"I don't know. Maybe."

Mel flopped into the seat next to Alex.

"Who's Andrei Volkov?" said Pedro.

"Kaito's ex," said Mel, as she feared the repercussions of that one piece of information. "I was her shoulder to cry on, years ago, when they had a bad break up. I remember that he had a son from a previous relationship – that boy must be Ivan's age by now."

Mel thought back to the security footage and the sense of betrayal at watching Ivan use *her* code to access the cold store. He had kept his face turned from the cameras until that one mistake at the elevator, like someone with inside knowledge.

"What does this mean?" asked Pedro.

"I'm not sure," said Mel, hoping she was being drawn to the wrong conclusion. "But when I see Kaito, I'm going to make sure she tells me."

CHAPTER FIFTY-TWO

Hundreds had been expected to gather outside Hunter House, but thousands came, bringing with them their anger and a simmering sense of injustice. It rumbled through the crowd like their chattering voices, creating a mass of distrust and suspicion.

Mel, with her face hidden behind a scarf, was in the middle of it.

From the voices she could hear around her, many with valid food tokens had been turned away at ration queues during the day. A spate of forgeries was blamed, but rumors insisted it was an excuse to disguise the reality that there was no food. Some discussion offered an innocent explanation, that a hitch in the supply chain had meant ration parcels hadn't arrived on time. Other people said the rich and powerful were using bribes to procure the food for themselves.

Whatever the truth, the people were hungry and they were angry.

They had gathered in Central Plaza where the impressive

front elevation of Hunter House looked out onto the statue of its founder. It was a grand statement of a building, constructed to reflect the ancient architecture of some of the major cities on Earth. Its lofty stories reached up into the apex of the dome in a series of molded turrets echoing the angles of traditional carved stone, while the entrance consisted of two giant glass sliding doors set back from a set of ten steps leading up from the plaza. A line of nervous MSS officers with shockguns pointing into the crowd stood at the bottom of the stairs.

Around the edge of the plaza, MSS officers in body armor also aimed their shockguns. Despite their weapons, they were vastly outnumbered.

"Feed us! Feed us! Feed us!" came a cry from the back of the crowd.

More joined in: "Feed us! Feed us! Feed us!"

A surge from somewhere behind caused Mel to lurch forward. Her face squashed up against the back of the man in front of her, who was, in turn, pushed into the person in front of him. Screams erupted from those crushed at the end of the line.

"Move back!" cried someone. "Move back!"

MSS officers waved their arms and shouted for everyone to stop pushing.

A long, thin object – which could have been a metal piece of piping – flew over her head, turning end over end like a majorette's baton, heading toward one of the MSS officers on the steps. The officer jumped out of the way and it landed harmlessly near her feet. But it had been close.

More objects came flying. An officer at the top of the steps turned to avoid something the size of a baseball coming straight towards him, only to put his face into the path of a spinning metal pole thrown from another direction. He staggered backwards and put his hand to his cheek, where there was suddenly blood. A colleague turned to help him.

The chants of "feed us!" became sporadic and out of time with each other as they were overtaken by the shouts and screams of people either determined to cause violence or afraid they were going to get caught up in it.

A public address system, hidden somewhere in the fabric of the dome or the buildings, resonated through the air. *"Return to your homes. For your own safety, please return to your homes. Peacefully and quietly… "*

But no one was listening. No one had come to Central Plaza on that day hoping to find peace and quiet.

Another surge swelled from behind and Mel was propelled towards Hunter House. Officers on the stairs fired indiscriminately into the crowd and shockdarts zipped through the air. The man in front of Mel was struck in the chest. He yelled and reached to pull the projectile out of his body. But the dart unleashed its paralyzing power before he could even touch it and he fell to the ground with his body convulsing.

Mel was pushed forward in the ensuing panic. She fell over his body and reached out her hands to protect herself from the fall. Her palms slapped hard on the tiles. People kept surging forward. Someone stepped on her fingers, crushing them painfully into the ground. She screamed, but her cry was lost in the cacophony of the crowd.

Somehow, Mel found a gap in the advancing bodies and scrambled to her feet before she was trampled.

Ahead of her, the mob had overrun the MSS officers on the stairs and was pushing at the doors to Hunter House. Even with all of that weight pressing on them, the doors held fast.

Someone began counting. *"One. Two. Three!"*

On three, the mass rammed the doors with a single force. The glass panels edged open a crack, but did not give way.

"Again!" shouted the voice, even louder. *"One. Two. Three!"*

On the second surge, the doors were ripped from their frames and crashed to the ground.

The crowd trampled over them, cheering and shouting as they poured inside. Mel rushed up the steps to follow.

Jumping over a set of security barriers, she landed in a grand entrance hall with two sweeping staircases curving down from the upper floor like two halves of a heart. On either side of her, screens on the walls showed information about Hunter House and the history of Deimos City itself.

A man brandishing a metal pole ran past Mel and took a swipe at one of the screens. He whooped with delight as historic images of Deimos crashing into Mars to form the crater where the city was built, disappeared in a shower of sparks.

As he ran off into the building, Mel realized her chances of getting near Kaito were next to zero. She had planned to slip quietly into Hunter House, not invade it with a mob of demonstrators. Security around the news briefing would be tight to the point of impenetrable.

She contemplated giving up altogether and considered taking her chances back out in Central Plaza. Then she heard a groan from under the stairs.

An MSS officer was lying on her back, semi-conscious, with a shockdart sticking out of her leg.

Mel smiled. This could be her way in.

She took the officer by the arms and dragged her to the other side of the hall and the privacy of the women's toilets. Apologizing to the woman, as she slipped into complete unconsciousness, Mel relieved her of her uniform and left her in one of the cubicles in her underwear.

Mel changed in a separate cubicle and dumped her clothes in a corner. When she stepped out, she looked in the mirror to see that she appeared to be every bit an MSS officer. The uniform gave her authority and it also added another layer of disguise. When a person wore a uniform, they took on the identity of that uniform and most people wouldn't even look at the face of the person wearing it.

Leaving the toilets, Mel double checked a map of the building on one of the screens and found that the media room, where the news briefings were held, was on the fourth floor. Then she found the elevator.

Holding her breath, she tried to be prepared for anything as the elevator reached its destination and opened the doors.

They revealed only the blank opposite wall of a corridor.

Stepping out, she noted the entrance to the back stairs to her left and, to her right, a long corridor with doors leading off it. According to the map, the door to the media room lay halfway down the corridor. To confirm it, two MSS officers stood on guard at either side.

She approached, her heart thumping while she tried to look like she had the right to be there. The officers glanced in her direction, but on seeing her uniform, they appeared unconcerned and returned to face forward.

When she was halfway, a Mars-born man in civilian clothes

exited the media room and turned in her direction. She tried to act perfectly normally and smiled at him as he acknowledged her with a nod. He glanced away and she kept walking. Then he seemed to have second thoughts and looked again.

Their eyes locked and Mel saw recognition spread across his face. At the same time, she recognized him.

"Doctor Erdan?" It was Inspector Deverau's sergeant.

His surprise gave her a moment to turn. But not before she saw him pull a shockgun from his belt. She ran.

"Doctor Erdan! Stop!"

The back stairs were almost in reach.

She heard the shockgun fire and, almost instantaneously, a sharp stab struck her back. She cried out as the *click, click, click* of the shockdart discharged its electricity. Every muscle tensed. Her brain willed her legs and arms to move, but they ignored her.

Gravity claimed her body and pulled her to the floor. She tried to move, but all she could do was quiver to the continued *click* of the dart until she fell unconscious.

CHAPTER FIFTY-THREE

Mel opened her eyes to a blue blur. Focusing, she saw she was looking at the weave of the fabric of the shirt she was wearing and realized she was sitting with her head flopped forward. It was an awkward position, resting her weight against her arms behind her which pressed into the bruise made by the shockdart in her back. She went to move them, but something was holding her wrists together. She tugged harder and the restraints cut into her skin.

Lifting her head, the wooziness of induced unconsciousness blurred her vision again. She took a moment to settle herself, with aches running up and down the muscles of her neck, until she could see a figure in front of her.

It steadily coalesced into Inspector Deverau.

With a start, she tried to stand, but with her hands cuffed behind her and still groggy, she barely lifted herself a centimeter before she fell back onto the chair.

"Good morning, Mel."

Deverau's voice had a sarcasm about it which suggested

it was not, in fact, morning. What little she knew about the effects of shockdarts suggested it was still afternoon. Between five and twenty minutes since she'd been shot.

"How are you feeling?" he asked.

"Like someone fired a shockdart into my back," she said.

Her mouth was dry. She must have breathed through it while she was unconscious.

"You'll have to forgive Sergeant Jones," said Deverau. "He tends to be a shoot first, ask questions later kind of person."

She wasn't in an interrogation room. She wasn't even in MSS offices, as far she could tell. The windowless walls, apart from a small gap at the door behind Deverau, were draped in heavy, black curtains. They deadened the sound and made the room feel dark, despite the bright lights from above.

She craned her aching neck to see behind her and caught a glimpse of a podium similar to the one Kaito used on her news briefings.

"Am I still in Hunter House?"

"We had a little crowd trouble," admitted Deverau. "I'm waiting for the all clear to leave the building."

"Where's Kaito?"

"Kaito Tanaka isn't here. She never was here. She moved all her operations to Noctis City more than a week ago. They have better security arrangements there and it's where the Terraforming Committee is based, so it made sense. The scheduled news conference went ahead without interruption."

Mel's defeat was complete. She had risked her freedom on getting into, not only the wrong building, but the wrong city.

"What are you going to do with me?" she asked.

"I thought you and I could have a little talk."

There was something sinister in the way he said it. She knew that inside MSS buildings, interviews were recorded and conducted under strict rules. In a room alone with him, things might happen which no one would know about. She shuddered at the fear of it. "You're not going to beat a confession out of me?"

"Who do you think I am?" said Deverau, appearing to be genuinely offended.

"I don't know anymore." So many of her expectations had been undermined over the past weeks that nothing would surprise her.

"You have the right to say nothing, if that is what you prefer. All the same, I'm curious to know: why did you send me that footage of Ivan Volkov stealing from your lab?"

"I wanted to show you I'm not guilty."

"Did you know he came into a sizable amount of money at around the same time?"

"No." She studied Deverau's face to try to understand why he was giving her that information. "Did Teractor pay him?"

"Good guess, but no," said Deverau. "I don't think a corporation would have been so brazen as to hire the leader of a street gang."

"Why are you telling me this?" said Mel, still suspicious.

"I thought I could tell you a little bit about what I know in return for you telling me a little bit about what you know."

Mel said nothing. She had no reason to trust him.

"Ivan tried to hide where the money came from, but that didn't stop him splashing his new-found wealth around," Deverau continued. "His downfall was buying a very expensive holographic simulation unit. There are few of them in private hands on Mars, so it was easy to find out where he bought it. We traced the payment to a secret account which included two large deposits made around six and seven months ago. The person who paid him tried to cover up the transaction, but they are an amateur, whereas the MSS has a team of specialists who uncover this sort of thing every day."

He paused. Whether it was for dramatic effect or whether he wanted her to fill in the blanks, she wasn't sure. But she had to know. "Who paid him?"

"Doctor Kaito Tanaka."

With each syllable of Kaito's name, Mel's heart sank a little further. She leaned against the back of the chair as best she could with her arms secured behind her and stared up at the ceiling. So it was true. Kaito had been the one who betrayed her.

"You don't seem that surprised," he said, almost sounding disappointed.

She sighed. She no longer had a reason to hold back. "Kaito used to date Ivan's father. A long time ago. She must have thought no one would connect them."

Deverau smiled, indicating this information was new to him. He lifted his WristTab. "Sergeant Jones?"

Mel deflated. So that was it, despite evidence pointing towards Kaito, she was still going to be carted off to an MSS cell.

"Here, Dev," came the answer from the WristTab.

"Find out where Doctor Kaito Tanaka is at the moment, will you?"

"She'll be in Noctis City," said Jones. "That's where the news conference came from."

"Just check," said Deverau.

"No problem."

Deverau lowered his WristTab and looked back at Mel.

She tried to see in his expression, whose side he was on, but he was giving nothing away. "You haven't questioned Kaito about this?"

"She's an important person now," said Deverau. "Her office keeps giving me the runaround, I'm told I don't have enough evidence to arrest her and even my own security has been told to prevent me getting access to her at the news briefings. This last piece of information about Ivan could be what I need."

Jones came back on Deverau's WristTab. "Doctor Tanaka's left Noctis City over some report that a gang of people has broken into one of the farms."

Mel shifted on her chair and winced at the renewed pressure on the bruise on her back. Pedro and Alex must have triggered the report, which meant they were about to be caught.

"I assumed they were stealing food," Jones continued. "But it's one of the farms that was being sterilized ahead of planting more crops. It's completely empty."

"Why would someone break into an empty farm?"

"The sergeant at Noctis assumed they didn't know it was empty, but he said Doctor Tanaka rushed off when she heard."

A shiver of realization passed through her. Kaito was probably the reason the Science Board refused permission for the scientists at Squyres to plant the potato crop.

"Is there a problem?" said Jones.

Deverau's gaze alighted onto Mel. She stared back at him,

trying to work out if telling him could help her friends or put them more in danger.

"Not yet. Meet me back here in five minutes." Deverau terminated the call.

Mel glanced at the door – the only way out of the room – wondering if she dared try to push past Deverau to reach it, even with her hands secured behind her.

Deverau walked up close and bent over so their noses were almost touching. His intimidating breath brushed at her face. "You know what's going on, don't you?"

"How do I know I can trust you?"

He straightened up again, reached into his pocket and pulled out an electronic fob like the one she had used to release her handcuffs on the train. He tapped a series of keys and, with a *click*, the pressure on her wrists eased and the handcuffs clattered to the floor.

Mel brought her arms round to her front and a wave of relief spread across her shoulders.

"Well?" said Deverau.

Even if she said nothing, Pedro and Alex were already in trouble. She took a breath and decided to take the risk. "They're planting a crop which we think will help end the food crisis. My guess is, Kaito's gone to stop them."

The door opened. Mel jolted at the interruption. It was Sergeant Jones.

"Was that really five minutes?" said Deverau.

"I thought you meant a generic five minutes, not an actual five minutes," said Jones.

Deverau sighed. "It doesn't matter. I need you to get Mel back to the station, then follow me out to the farm."

"You can't do that!" said Mel, fearing she was about to be locked away and unable to help anyone. "I need to stop her."

"The MSS will prevent her from breaking the law."

"But she's *making* the law – that's the point!" said Mel. "What are you going to do if she orders you to back away?"

Deverau tapped his fingers against the back of the electronic fob as he considered.

"Dev, you're not seriously thinking of bringing the prisoner with us?" said Jones.

"Please," said Mel. "I've known Kaito since she first came to Mars. If anyone can get the truth out of her, I can."

"Stand up," he ordered.

Mel, uncertain about what he was doing and unsteady on her legs, pulled herself to standing.

He regarded her doubtfully. "That uniform's going to be a problem."

She looked down at herself. She had forgotten she was still wearing the MSS uniform she had stolen from the unfortunate woman under the stairs.

"On second thoughts, it'll be fine," he said. "Do you have a sister?"

"No," she stuttered. It was an odd question. "A brother."

"From now on, you also have a sister and she is you. If anyone asks, you are Mel Erdan's sister and it's embarrassing that you keep being mistaken for her."

He was actually trusting her. After all the time she had spent running from him, she didn't know whether to be excited or terrified.

"Sergeant Jones," said Deverau, standing aside so she faced his sergeant. "Meet Officer Walker."

Jones regarded Mel suspiciously. Mel returned the look, remembering the paralyzing pain of the shockdart he had fired into her back.

"Dev, are you sure this is a good idea?" said Jones.

"No," said Deverau. He turned back to Mel. "Understand, if you make me regret this, I will ensure you serve a significant amount of jail time. Even if you are innocent of causing the food crisis, there are plenty of things I can charge you with."

Mel nodded. She had nothing to lose. "Understood."

CHAPTER FIFTY-FOUR

Alex followed the hopper of seed potatoes from the delivery vehicle supplied by Isaac and watched it take up its position next to a row of five others at the top of the field. Laid out in front of them were the stacks of empty soil trays waiting to accept their next crop. In the aisle that ran between them, the farm workers who Kurt had persuaded to help were preparing the field to be planted. Among them was Kurt himself, who came jogging up to the top of the field as he saw Alex.

"Is that the last one?" he said, glancing over at the hopper which brought itself in on the automated track.

"Yeah." Alex nodded.

"If this works, it's going to be a hell of a thing," said Kurt.

Pedro appeared from around the back of the stacks of trays. He looked both amazed and troubled.

"Kurt!" Pedro waved as he saw him. "I want to thank you for all you're doing."

"Don't thank us yet," said Kurt. "Not everyone agreed to work, so we're a bit under strength compared to what we're used to. But potato planting has a reasonable amount of automation, so we're confident we can get it done in one shift."

"I want to make sure all the growing conditions are optimized," said Pedro. "Because of the accelerated growth, there's not as much leeway for the plants to cope in less than ideal conditions."

Pedro lifted his WristTab to consult a data sheet.

"Pedro!" Kurt slapped him on the back like he had been a lifelong friend. The scientist shuddered under the sudden thump from his strong hand. "We've discussed this. You can look over my shoulder while I program everything in if it makes you feel better. But let's get these things in the soil first – before some officious so-and-so realizes we're not supposed to be in here."

Kurt clapped his hands to draw everyone's attention and told them to get ready. The last of the remaining farm workers scuttled to the top of the field.

Alex was so pleased he was able to rely on Kurt. His skills at organizing and handling people were far better than Alex's. One day, Kurt would probably be running a farm, if not a whole series of them.

With all of the people clear of the field, Kurt set the first of the forklift robots running and it trundled down the aisle to the far end, where it turned to face the empty trays. Its prongs elevated to the height of two fully grown Mars-borns and slid beneath the top tray on the furthest rack on the left-hand side. It turned, brought the tray down to a human's waist level and trundled back to the top of the farm where Yule and Langi were waiting.

They helped the robot line up the tray onto the waiting conveyor belt. The belt sensed the weight of the object and propelled the tray into the potato planter. The machine's tiller blades turned the soil to make a trench for the seed potatoes which were dropped from a funnel and covered up with soil by a second set of blades. The forklift collected the tray from the conveyor at the other end and trundled back to return it to its place on the stack. Ready to begin the growing cycle.

Kurt grinned widely. Pedro still looked worried. Alex turned to the hopper and, by hand, helped Kieran fill a container to replenish the potato planter. It was heavy work and they would have to rotate tasks every twenty minutes to avoid over-tiring themselves. Meanwhile, a second forklift was set running and the robots entered into a planting relay.

Alex was carrying a heavy basket of potatoes to the planter when he noticed the door to the field sliding shut.

The embarkation room acted like an airlock to maintain environmental integrity. If the door to the inside was closing, it meant someone from the outside was trying to get in.

"Kurt!" he shouted and dumped the basket on the conveyor.

Alex rushed to place his hand in the closing gap between the door and the frame. He knew safety measures wouldn't let it shut if a human was in the way. But, as he reached out to the narrowing gap, it became too small to fit even his fingertips. He nails scratched uselessly at the surface and the door sealed itself into the frame.

"What's going on?" said Pedro.

"We've got unexpected visitors," said Alex, powerless to prevent whoever it was coming to stop them.

"Who?" said Pedro.

Alex dared not imagine the answer.

•••

Deverau sat in the back of the rover traveling from Deimos City to the farm, keeping an eye on Mel while Jones sat in the driving seat. As the dark of night claimed the landscape outside of the windshield, he asked her to explain more about what she had learned and why people had broken into one of the farms. In return, he told her about his encounter with Kaito at Teractor.

He knew it was rash to have removed Mel's handcuffs and allowed her to come with them. He could sense Jones disapproved, even when he told him his reasoning. Deverau was, he had to admit, betting his career on the integrity of a botanist.

The forklift robot stood in suspended animation at the end of the planting machine, it's arm-like prongs held out as if begging for something it was not going to receive. The machine had been stopped while the farm workers stood waiting for the inner door of the embarkation room to open.

In the quiet of nervous anticipation, Alex heard the locks release and the gentle hiss of gas equalizing between the pressurized environments. The sliding door revealed a uniformed MSS officer standing ready with a drawn shockgun.

Gasps rose up from some of the farm workers. Others murmured their anxieties. Alex ran through a host of possibilities in his mind, each one more terrible than the last.

The door continued to slide, revealing even more armed officers. Eight in total. Standing in front, like a commander in a blue suit, was Kaito Tanaka. She was the only one without a gun. Unless the authority entrusted in her by the Terraforming Committee was considered a weapon, in which case she commanded the most power of all.

It was the worst possibility of all – they were about to get shut down and arrested.

Kaito regarded them with a stern, disapproving and uncompromising face. "All work here is to cease and this farm must be evacuated!"

"But we're working to feed Mars," said Kurt. "Everyone here is willing to work overtime to ensure it happens."

"Not with untested, experimental crops, you're not," insisted Kaito.

Pedro stepped forward, holding out his hand to introduce himself. "I'm Doctor Pedro Serrano from the Squyres Research Outpost." Kaito didn't even look down at his hand, let alone attempt to shake it. "We have an exciting opportunity to get food on the tables of ordinary people on Mars far quicker than if we rely on standard crops. I have prepared a full report, if you would care to consider…"

But Kaito had already stopped listening. She turned to an MSS officer standing to her right. "Sergeant, get these people out of here."

"Yes, doctor," replied the sergeant and waved forward the rest of the officers.

Dark blue uniforms invaded and voices of protest filled the field. The strong hand of an MSS officer grabbed Alex's upper arm.

"You can't do this!" shouted Alex at Kaito. He tried to pull his arm free, but it was held tight.

Alex continued to struggle. "Kurt!"

He looked to his friend for some kind of help, but saw the broad, muscular farm worker had all but given up. He allowed an MSS officer to pull his arms behind his back and cuff him.

If Kurt – physically the strongest of them all – could not fight back against the MSS, then all hope was lost.

Pedro was led away at the point of a shockgun. "Doctor Tanaka, let us try it in one farm," he pleaded. "Just one – and if it doesn't work, then you have lost nothing. But if we are successful, think how valuable it will be to Mars."

Kaito did not waver from her stern, disapproving and un-compromising expression. "The answer, Doctor Serrano, is no. We need all fields to grow reliable food. I'm not going to be the one to look into the eyes of starving children and tell them there's nothing to eat because we let a scientist play around in one of them."

Pedro was pushed into the embarkation room and Alex was pushed in afterwards. They stood with the other farm workers, some in handcuffs, some not. But all surrounded by armed MSS officers.

Through the gaps in the row of people in front of him, he watched Kaito at the conveyor belt. She picked up one of the seed potatoes from the basket he had left there. She turned it in front of her eyes like it was a curious artifact. Then discarded it.

She glanced across at the embarkation room and nodded to the officer standing in front. "You go ahead," she said, evidently deciding against stepping inside the crammed space with the rest of them. "I'll join you in a minute."

The door began to close and Alex wondered how Kaito had arrived at the farm so quickly. Then he thought of the few people who hadn't turned up to take the bus to work the shift. One of them, he realized, must have leaked the information.

CHAPTER FIFTY-FIVE

Deverau entered the walkway of the farm complex to see the unmistakable figures of eight MSS officers in uniform leading a group of forlorn-looking civilians. One was Pedro Serrano and another looked like Alex Pawlikiewicz, the farm worker from Ivan's gang who had evaded arrest. They had to be the farm workers Mel had talked about in the rover.

With Jones and Mel behind him, he approached, but saw no sign of Doctor Kaito Tanaka.

Deverau lifted his WristTab to broadcast his credentials to all MSS officers in the vicinity. As he approached them, some checked their WristTabs and he heard his name whispered to the ones who hadn't.

He stopped in the center of the corridor with Jones and Mel on either side, so they blocked the way. Leading the officers was an Earth-born woman with a sergeant's insignia who Deverau didn't recognize, which suggested she came from Noctis City.

"I'm Inspector Deverau of the MSS at Deimos City. This is Sergeant Jones and…" he took a second to remember Mel's alias, "… Officer Walker."

"Sergeant Chiang from Noctis," she replied.

"What's going on, sergeant?"

"These people were caught breaking into the field, sir."

Deverau raised his eyebrows, firstly because he wanted to suggest that he had no prior knowledge as to what was going on and secondly because she called him 'sir', which was a rare honorific mostly used by people pretending to be respectful when they were, in reality, nothing of the sort. "I want you to let them go, sergeant."

"I can't do that."

"I order you. As an inspector, I outrank you."

"But I was given orders by Doctor Tanaka, who works for the Terraforming Committee and, therefore, outranks you."

Deverau knew he was on dodgy ground with the tit-for-tat game of hierarchy and decided to act like he was in charge anyway. "Where is Doctor Tanaka?"

"She's still in the field. She didn't want to share an embarkation room with… these people."

Deverau glanced over to Mel. "Officer Walker – go wait for her."

"Yes, inspector," said Mel, expertly playing her part.

She strode past them all. Several turned their heads to watch and, by the looks on their faces, some might have recognized her, but were confused by her uniform. Deverau needed to distract them while he came up with some kind of plan.

"Sergeant, I think you'll find there has been some sort of mistake," he said, noticing Mel doing something at the controls while trying not to let on. "These people are working to feed Mars. They should not be considered prisoners, but heroes."

"They still broke into a field without permission, sir."

"Sergeant!" One of the officers shouted from the back. "Should she be operating the embarkation room?"

Everyone – MSS officers and farm workers – turned to see Mel had opened the door and slipped inside.

Sergeant Chiang glared at Deverau. "What is she doing? The door has to be sealed this side for Doctor Tanaka to get through."

Deverau made a play of looking worried. "I'll deal with this!" He strode past the increasingly uneasy officers.

"Officer Walker!" yelled Deverau, pleased to have an excuse to get past the others, but making up his plan on the fly. "I said *wait* for her, not *fetch* her!"

The door to the embarkation room was closing again, but there was still enough time to slip through the gap before it sealed shut.

Deverau stopped at the door in a moment of indecision. His police officer training told him he should not allow Mel to be alone in the field with Kaito. But the reality was, if he went in there with her, it would leave only Jones to stop Chiang and her officers following them in.

Mel stared out at him through the narrowing gap, as if pleading for him to let her go.

"Inspector Deverau, what's going on?" he heard Chiang shout behind him, followed by her angry, approaching footsteps.

He took off his WristTab, set it to record and threw it into the embarkation room. If he couldn't be a witness to what was going to happen, he had to ensure he had the next best thing.

There was no longer space enough for his body to fit, but he could still thrust his arm inside to stop the door closing. As Chiang would well know.

"Remember what happened on the train," Mel whispered.

It refreshed the memory of that last time they had been separated by a door. He pulled his shockgun.

He aimed it directly at her. "Officer Walker, stop!"

He saw the fear in her eyes as he fired – but deliberately too far to the right. The shockdart struck the surface of the door, pinged off and dropped to the floor.

Mel disappeared behind the closing door and it connected with the frame.

But he kept up the pretense. "I said stop!"

The door's lock clicked into place. Deverau fired again. This time, deliberately too far to the left. The dart struck the controls by the side of the door and discharged. Arcs of electric blue sparked through the workings.

Chiang, her face red with fury, was suddenly there. "What's your officer doing?"

"I apologize," bluffed Deverau. "I don't know what's got into her."

"You hit the controls!" Chiang went to touch the panel by the side of the door, but a spark flew out and she pulled her hand back.

"Again, I can only apologize." Deverau turned the shockgun over in his hand as if it were some strange, unfamiliar object. "I'm rather out of practice with these things."

Chiang pulled her sleeve down over her fingers and tried to operate the controls, but they were completely fried. Deverau allowed himself a moment of satisfaction, but maintained a straight face.

"Get this door open!" Chiang demanded.

"There must be some kind of emergency override," said Deverau, trying to sound like he was being helpful while actually being the opposite. "These things are probably operated from central control, but I don't think there's anyone there at night."

Chiang spun round to face her officers and the farm workers. "Which one of you can override this door?"

Deverau stared out at the farm workers. None of them said anything. Either they understood he had shot out the controls for a reason or they simply didn't know.

Chiang was incensed. She yelled at one of her officers, ordering them to find someone in charge who could release the door. They pulled up their WristTab and started searching.

He hoped he had done the right thing in allowing Mel to go after Kaito on her own. If he hadn't, he had just made a very impulsive, dangerous and career-ending move.

CHAPTER FIFTY-SIX

The door to the field slid open and revealed Kaito standing behind the automated planting equipment, waiting. She must have been expecting one of the MSS officers.

Her eyes widened when she saw Mel.

Looking at her former friend, an unexpected sadness came over her. It was almost a bereavement at the loss of what they once had. Behind Kaito was the abandoned field which Mel had hoped would grow a crop to pull Mars back from the brink. Most of the seed potatoes lay unplanted in hoppers, the forklift robots stood idle and, although the conveyor belt moved, it had no tray of soil to offer up to the planter.

Kaito regarded Mel's stolen MSS uniform with contempt. "What are you doing wearing that?"

Mel ignored the question. "You set me up."

"It was *your* crops that died in farms across Mars. *I'm* the one trying to put things right."

"Don't lie to me, Kaito."

Mel stepped out of the embarkation room and Kaito,

suddenly alarmed at her approach, backed away. "I'm your friend, Mel. I wouldn't do anything to hurt you."

"Did you pay Ivan Volkov to steal my experiment?"

"Who? No!"

Mel advanced and Kaito took another nervous step backwards.

"Did you think no one would connect you to the son of your ex-boyfriend? You forgot, Kaito, that I know all about Andrei Volkov – you're the one who told me."

"Then you know I've had nothing to do with Andrei for years. I despise the man."

Mel took another step and Kaito doubled back around the conveyor belt and into the embarkation room.

Mel hoped Deverau had understood her whispered instruction. If he had, then Kaito had nowhere to run.

Kaito shouted at the controls and hit it with her fist, but the embarkation room did not respond. She turned to Mel with suspicion. "What have you done?"

"It's just you and me in here," said Mel. "I know all the pieces, I just need you to put them together. I know the dead crops were potatoes derived from my stolen experiment and I know it was Teractor that delivered them to the farms. Was that side of the operation handled by your new boyfriend, Felix?"

"You leave Felix out of it! He has nothing to do with this!"

As soon as the words were out of her mouth, Mel saw Kaito's regret that she had given herself away.

"If you know it wasn't Felix, then you must know who it was."

Mel approached the embarkation room. She assumed Kaito would back away again, but instead she made a break for it. She ran past the conveyor belt, swiping her arm at a basket of potatoes left there by one of the farm workers. The crop scattered across the conveyor and cascaded to the ground where the potatoes bounced and rolled like misshapen balls.

Mel ran after her, but trod on one of the potatoes and her ankle turned sideways. Crying out as the ligaments stretched, she reached out to the conveyor to stop herself from falling. But the belt was still moving and her hand shot away from her and she fell onto her hands and knees.

Kaito ran down the aisle, stopping only to set the forklift robots in motion. They trundled away on their pre-programmed pattern, resuming where they had left off.

"Where are you running to, Kaito?" shouted Mel. "There's literally nowhere to go."

Mel stood and tried to put weight on her ankle. A sharp pain shot up her leg. She was sure she had strained it, not broken it, but it was going to make it harder to chase Kaito. If her former friend was going to insist on playing that senseless game.

Kaito had disappeared behind the stacks of soil trays.

"What I don't understand is *why*," Mel shouted out to wherever Kaito was hiding. "If you were working for Teractor, why did they want to cause a famine on Mars?"

"No one knew your experiment was going to fail." Kaito's voice came from behind the stacks. "Even you thought it would be a success."

Mel turned to face the direction of her voice and a tray shot out from the stack – pushed from behind. Mel jumped sideways as it plummeted to the ground. A mound of soil tipped out by her feet.

Limping on her strained ankle, Mel approached the bottom of the field, listening for the sounds of movement and looking between the stacks for signs of Kaito. She caught a glimpse of Kaito's jacket, but kept walking to pretend she hadn't noticed.

When Mel had gone past, Kaito did exactly what Mel had hoped she would. She dashed out to make a run for it. But Mel was ready. She swiveled, ignoring the pain in her ankle, and gave chase.

Kaito ran with the frantic desperation of someone afraid of being caught. Mel's determination made her faster, but even as she gained ground, Kaito remained two steps ahead of her, with her unfastened jacket billowing out behind.

It gave Mel a new target. Mel reached out for the material and grasped. With a jerk, she tugged the jacket backwards and pulled Kaito with it.

Kaito stumbled and fell into Mel's arms. Mel locked them around Kaito and held her tight. Kaito struggled, but her writhing was no match for the strength of Mel's anger and sense of betrayal.

They stood in the central aisle with an innocent forklift robot trundling towards them. Mel thrust Kaito in front so she faced the machine's two advancing prongs.

"Mel! What are you doing?" The fear in Kaito's voice meant she understood that Mel was desperate enough to keep her there until she was speared by the forklift.

"Tell me what this is about, Kaito!"

"There's nothing to tell."

"Start with what you were doing at Teractor," said Mel, ensuring any attempt by Kaito to break free was subdued by her locked arms.

The robot, oblivious to the women in its path, continued to trundle forward.

Kaito swallowed. "When Teractor expanded into agriculture, they realized Mars was going to face a food supply problem," she said, fear causing her voice to falter. "Because they'd drawn up all the legal contracts which were bringing migrants from Earth, they knew the farms would soon be unable to meet demand. They needed someone with expertise in food crops and they took me on as a consultant – off the books, so EcoLine wouldn't know. If I impressed them, they were going to offer me a better job."

"You impressed them by plunging Mars into a crisis?"

"I thought I would be *preventing* a crisis! Enhanced potatoes had the potential to feed millions of people far more efficiently than fields of wheat or corn. The Science Board wasn't going to approve it until all the trials and checks were complete – we were talking years and more migrant workers were arriving in months."

Kaito began to tremble as the forklift closed in. "Mel, *please!*"

But Mel wasn't finished with her. "Why not come to me? Why pay Ivan to steal my experiment?"

"You wouldn't have agreed to it and the technology was owned by EcoLine," gasped Kaito between frightened breaths. "I needed an unofficial way to get it out of the lab so Teractor could claim they were offered the technology in good faith. I thought, once it was a success, no one would care where it came from. I remembered Andrei's son when he was twelve and knew he would do almost anything for money. I hadn't seen him in ten years, I didn't think anyone would trace him back to me."

"So when it all went wrong, you set me up to take the blame. It was you who told the MSS what happened to my field trial, wasn't it?"

"I didn't think you would get into trouble, Mel. Believe me. I thought they would question you and let you go. I'm sorry."

The hypocrisy of her apology rang hollow in the field of unplanted soil trays.

The prongs of the forklift were seconds away.

"You could have told the truth at any point," said Mel. "You had the power to do anything when the Terraforming Committee put you in charge of the food crisis, but instead you continued to lie."

"I was in so deep, Mel," Kaito cried. "I didn't know how to get out."

Kaito screamed as the forklift was about to spear her. She turned her head to shield her eyes from the moment of impact.

The machine shuddered to a halt.

The whirr of its motor ceased and its wheels stopped turning centimeters before her body. The sensors had detected a person in the way and simply stopped.

She let go of Kaito's body and she slumped to the ground, a wreck of a human being.

Mel leaned back against the nearest stack of soil-filled trays. The relief was dizzying.

At the top of the field, the door to the embarkation room opened. Four MSS officers spilled out. They took in the scene quickly and rushed to help Kaito.

Following them, at a composed pace, was Sergeant Chiang and, behind her, Inspector Deverau.

Kaito pointed at Mel. "It's Mel Erdan!" she screamed. "The one who caused the crops to die!"

A sickening feeling rose in Mel's stomach. Even after her confession, Kaito was still passing the blame.

Confused, the officers looked at Mel in her stolen MSS uniform and hesitated.

"Sergeant Chiang!" shouted Kaito. "It's Erdan – arrest her!"

Chiang nodded across to them.

Mel went limp in defeat as two officers grabbed her, turned her around and threw her against the stack. One spoke the rehearsed, perfunctory words that comprised her rights, but they were just noise reaching her ears. Her face was squashed against the soil trays, her arms forced behind her and she, again, felt the metal of cuffs encase her wrists.

When they spun her back round, Deverau was standing in front of her.

"You're arresting me?"

Mel wondered what Deverau and Chiang had discussed after she left them. She scoured his expression for some kind of hint of whether he was her ally or not, but he remained impassive.

"I can't stop them," said Deverau. "Your arrest warrant is still valid."

"But she told me everything!" Mel said in frustration.

Deverau pulled his WristTab from his pocket and made play of fastening it to his arm. "It was a good job I was recording it, then."

Kaito, holding onto the two MSS officers on either side of her, found enough strength to spin round and glare at them. "That means nothing. Everything I said was under duress."

"It might be inadmissible in court," suggested Deverau with an air of smugness. "But it'll still make an interesting listen."

The MSS officer who had cuffed her grabbed Mel by the arm. Pain shot up her leg from her strained ankle as Deverau stepped aside and allowed her to be led away.

With Kaito free and her under arrest, she feared it had all been for nothing.

"At least let them back in here to plant the crop!" she called back. "If you won't save me – at least save Mars!"

CHAPTER FIFTY-SEVEN

A night in an MSS cell had been a frightening thing. Not because Alex feared what they would do to him, but because he feared it was a glimpse into the rest of his life.

The following day, he had been allowed to return to the field with the rest of the farm workers to plant the potatoes. He didn't know what Inspector Deverau had done – something to do with his case against Kaito Tanaka – but he had managed to persuade someone in authority to allow them to continue planting.

Once it was all over, Alex stood at the head of the field, behind the conveyor, watching his colleagues clear up the last of the equipment. The stacks of trays, full of seed potatoes, were already being watered by the irrigation system and the smell of damp soil was fresh and soothing. It was going to be his last opportunity to experience that smell for a long time. In all probability, many years.

Inspector Deverau joined him. Not to congratulate him for a job well done, but to formally place him under arrest.

"I hope the scientists are right," said Deverau. "The people of Mars need this to work."

"It'll work," said Alex.

Even if Pedro's enthusiasm for the technology hadn't been convincing, Alex had seen with his own eyes how the potatoes grew successfully at the research outpost. He was sure, when the field was ready to harvest, it would prove the crop was viable. Some of the potatoes would be eaten while others would be saved to seed yet more farms. With more being propagated at Squyres, it would be only weeks before dozens of farms across Mars were harvesting enough potatoes to feed the whole population.

Alex only regretted he would not be there to see it.

He gazed out in the field where Yule – the girl who had once offered him a seat on the bus – was setting a cleaning robot to clear up the scattering of soil that had been spilled on the ground. He wondered, if he had made different choices and hadn't been misled by Ivan, what would have happened if he had asked her out.

"Are you ready to come back to the station?" said Deverau.

Alex swallowed, feeling his last moments of freedom slip away. "Will I have to testify against my friends?"

Alex thought of Elea, Pete, Sammi – and even Ivan. He remembered their smiling faces as they talked, laughed and messed around in the lake in Central Plaza and tried to understand how it all went wrong.

"If you tell the truth, it will be taken into consideration when you are sentenced," said Deverau. "But they must answer for their own crimes. Nothing you can say or do can prevent that."

"And me?" said Alex. "You said there's a rehabilitation program? I could work in space like my father?"

"You will still have to serve a prison sentence, but I can recommend that you are considered for the rehabilitation program for young people. You might be offered a placement in space, but that's up to the parole board."

Alex took a deep breath. He had to find the courage inside of him to face whatever was to come. "OK," he said.

Deverau nodded and led him to the embarkation room.

Glancing behind, Alex saw Kurt place the last of the empty hoppers in a stack in the corner of the field. Kurt smiled and gave him a wave.

Alex had no smile to return. He turned to hide his tears and kept walking.

CHAPTER FIFTY-EIGHT

Mel watched Kaito intently as she stood in the dock of Mars' highest court in Noctis City. Kaito had lost weight during the weeks of testimony, so her body was overwhelmed by her drab gray suit. Hanging her head, she kept her gaze from the people packed inside and eager to hear the judgment against her.

A hand-picked sample of the aggrieved and curious jostled around Mel in the public gallery. She, like the others, had abandoned her seat and was pressed up against the balustrade of the balcony overlooking the court. Below, lawyers from both sides sat divided by an aisle that led to the dignitaries and journalists who had been given a front row seat. Around them buzzed the rotors of hovercams, recording every minute detail for a scarred planet ready for vengeance.

Presiding over the proceedings was Honorary Judge Bublik, a former chief administrator with the Terraforming Committee who had a legal background and had been brought out of retirement for the inquiry. With no ties to

Teractor or any other corporation, he was considered to be the closest thing to independent it was possible to be and his judgment was expected to be fair.

Anticipation hung in the courtroom. So thick that Mel tasted it with each nervous breath.

Bublik rested his elbows on the bench in front of him, interlaced his fingers to make a bridge with his hands and turned to Kaito with somber eyes.

"Doctor Kaito Tanaka, this inquiry has heard how you brought unnecessary fear and uncertainty to the people of Mars. You put one of humanity's prime requirements for survival – the supply of food – at risk. You state that your motive was to do the opposite, to feed an increasing population. Although this may have been true initially, it was overridden by a persistent and increasing desire for self-gain."

Bublik paused to look down at his notes. If anyone in the courtroom dared to breathe, they kept their breath silent so the only noise was the gentle whir of the ICN hovercams.

"When your plan failed, you compounded that failure by blaming a lifelong friend. You then accepted a position as the science lead for the food crisis where you attempted to control the flow of information to the public."

Kaito's shoulders sagged under the weight of his words.

"I would like to take this opportunity," Bublik continued, "to praise the actions of that friend, Doctor Melanie Erdan."

He glanced up into the public gallery and looked directly at her. Mel felt herself blush as everyone in the courtroom, except Kaito, turned to do the same. Two hovercams flew over to catch her embarrassment in close-up.

"Her investigations, although not entirely within the law,

helped uncover the serious injustice being committed on this planet. It should be an embarrassment to the authorities that it took an accused scientist to uncover the truth. In light of this, I hereby fully exonerate Mel Erdan for any misdemeanors she may have committed in this endeavor and offer her the sincere thanks of both this court and of Mars."

Mel's legs weakened at the relief and she put out her hand to the balustrade to steady herself. On either side of her, the cameras captured every nuance as she thought of what it meant for her future. Now that there was a future to have.

"As for you, Kaito Tanaka," Bublik continued. "This court acknowledges your admission of guilt, but doubts your testimony that no one else was involved. I find it incredible that you arranged for technology to be stolen, secretly propagated in a Teractor facility and distributed to farms without anyone else being aware of – and, indeed, complicit in – what you were doing."

Bublik looked out into the court and his gaze settled on some of the dignitaries, including Teractor officials, sitting behind the lawyers. The cameras swooped to catch their reaction.

"This inquiry is not a criminal trial. My role has been to examine what happened and to make recommendations for the future security of Mars' farming industry – which I shall do in my report.

"However," he returned his attention to Kaito. "For your crimes of conspiracy to steal and endangering the food supply, it is my recommendation that you, Kaito Tanaka, serve a prison sentence of no less than ten years."

Gasps rose up all around her, but Mel stayed silent. She had expected to be pleased to see Kaito punished for what she had done. Instead, all she felt was pity.

Kaito had been foolish, ambitious and self-serving, but she had never meant to lead Mars down the road to starvation. Her mistake had been to allow one bad decision to dictate her every subsequent move until she had dug herself into a hole so deep she was unable to climb out.

Kaito stared ahead at nothing. As if blocking out the reality of the judgment against her.

Only when a court official took her by the arm to lead her away, did she blink herself back into the moment.

Kaito glanced up into the public gallery as she left the dock and Mel saw sorrow in her eyes. Whether it was remorse for what she had done to Mel, remorse for what she had done to Mars or regret over what she had done to herself – it was impossible to tell.

Mel returned her stare without sympathy. She hoped Kaito understood that no amount of sorrow would ever erase the contempt she had for what Kaito had done.

Mel emerged onto the steps outside the court building and was instantly surrounded by a crowd of journalists, hovercams and members of the waiting crowd.

She garbled a statement welcoming the judgment, avoiding any personal opinion about Kaito and expressing hope that Mars could move on from the trauma of the food crisis.

When it was clear she was going to say no more, the crowd spotted Inspector Deverau leaving the court further along the steps and rushed over to berate him with their questions instead.

Isaac and Daniel stood patiently waiting for her at the bottom of the steps. The little boy, standing under his own strength and hanging on tightly to his father's hand, gave her a big smile and waved.

The joy at seeing them, enhanced by the knowledge that no judge, court or law would take her away from her family, lifted her so she felt she was flying, not running, down the steps.

She embraced Isaac. She embraced Daniel. They both embraced her.

"Mommy, you're squashing me!" Daniel complained.

She laughed. "I'm sorry, sweetheart."

She ruffled his hair and he grimaced while patting it down again.

"Hey, Mel."

Mel turned to see Pedro approaching from behind. Overwhelmed by the emotion of it all, she hugged him too.

"Pedro! I thought you were going to be in court."

"People were camping out overnight to get in the public gallery and I wasn't given special status like you."

"Really? After everything you did?"

"You're the one who made the science work, Mel," said Pedro. "I only got it over the last hurdle."

"Why don't we go celebrate?" said Isaac. "I've booked a restaurant around the corner. Now that regular food is returning to the supply chain, they're promising not to serve a single potato."

Pedro laughed. The crops had been a savior for Mars, but there wasn't anyone on the planet who wasn't fed up with eating them.

Mel wasn't yet ready to leave. She looked to where the

crowd had gathered around Deverau. "Wait a minute," she said to her husband.

As she approached, she heard the last of Deverau's prepared speech. "... vindicated by the judgment handed down today. I look forward to Judge Bublik's report and hope that both Mars and the MSS can learn from his findings. Thank you."

Journalists shouted questions, but Deverau said nothing more.

Eventually, they dispersed and Mel was able to catch Deverau's eye.

He smiled as he came over. "It was a good result today," he said.

"Yes," said Mel, still coming to terms with the reality that it was all over.

"So, what are you going to do now?"

She shrugged. "I don't know. Me and Pedro are fielding a lot of inquiries about our accelerated growth and viral enhancing technology. There's the possibility we could improve and adapt it to other uses on Mars. The problem is, EcoLine owns my bit of the science and Tharsis Republic owns Pedro's. The corporations are talking about solving the issue by selling the whole lot to Splice Tactical Genomics, with an option for me and Pedro to continue the research. I haven't decided what I'm going to do yet – like the rest of Mars, I'm a bit tired of potatoes."

Deverau nodded his understanding.

"What about you?" Mel asked.

"The MSS aren't sure whether to praise me or punish me for helping you," he admitted. "So they've opted to leave me alone in my current job for now. Which is fine by me."

"We're going out for a meal to celebrate," said Mel. "You're welcome to join us."

"No, I promised Jones I would see him back at the station."

"If you're sure I can't tempt you..."

"It's a celebration for you and your family. You don't want me there."

Mel felt something touch her leg and glanced down to see Daniel had run over. Still a little unsteady on his feet, he hugged tightly onto her knee.

"Mommy! I'm *hungry!*"

When she looked up, Deverau was backing away. "Good luck, Mel!" he said. "I don't expect we'll see each other again."

"Yes, good luck!" she called after him as he turned and walked off down the street.

She watched him go until she was joined by Isaac and Pedro.

"Ready now?" said Isaac.

She picked Daniel up, sat him on her hip and felt how heavy he had become. "I'm ready."

They walked to the restaurant with Isaac reading out all the amazing-sounding options from the menu on his WristTab. By the time they got there, they were eager to eat the most long-awaited meal of their lives.

ACKNOWLEDGMENTS

I would like to thank Professor Johnathan Napier of Rothamsted Research for taking the time to talk to me about genetics and plant biology with regard to the modifying of food crops. Especially for his valuable comments on some of the issues which emerged in the writing of this novel. If any scientific inaccuracies have slipped through, however, that's entirely my responsibility.

ABOUT THE AUTHOR

JANE KILLICK is an author and journalist who juggles working for BBC Radio with a lifelong passion for science fiction. Alongside several series of original SF novels, she has also written numerous behind the scenes books, including *Stasis Leaked Complete*, a guide to TV show *Red Dwarf*, and a series on *Babylon 5*.

janekillick.com // twitter.com/janekillick